DOC
CL

The
The

DOCTOR WHO CLASSICS

The Dominators
The Krotons

Based on the BBC television serials by Norman Ashby
and Robert Holmes by arrangement with the British
Broadcasting Corporation

IAN MARTER

TERRANCE DICKS

A STAR BOOK
published by
the Paperback Division of
W.H. ALLEN & Co. Plc

A Star Book
Published in 1988
by the Paperback Division of
W.H. Allen & Co. Plc
44 Hill Street, London W1X 8LB

The Dominators novelisation copyright © Ian Marter 1984
Original script copyright © Norman Ashby 1968

The Krotons novelisation copyright © Terrance Dicks 1985
Original script copyright © Robert Holmes 1968

'Doctor Who' series copyright © British Broadcasting Corporation,
1968, 1984, 1985

This dual edition published 1988

Printed in Great Britain

ISBN 0 352 32265 9

CONTENTS

1 Island of Death 7
2 The Radiation Mystery 19
3 The Assessment 31
4 Heads in the Sand 41
5 Slavery 55
6 Fighting Back 69
7 Buried Alive 79
8 Clues 91
9 Last Chances 101
10 Desperate Remedies 115

1

Island of Death

A huge crescent of brilliant pinpoints of light sliced through the unimaginable emptiness of space near the edge of a remote spiral galaxy. Like a colossal scimitar, it flashed in a relentless sweep towards an insignificant little planet which orbited an isolated minor star. Suddenly the very tip of the nearer point of the crescent separated itself from the rest. It decelerated into a tight curving path which gradually spiralled closer and closer to the pale, ochre-coloured planet. Far above, the gigantic blade of lights swept on through the galaxy, leaving the meteor-like object to burn its deadly way down through the hot dry atmosphere towards the barren waste shimmering below.

A vicious whirlwind of sand and rock splinters was sucked into the air around a vast dune-covered basin at the foot of rugged sandstone cliffs. A sickening throbbing sound vibrated through the dense clouds as an enormous circular shadow darkened the swirling hollow. Slowly a massive silver disc descended and hovered a few metres above ground. Its upper surface was a shallow dome with cowlings radiating from the centre like flattened tubular spokes. A band of circular ports pulsated in rapid sequence round and round the rim, giving the impression that the saucer was rotating as it slowly gyrated and steadied itself while emitting a piercing rhythmic whine. After a few seconds, a broad silver shaft emerged from the underside and extended itself to the ground forming a central support.

For several minutes the whirlwinds raged around the weird craft and the oscillating whine reached a deafening climax. Then gradually the noise decreased, the pulsation of the rim slowed and stopped, and the shrieking sandstorm subsided. An eerie silence enveloped the giant metallic mushroom as the thick dust settled and the ground ceased to tremble. Then from far in the distance came the faint sound of waves monotonously breaking. For a while nothing happened.

All at once a curved panel at the base of the central shaft hummed smoothly open and something stirred in the dark interior. Two massive figures strode menacingly into the hot air. They were human in form but towered more than two and a half metres in height. Their leathery features were starkly chiselled, with thin bloodless lips and deeply set red-rimmed eyes which burned with a cold green light beneath heavy brows. Their short hair was black and sleeked back, like a skullcap, from their shallow foreheads. The creatures were clad in protective suits consisting of black quilted material like rubber, armoured with small overlapping plates and built up around the shoulders so that they appeared to have no necks. Massive boots encased their long thick legs and their hands were concealed inside huge padded gloves which creaked when they moved their fingers.

The two figures stalked cumbersomely around under the saucer, surveying the arid landscape with piercing emerald stares.

'Is flux absorption complete, Toba?' one of them suddenly rapped in a hard imperious voice.

The other checked a small instrument he was carrying. 'Affirmative, Navigator Rago,' he announced. 'Energy now transferred to fuel fields. But we require much more.'

Rago waved his big arm impatiently. 'That is the purpose of our visit, Probationer Toba.'

Like two giant turtles on their hind legs, the figures marched slowly through the soft sand.

Toba glanced sideways at his superior. 'With respect, I still submit that we should continue to Epsilon Zero Gamma. This planet has not been fully evaluated ...'

Rago drew a hissing breath and his eyes reddened. 'This planet is ideal,' he retorted sharply. 'At this location, crust parameters are optimum. Also an intelligent life-form is present.'

8

'But the species might be unsuitable,' Toba objected. 'It might be hostile.'

Rago's gloves creaked ominously. 'If necessary we shall destroy it, Toba.'

A trace of a ghastly smile buckled Toba's iron features. 'Yes we shall destroy ...' he rasped eagerly.

Rago glared contemptuously at his subordinate. 'Commence the preliminary survey at once,' he ordered.

'Command accepted,' Toba replied submissively. Turning towards the dark hatchway at the foot of the shaft he rapped out a harsh summons: 'Quarks!'

Instantly an excited whirring and chattering sound issued from within, a noise that was part human and part mechanical. Something glinted and sparked in the shadows. And then the Quarks emerged ...

On the far side of the parched plateau stretching back from the ridge of sandstone cliffs, lay a vast grey sea covered with a smoky mantle of fog. Across the gently heaving, murky water a large hovercraft shaped like a flat beehive was gliding towards the shore. Its hull was composed of concentric rings rising from a broad base and tapering to a small dome and several faintly illuminated panels glimmered around its middle ring. Otherwise the vessel was featureless, looming through the cloud with a low-pitched grinding sound.

In the cool, softly lit interior, four people were lounging in padded seats set in a semicircle around a well-worn instrument console. They were staring up at the large display-screen suspended at an angle above them, which showed a clear image of the approaching land, while through the observation ports the thick vapours writhed and swirled outside. The four travellers – three male and one female – wore sleeveless garments like togas, cut low around the neck but with curiously bulging pleated waists. Their legs were bare and their feet were clad in thong sandals reaching to their ankles.

A slender but athletic young man with fine bronzed features and wavy blond hair turned to his companions with a wry smile. 'This really is a terribly primitive way to travel,' he exclaimed.

'Well, we wanted some excitement for a change didn't we, Tolata?' replied a second youth with dark curly hair, turning to the beautiful fair girl beside him.

Tolata nodded eagerly. 'An adventure. That is why I came, Etnin.'

The blond youth gestured round the shabby cabin. 'Excitement? What's exciting about sitting for hours in this obsolete old tub?' he demanded. 'In a capsule we'd only have taken a few minutes.'

Just then the fourth traveller – a short balding man with a plump body and a mischievous expression – sprang up to adjust some controls. 'Not without a permit, Wahed!' he retorted. 'You seem to forget ... all this is extremely illegal.'

At that moment the craft shuddered and lurched violently from side to side. The helmsman smiled at his passengers' gasps of dismay. 'You can hardly complain. You've travelled hundreds of kilometres by sea with a real live navigator ...'

The vessel lurched again.

'Well, Kully, perhaps that does add a little zest,' Wahed admitted doubtfully.

Kully gestured up at the scanner. 'The Island of Death!' he announced dramatically. 'Uninhabited for 170 annos. Nothing could survive in this poisoned wasteland ...'

The passengers stared at the brownish coastline and distant cliffs. There were no signs of life of any description.

Eventually Wahed shrugged. 'It's not so impressive. There's a regular visit by the Monitoring Unit and ...'

'And sometimes Students are allowed to see the effects of atomic radiation there ...' Tolata added, her large blue eyes wide with fascination.

Kully snorted dismissively and jiggled his controls. 'But all that's organised by the Council,' he cried. 'This is the *real thing*!'

Wahed frowned at the screen. 'It looks like the images on my video at home,' he objected. 'You could be cheating us, Kully.'

Kully shook his pinkish round head impatiently. 'This is real. You're actually here,' he protested.

Etnin rose to his feet. 'Why don't we land on the Island ... and see for ourselves?' he suggested in a hushed voice.

Kully stared at him in horror. 'You can't.'

'Whyever not?' demanded Wahed, standing up on the other side of their perspiring little guide.

'Yes. Why not?' Tolata joined in excitedly.

Kully gripped the control console and swallowed nervously. 'Without protective suits?' he murmured. 'It would be madness.'

At that moment, warning systems started buzzing and flashing urgently.

Kully went pale. 'Radiation hazard ... Radiation ...' he stammered, gazing in panic at his instruments.

Suddenly they were thrown violently sideways.

'Kully ... do something, Kully ...' Tolata screamed as the ship swung abruptly to and fro and then shuddered to a stop, its propulsion systems grinding in protest.

Kully struggled to regain control, but the systems whined and squealed uselessly. The craft would not move. 'We've run aground,' he admitted in a whisper. 'The drives are completely stuck.'

There was an appalled silence.

'You mean permanently?' Wahed asked uncertainly.

Kully nodded miserably, falling back into his seat and covering his face in his hands.

'This certainly is exciting!' Etnin murmured, clutching Tolata's arm nervously.

'Running aground on radiation-contaminated islands isn't my idea of excitement,' Kully wailed.

Suddenly Wahed pointed to the instruments. 'Look, the radiation detectors are indicating zero!' he exclaimed.

Kully peered through his stubby fingers. 'Zero? But they can't be.'

'So much for your real live navigation,' Wahed laughed. He turned to the others. 'Wherever we are, this can't be the Island of Death,' he scoffed.

Kully roused himself and thumped the console. The detectors continued to register zero radiation. 'It must be a malfunction,' he protested defiantly.

Behind his back, Wahed had reached across and craftily operated a series of switches.

'Hey, what do you think you're doing?' Kully shouted angrily as a hatchway rumbled slowly open somewhere in the vessel.

Wahed grinned. 'Let's go and see where we *really* are,' he suggested mischievously.

Kully stared at him incredulously. 'Go out there?' he echoed. 'But you'll all be cooked to a frazzle in seconds!'

Ignoring him, Wahed gestured to Tolata and Etnin to follow and walked fearlessly out of the cabin.

For a moment Kully could only watch in horrified silence as Etnin disappeared after him. Then his shiny face puckered with rage. 'Don't complain to me if you all kill yourselves,' he shouted, 'because I don't refund money to ...' He clutched his sparse hair in panic. 'Refund? What am I saying? You haven't paid me yet. Come back!'

He darted forward and seized Tolata's arm as she was about to follow the others. 'Don't be a fool. This is the Island of Death!' he screamed. 'The detectors are malfunctioning ...'

The tall girl shook herself free, reached the hatchway and jumped elegantly down into the shallows. 'You are a rogue, Kully!' she cried setting off eagerly up the beach through the thinning mist. 'This can't be the Island of Death.'

'I tell you it is!' Kully yelled after her. 'And I must insist that you pay me the agreed price ...'

Just then, Wahed appeared over some nearby dunes and ran down towards them. 'People ... up by the cliffs!' he shouted triumphantly.

'That settles it, Kully,' Tolata said over her shoulder. 'There would be no people on the Island of Death.'

'Only the Monitoring Unit,' Kully gasped, cowering in the hatchway as Wahed splashed towards him.

'The two I just saw are not wearing radiation suits,' Wahed retorted smugly.

Suddenly Etnin appeared, waving his arms excitedly. 'They've got robots with them!' he cried.

Reaching up, Wahed grabbed Kully's podgy hand and pulled him into the shallows. 'Robots,' he exclaimed. 'Come on, Kully, perhaps we can persuade them to assist us.'

Dragging Kully behind him he set off towards the dunes.

Kully glanced back at his marooned ship listing drunkenly in the soft sand. 'Robots!' he muttered scornfully and stumbled reluctantly after the others.

Beyond the dunes, at the foot of the towering cliffs near the saucer, two Quarks were being programmed by Probationer Toba. Each Quark stood about two metres tall. It consisted of a squat 'body', like a heavily armoured box mounted upon two stout extendable 'legs' and surmounted by a large spherical 'head'. This head was covered with a network or eyes and sensors, and resembled a crystal-studded ball. From it protruded five antennae shaped like elongated glass pyramids – one each side, front and back, and the fifth projecting vertically from the crown. For 'arms', each Quark possessed two extendable probes hinged across its 'chest' and ending in a complex 'hand' bristling with sensors, sockets and implements.

The robots acknowledged Toba's instructions with a continuous metallic chuckling sound, eerily resembling the laughter of small children. Around their sharp-edged and pointed antennae, the air buzzed and crackled menacingly.

'Drilling targets will be established at the five vector nodes and depth parameters calculated for each target ...' Toba ordered.

Suddenly one of the Quarks emitted a vicious sparking between the points of its antennae. Toba wheeled round and saw three distant figures running across the dunes towards the saucer, shouting and gesticulating. He watched them impassively for a moment and then a kind of smile cracked around his hard mouth. He glanced furtively towards the saucer and then rasped out an order. The Quarks immediately turned, deploying their probes and aiming at the approaching figures.

'Destroy them,' Toba hissed, in an obsessive whisper.

There was a brief wailing and bleating sound, followed by a series of whiplike cracks as bolts of ultrasonic energy burst simultaneously from the Quarks' probes. Wahed, Tolata and Etnin were flung into the air like helpless puppets before

13

collapsing in shapeless broken bundles in the sand.

'Recharge force units!' Toba rapped, licking his thin dry lips with relish.

The Quarks chuckled harshly in anticipation.

'Is there trouble, Probationer Toba?'

Toba started guiltily as Rago strode out of the access hatch at the base of the shaft.

'I have dealt with three alien beings, Navigator Rago,' he reported, smartly recovering his composure.

'Dead?'

'Affirmative.'

Rago strode menacingly over to him. 'That was unnecessary, a waste of vital energy reserves,' he hissed. 'Resume your proper functions immediately.'

'Command accepted,' Toba acknowledged. His eyes glowered with resentment and he resolved to avenge his humiliation as he watched Rago marching off to examine the remains of his victims.

Some distance along the wandering ridge of the sand-cliffs, Kully lay among some boulders, paralysed with horror at what he had just witnessed and stunned by his miraculous escape. Now he was stranded on the Island, alone and defenceless against an unknown enemy. Eventually pulling himself together, he massaged the wrenched ankle that had made him fall behind the others – ironically, saving his life – and tried to think.

All at once the rocks started trembling and clattering together around him. Holding his breath, he listened as a raucous screeching and groaning rose from somewhere below him. Then he scrambled to his feet and frantically clawed his way up the cliff-face whimpering with terror.

Below, a shabby, rickety structure topped by a flashing yellow beacon gradually became visible against the cliff. After a few seconds the beacon stopped flashing, the ground ceased to vibrate and there was silence ...

After a while the door of the police public call-box creaked open and a short dark-haired little man ambled out, yawning and sleepily rubbing his eyes. He was wearing grubby

14

checked trousers, a kind of frayed frock-coat and a threadbare and none too clean shirt, with a bootlace tie negligently knotted under his jutting chin. His shoes were scuffed and down-at-heel and his manner was carefree and unassuming. Stretching, he shook himself and looked keenly around with dark humorous eyes, sniffing at the air expectantly.

'Ah yes ... indeed yes ...' he muttered happily.

'Are ye all right, Doctor?' demanded a gruff Scots voice as a tough-looking young lad dressed in a kilt complete with sporran, sleeveless furry jacket and knee-length socks with heavy boots emerged behind him, brandishing a folded deckchair.

'Just a little tired, Jamie,' the Doctor replied. 'Mental projection can be an exhausting business, you know.'

Behind Jamie, a lively teenage girl with a round face and short black hair dressed in slacks and a tee-shirt peered round the police-box door. 'You need a rest, Doctor,' she announced firmly.

'My dear Zoe, we all do,' the Doctor agreed. 'That's precisely why we came to Dulkis. This is a splendid little planet.' He took the deckchair from Jamie and set it up on the sand.

Jamie grunted sceptically. 'Och, we've heard that one before.'

'You mean there won't be any Cybermen or Daleks?' Zoe complained, wrinkling her nose in disappointment as she stared around them. 'Is the whole planet as dreary as this?'

The Doctor settled himself comfortably in the deckchair. 'Dear me, no,' he chuckled patiently, 'this is just a small island. The main cities are quite extraordinary and you'll find the Dulcians are an extremely advanced people, gentle and friendly and very ...'

A tremendous explosion drowned the rest of the Doctor's words. He leaped out of the deckchair, which collapsed in a heap.

'Whatever was that?' exclaimed Zoe, covering her ringing ears.

'It came frae over this way!' cried Jamie, running off along the base of the cliff.

The Doctor and Zoe set off in pursuit. Eventually they came upon the wreckage of a low L-shaped building, half buried in the sand in a kind of horseshoe indentation in the cliff. Shattered concrete slabs and twisted metal framework were scattered everywhere. A gaping hole in one wall held charred window frames and the remains of a heavy door.

'What were you just saying about the gentle, friendly Dulcians, Doctor?' Zoe teased as they surveyed the ruin.

'But that explosion couldna have caused all this ...' Jamie observed.

The Doctor frowned and deep lines formed at the corners of his nose and ran down each side of his mouth. He picked up a fragment of concrete and crumbled it thoughtfully. 'Quite right, Jamie. All this happened many years ago,' he murmured. 'Probably the result of an atomic explosion ...'

Jamie and Zoe exchanged anxious glances as the Doctor cautiously approached the dark hole and ventured inside the ruin. With the recent detonation still throbbing in their ears, they tentatively followed.

'I just don't understand it ...' the Doctor was muttering as he peered around. Against the walls stood large display-cabinets made of a kind of thick perspex material, dusty but completely undamaged. They contained all kinds of sophisticated devices, some of which were obviously very old, while others looked new and unused.

'Looks like some kind of museum,' said Zoe, wandering through the gloom and round the angle into the shorter arm of the building.

'Exactly. A war museum,' agreed the Doctor.

Jamie had lifted a slim rifle-like weapon out of its case and was squinting into its electronic sight. 'But you said the Dulcians were a peaceful lot, Doctor,' he protested, waving the gun carelessly about.

'Oh, these are very ancient weapons,' the Doctor explained. 'They banned these gadgets decades ago.'

At that moment an intense beam of energy shot across the building and, with a crack, punched a hole in the remains of the door.

'Careful Jamie,' the Doctor yelled, lunging forward and

16

snatching the deadly laser from him.

Jamie went pale and giggled nervously as the Doctor replaced the thing gingerly on its stand. Then a fearful shriek made them both spin round.

'Zoe ...!' the Doctor cried, rushing across to the right-angled corner of the building with Jamie at his heels.

Zoe came towards them in the half-light, backing slowly away from a spine-chilling scene at the far end of the room. Four figures were seated around a circular table, their bodies frozen into grotesquely contorted positions. Their clothing was charred and rotten, here and there fused into a glassy lump with their roasted and flayed flesh. The eyeless faces were burned beyond recognition.

Jamie put his hand to his mouth. 'What ... what happened to them?' he gasped, his stomach rising.

Signing to his young companions to stay put, the Doctor slowly approached the nightmarish tableau. Then as he drew near he began to shake with laughter. 'Oh dear me ...' he chuckled, shaking his head. 'Of course ... of course ...' He beckoned them over.

Zoe and Jamie stared at each other in astonishment and then reluctantly crept forward. Just as they reached him, the Doctor gave the nearest figure a sharp nudge. It slumped sideways and its head twisted off and rolled across the table before bouncing onto the floor. They gaped at their smiling friend in horrified disbelief.

'Well, don't you see?' giggled the Doctor. 'They're dummies. Just dummies!'

'But why? What are they here for?' Jamie demanded after a shocked pause, still not convinced.

Without replying, the Doctor thrust his hands deep into his pockets and started shuffling round and round the table muttering quietly to himself.

Zoe was still staring fixedly at the macabre tableau in front of her. 'Doctor, did you check the radiation levels before we left the TARDIS?' she demanded.

The Doctor stopped in his tracks. 'Zoe, that's just what I was trying to remember. I'm sure I did.'

Zoe shuddered slightly. 'This place reminds me of those

17

old atomic test ranges on Earth,' she said nervously.

The Doctor nodded thoughtfully. 'Yes, Zoe, I think you may be right. But why on Dulkis?'

Jamie looked puzzled. 'But you said the Dulcians ...'

'Oh, they certainly outlawed war ...' the Doctor agreed.

Zoe moved back into the other half of the building. 'I think we ought to get back to the TARDIS and check the radiation levels again, Doctor,' she urged him.

'There must be some other explanation ...' the Doctor murmured, shaking his head in perplexity as he and Jamie followed.

There was a fearful gasp from Zoe. Jamie and the Doctor looked up sharply. Three tall figures in dazzling white protective suits with smoked-glass visors were looming among the display cases, their heavily rhythmic breathing hissing and roaring through the respirators. Very slowly the three apparitions raised their large gloved hands and advanced towards them.

2

The Radiation Mystery

Still badly shocked after seeing, first, his three companions cold-bloodedly murdered and, now, his stranded hovercraft blown to smithereens by the alien robots in a gigantic explosion, Kully had been scrambling among the cliffs desperately trying to find out what was happening. Grubby and exhausted, he edged cautiously round a crumbling sandstone bluff towards the strange blue box-like structure he had just discovered. Before he reached it, he suddenly came across what looked like a huge black spider flattened into the sand. Stifling a squeal of alarm, he pulled himself together and knelt to examine the five-pointed star shape, about a metre in diameter, burnt into the ground. Something about the weird symbol sent a spiky sensation crawling up his spine.

All at once, harsh angry voices burst out nearby. Kully scuttled away in panic and hid behind the police box ...

'So you destroyed the ocean craft?' Rago was saying accusingly. 'You continue to allow your destructive instincts to interfere with prime objectives.'

'Censure not accepted,' Toba retorted as the two huge figures reached the black star symbol and stopped. 'The target survey is completed. This is perimeter two. Atomic analysis is also completed.'

'Report,' Rago snapped.

'Atomic activity on this planet located only on this island. Radiation released 17.2 decades ago.'

Navigator Rago nodded approvingly. Then he noticed the TARDIS under the cliff. 'What is that artefact?' he demanded suspiciously.

'A primitive native structure,' Toba answered, his eyes gleaming expectantly. 'Shall I summon a Quark to destroy it?'

'Negative!' Rago rasped contemptuously. 'Such action would waste energy. It does not obstruct our work. We will examine the remaining targets.'

'Command accepted,' Toba gruffly acknowledged. 'Central bore is next.'

As they strode off heavily, Kully crept out from behind the TARDIS and trailed them along the base of the cliff, his heart hammering almost audibly. Eventually they reached another spidery star melted into the sand close to the ruined building. Kully took refuge among some shattered concrete slabs and watched.

'Primitive technology,' Toba sneered as he and Rago entered the ruin and glanced around at the exhibits.

'Every culture develops,' Rago retorted coldly.

Toba picked up the laser gun that Jamie had toyed with earlier. He aimed at the wall and fired. There was a piercing whine and a jagged hole was blown clean through the concrete. Just for a second, a tremor of pleasure seemed to ripple through Toba's massive frame. Then he dropped the weapon uninterestedly. 'All this is obsolete,' he shrugged. 'There is nothing to threaten us here.'

Rago stared at his operative in despair. 'It is unwise to base your assessments on the past,' he rapped. 'Do you not conclude that more advanced weapons must have been developed since these?'

'Affirmative.'

With a viciously slicing fist, Rago thumped a nearby display cabinet which cracked all over without splintering. 'Probationer Toba,' he raged, 'because of your precipitate act of self-gratification in destroying the three inhabitants, it will be necessary to locate other specimens and to investigate and assess them in accordance with our objectives.'

Toba followed his superior outside to examine the target mark.

'This debris must be cleared away from the bore area,' Rago ordered. 'When we have completed perimeter target checks, you will prepare a preliminary assessment and communicate to Fleet Leader.'

The Doctor, Zoe and Jamie stared helplessly at their white-suited captors through the thick glass observation-panel. They were confined in a cramped airlock chamber and surrounded by a hot steamy vapour which was choking them and threatening to boil them alive. Through the glass, the three tall figures – who had removed their protective helmets – peered in at them from time to time, discussing something animatedly and then hurrying over to make adjustments on a large and complex instrument panel.

'Well, they seem ... seem genuinely concerned abut our welfare ...' the Doctor managed to croak in a strangled attempt at reassurance, 'but I fear they're going to kill us with kindness in a minute ...' He broke off to mouth a desperate plea to the silver-haired and bearded figure who at that moment was squinting through the scalding haze at them. But the distinguished person turned back to his two young assistants and the Doctor could only resort to thumping the glass feebly.

'I do hope we are not too late, Kando. How badly were they affected?' the silver-haired man aked the tall fair girl at the instrument panel.

'I cannot tell, Educator Balan,' she replied. 'The radiation level still reads zero.'

Balan turned gravely to the slim young man beside her. 'Teel?'

'Zero confirmed,' Teel announced in a puzzled voice. 'I do not understand it.'

Balan glanced anxiously across at the three figures sagging limply against the observation port, their tongues hanging out and their eyes rolling. 'There must be an instrument malfunction,' he murmured. 'They had no protection at all. The count cannot be zero.'

'We cannot leave them in there much longer!' Kando warned him.

After a moment of agonised indecision, Balan leaned over and touched a switch. The airlock chamber door swung open

21

and the three sweating, gasping victims stumbled out into the clinical and complex laboratory.

'What ... what the divil are ye trying to do, ye Sassenachs ... cook us?' Jamie spluttered. 'Cos I'm no haggis ...'

The Doctor restrained him as best he could and staggered angrily over towards Balan who backed away from him pointing a small Geiger counter at arm's length.

'All totally un...unnecessary,' the Doctor panted, brushing the instrument aside. 'There's not a trace of contamination on any of us.'

Calmly Balan checked the reading. 'Strange, is it not? The whole island has been lethally radioactive for 172 annos,' he said in a cultured voice.

'Well, it isn't now!' Jamie snapped rudely, clutching his head.

'Of course it is,' Kando corrected him politely.

'I suggest that you check,' the Doctor advised Balan firmly.

'We have only just arrived here,' Teel explained. 'The annual environmental audit will be conducted during the next few days.'

The Doctor moved closer to Balan and addressed him with confidential urgency. 'I insist that you order a check immediately. It could be of the utmost importance.'

Balan stared impassively at the dapper stranger for a moment. Then he turned and nodded to Teel. The young Dulcian picked up the Geiger counter and his helmet, and hurried out.

'What is happening here?' Balan suddenly demanded, glancing at Zoe and Jamie. 'I was not aware that any other persons were permitted to work on the Island.'

'Neither was I,' bluffed the Doctor, smiling courteously. 'We were rather hoping that you might be able to enlighten us.'

Zoe stared at the formidable array of equipment around them.

'Why is the Island supposed to be so dangerous?' she asked, wincing from the dull headache her recent ordeal had given her.

Balan frowned in surprise. 'Everyone is aware of the atomic

22

test ...'

'But I thought you had abolished such research here on Dulkis,' the Doctor exclaimed.

Balan shook his head. 'You seem very poorly informed about your own planet.'

'That's because our own planet is ...' Jamie clammed up as the Doctor kicked him sharply in the ankle. But it was too late.

The Doctor looked furious, but simply shrugged. 'As Jamie was about to reveal, we come from a different planet ... indeed from a different time,' he admitted.

Balan seemed completely unmoved. 'Really? Not from Dulkis. I must record that in the bulletin,' he said. Then he smiled indulgently: 'That explains why you exposed yourselves to the dangers on the Island. No Dulcian would be so foolhardy.'

'Then what the divil are *you* doing here?' Jamie demanded roughly, turning to Kando.

She drew herself up with elegant pride. 'We are members of Educator Balan's university research group.'

The Doctor intervened hastily. 'When I visited Dulkis before, it was a civilised and peaceful place,' he remarked gently.

Again Balan looked singularly unimpressed. 'This is not your first visit. I must note that in the bulletin.'

'But what has happened here?' the Doctor inquired impatiently. 'Why are you conducting atomic tests?'

Balan smiled and turned to Kando. 'The Seventh Council ...' he prompted her.

There was a brief silence while Kando muttered parrot-fashion under her breath about fifth and sixth councils and the Doctor shuffled restlessly from foot to foot, nodding encouragement.

'... the Seventh Council under Director Manus initiated research into atomic energy, using this Island as a test site for the device, the results of which can be seen today ...' Kando recited tonelessly. 'Thereafter all such projects were prohibited. The Island is preserved as a museum and as a warning to future generations.'

'She's certainly done her homework!' Zoe remarked, with a

sarcastic grimace at Jamie.

Oblivious, Balan beamed at his pupil approvingly. Meanwhile the Doctor had wandered off around the laboratory, shoulders hunched, hands deep in pockets.

'Atomic weapons or no atomic weapons ... that was quite a bang we heard,' he murmured. Then he stopped in his tracks, face to face with Balan. 'So what has happened to all that radiation?' he demanded. 'I do hope you don't suspect that its disappearance has got anything to do with us!'

As soon as Rago and Toba were out of sight, Kully emerged from his cramped niche among the debris and scurried over to look at the sticky black markings in the sand, not far from the wall of the museum. Then he noticed several sets of regular rectangular tracks and shuddered at the memory of the ruthless robots he had seen earlier.

A sudden movement behind him made him jerk round with a gasp. A tall faceless white figure was clambering over the wreckage towards the ruin. Springing up, Kully started to run as fast as his short plump legs would carry him, away towards the dunes.

'Kully ... Kully!' rasped an echoing metallic voice. 'What are you doing here?'

Kully stopped but dare not turn round. 'Who ...who is that?' he shouted, as heavy footfalls thumped up behind him.

'It is Teel. I am with the survey group.'

Kully spun round, almost crying with relief as the suited figure ran up to him. He peered into the dark visor, but saw only his own terrified bulbous face reflecting back at him.

'Surely you remember me?' rasped the voice through the helmet speaker.

'Survey group!' Kully gasped, gripping Teel's arm. 'Take me there. Quickly, take me there.'

'But what are you doing out here like that?' the voice demanded in astonishment.

Kully tugged frantically at the thick suit-sleeve. 'Don't argue, just take me there,' he pleaded.

As Teel led the way swiftly back to the survey module, Kully trotted along beside him endlessly jabbering about aliens and robots and giant wooden boxes, until Teel began to fear that either the frenzied Dulcian had lost his sanity or he was suffering from some kind of radiation sickness.

Meanwhile, back in the cool humming chamber of the survey module the Doctor was pacing agitatedly. 'But why should you think that we are responsible?' he objected.

Balan shrugged. 'It is possible that your craft ... your TARDIS has attracted the radiation somehow and absorbed it,' he speculated blandly.

'Nonsense. Quite out of the question,' the Doctor protested vehemently, running a critical eye over the module's instruments.

Zoe and Jamie were deep in conversation with Kando.

'Do spacecraft often visit Dulkis?' Zoe wondered.

'I believe that yours is the first,' Kando replied.

Jamie looked baffled. 'Well, ye dinna seem very surprised ta see us.'

Kando frowned at the strange young man's curious speech. 'We Dulcians are taught to accept fact,' she explained. 'You are here – that is fact. That you come from another planet I must accept as fact, since I have no evidence to prove otherwise.'

Jamie stared mischievously at her, trying to think up some way to shock the serene young Dulcian.

Suddenly the airlock hissed open and Teel entered, removing his helmet. 'Not a trace of local radiation,' he announced. 'But look what I did find!' he added, ushering forward a dusty, rumpled figure covered in scratches.

'Kully!' Balan exclaimed with a start. 'How do you come to be ...?'

'Never mind that now,' Kully cried, ignoring the Doctor and his two companions and seizing the Educator by the arm. 'We must get back to the Capitol immediately.'

'Impossible,' Balan retorted. 'We have not even begun our survey for the annual audit.'

Kully stared at him wild-eyed. 'You'll all be wiped out here!' he cried.

Teel laughed uncomfortably. 'He claims to have seen aliens

and killer robots and spacecraft,' he explained.

Balan turned to the Doctor. 'You did not mention that you had brought robots.'

Before the Doctor could reply, Kully babbled on recklessly. 'Listen, Balan, I brought three citizens to the Island in my hovercraft. The robots killed them and destroyed the ship.'

Balan started to smile and then broke into a deep resonant laughter as he turned to the Doctor, Jamie and Zoe. 'Three citizens ... I see. Really Kully, you and your three friends here should at least have agreed on the same story.'

The Doctor looked flustered. 'I have never seen this person before in my life,' he protested, gesturing at Kully.

Balan turned gravely to the dishevelled Dulcian. 'Kully, you may be the son of our distinguished Director, but you had no right to bring these people here without authorisation,' he said coldly.

Kully stared in turn at the three strangers. 'These aren't my clients. I've never seen them before,' he retorted. Then he grabbed Balan's arm again. 'Listen, you old fool, there's no time to lose. Call up my father in the Capitol ... at least he's not as senile as you are.'

Before the outraged Educator could find words to reply, the Doctor hurriedly intervened. 'You say that you saw a spacecraft?' he asked Kully.

'I've already told you!' Kully yelled in exasperation. 'And robots ... *horrible* things.'

The Doctor looked anxious. 'This spacecraft, it wasn't sort of square like a tall wooden box ...?'

Kully wrinkled his snub nose impatiently. 'No, no, no ... that's not the spacecraft. It's circular and flattish and silvery.'

Balan snorted scornfully.

'The blue box is somewhere else. By the black star,' Kully chattered excitedly. 'The aliens were there. They were talking about destroying it,' he shuddered.

'The TARDIS!' Zoe and Jamie chorused.

The Doctor turned urgently to his young friends. 'We'd better go at once,' he cried.

Balan raised a restraining hand. 'My dear sir, you will be wasting your time,' he warned.

26

'My dear sir, time cannot be ...' the Doctor stopped himself, turned and ran to the airlock. 'Come on, you two,' he shouted.

Jamie hurried over, but Zoe held back. 'I think I'd rather stay here, Doctor,' she murmured.

The Doctor nodded. 'We won't be long,' he waved, opening the hatch. Before Zoe could object, they were gone.

Filled with foreboding, Zoe wandered aimlessly round the module trying to ignore the fierce argument which had flared up between Kully and Balan, while Teel and Kando occupied themselves with an elaborate communications unit along the far wall.

'I am sorry, Kully, but I can take no action until I have contacted the Director,' Balan concluded adamantly.

Kully grimaced. 'We all know what the old man will say. 'Do nothing.'

Balan struggled to remain calm. 'Better to do nothing than to cause unnecessary panic in the community.'

'Vegetables. Just vegetables the lot of you!' Kully snapped.

'Show some respect!' Balan thundered. 'If not for me then at least for your father.' He swept over to the communications unit.

Teel indicated the useless strobing and flashing on the screen. 'There is powerful interference, Balan,' he reported apologetically. 'It is most unusual.'

'That'll be the robots ...' Kully muttered exhaustedly.

Zoe went over to the disconsolate little figure. 'You don't seem to be having much success convincing them,' she said sympathetically.

Kully pulled a grotesque face. 'Fossils. They don't really live, they just exist,' he despaired. 'At least your Doctor friend showed some interest.'

'He has a very enquiring mind, luckily,' Zoe said with a smile.

Kully grinned bleakly. 'Then he'll be as unpopular as I am.'

'Whatever do you mean?'

'Oh, I just don't fit the Dulcian mould,' Kully explained wryly. 'Their shapely civilised society. Everybody thinking and living alike.'

Balan suddenly clapped his hands. 'Quiet. We have made contact with Director Senex,' he announced.

They looked at the screen. A clear image was just beginning to form.

'Here we go,' Kully groaned. 'Words of wisdom from on high ...'

'Well, they've no harmed the TARDIS anyway,' reported Jamie after he had briefly inspected the dilapidated structure.

The Doctor was on his hands and knees near by, his nose almost touching the sand as he examined the tacky black markings scorched in the ground. 'Look at this, Jamie,' he muttered, 'most interesting.'

Jamie glanced at the five-pointed star. Then he noticed the sets of tracks. 'Hey, Doctor, what are these?' he cried excitedly.

Scrambling to his feet, the Doctor hurried over. Two pairs of rectangular prints led away among the dunes along the foot of the cliffs. The Doctor pondered a moment. 'Now who or what leaves footprints like these?' he murmured.

'Footprints ...' Jamie whispered, grinning uneasily as he looked warily around at the desolate landscape.

The Doctor sniffed the air expectantly. 'Come along, Jamie, let's follow them ... or it ... shall we?' He darted off nimbly over the brittle, ochre-coloured sandhills.

Reluctantly Jamie caught up and they followed the strange oblong tracks for about two kilometres. Eventually, climbing a short slope, they found themselves staring at the huge silver saucer mounted on its broad central column. Instinctively Jamie threw himself face-down in the sand, but the Doctor remained standing, shielding his eyes from the glare and gazing intently at the opening at the bottom of the shaft.

Slowly Jamie got to his feet. 'I reckon we ought to get back to Zoe now, Doctor,' he suggested nervously. 'She'll be worried.'

But the Doctor had already begun to creep forward towards the awesome machine gleaming menacingly against the cliff.

'You're not thinking what I think you're thinking ... are you Doctor?' Jamie whispered, clutching his sleeve.

'Most definitely,' the Doctor grinned, still staring in fascination at the open hatchway.

'Och no ...' Jamie pleaded, frowning at the hundreds of track marks criss-crossing the hollow in front of the ominously looming saucer. 'Can ye no keep oot a trouble just for once?'

They finally reached the curved hatchway and the Doctor stopped to admire the underside of the gigantic craft spread out above them.

'How absolutely splendid,' he murmured almost reverently. 'Yes, obviously an interstellar craft of quite sophisticated design, no doubt powered by some kind of ...' The Doctor paused as his arm was gripped painfully. 'Don't do that Jamie ...' he protested.

Jamie's gasp of horror made the Doctor jerk round. His jaw dropped open and his eyes widened in surprise and dismay. 'Oh dear. Oh Jamie. Oh my goodness,' he muttered, making Jamie wince as he gripped his arm in turn.

Two Quarks were standing a few metres away, cutting off their escape. The Doctor and Jamie stared at the squat, buzzing robots for a moment and then turned back in futile desperation towards the hatchway. The opening was filled by Toba's huge gaunt figure. His massive gloves creaked as he opened his hands in a gesture of ironic welcome on the threshold of the spacecraft.

'Do not move. Do not move!' bleated the Quarks, in a kind of crazed falsetto.

The Doctor and Jamie continued to stare into Toba's expressionless green eyes while behind them the Quarks chattered away, extending their probes and charging their weapon systems. An unearthly smile carved deep fissures in Toba's mask-like face and a livid pink tongue darted out momentarily to moisten his thin lifeless lips. Then his red-rimmed eyes lit up with a hypnotic gleam which seemed to be fired by hate and greed and lust and madness, all together.

'Quarks!' he suddenly rasped, his gloves creaking in eager anticipation. 'Prepare!'

3

The Assessment

Prodded viciously by the buzzing Quarks, the Doctor and Jamie soon found themselves entering the vast circular control centre at the heart of the alien ship. The chamber was filled with a ghostly glow from the fluorescent graphics and systems displays covering the walls. In the middle , on a raised circular dais, stood the main control column consisting of a mosaic of flickering crystal buttons set into a sphere which was mounted on a slim metal stalk, like some giant tropical bloom. Otherwise the chamber was streamlined and bare.

'Approach!' Rago ordered.

The Quarks propelled their captives across to the dais where Rago loomed over them, his emerald eyes glittering in the soft rainbow luminosity. Toba stood behind them breathing heavily.

'Who are you?' Jamie croaked, his throat dry with fear.

The towering figure glowered down at them. 'We are Dominators,' he announced, his voice echoing around the dome above.

'That's quite evident,' the Doctor muttered wryly.

Toba emitted a dangerous hiss. Jamie shivered despite himself.

'Assess the specimens,' Rago ordered tersely.

'Stand against the panel!' Toba rapped, whirling the prisoners round bodily and thrusting them towards a flat section of wall.

'I will not!' Jamie exploded, tearing himself free.

'Jamie ...' warned the Doctor, shuffling obediently to the panel.

'The Dominators are obeyed!' Toba roared.

Jamie stood his ground. 'Not by *me*,' he retorted.

'Quark!'

One of the robots whirred into action, its long crystal antennae glowing reddish white. There was a rapid throbbing sound and the young Scot was flung against the panel. He hung there dazed and limp for a moment. Then he feebly started to struggle.

'Help me ... help me, Doctor ...' he pleaded.

As soon as the Doctor responded, the staccato throbbing burst out again and he too was forced against the panel.

Rago smiled contemptuously. 'It is useless to resist. My Quark has bonded your bodies to the panel by means of molecular adhesion,' he boomed.

Toba touched some switches and Jamie's section of panelling immediately slid outward and then swung through 90 degrees to form a horizontal pallet.

'What are ye doing to me?' Jamie gasped, transfixed with terror as a transparent globular apparatus swung out and hung suspended over his body.

'Aliens are occasionally of use to us,' Rago explained coldly. 'We shall assess your physiological status. Quark!'

One of the robots tramped rapidly over and connected its two probes into sockets at the foot of Jamie's pallet.

Frantically Jamie tried to twist himself free, his eyes staring wildly and his white face glistening with sweat. 'Doctor ... can ye no do anything?' he panted.

'Activate!' Rago snapped, stepping down from the dais.

The Quark emitted a crazed giggling noise and the globular device above Jamie started to glow. Helplessly the Doctor watched as Rago took a kind of visor resembling an ophthalmoscope from Toba and slipped it over his head. Jamie was bathed in an eerie bluish aura as the Dominator bent over to examine him.

'Brittle skeletal structure ... calcium phosphate ... reasonable degree of flexibility and muscular strength ...' Rago murmured. 'Single heart ... superfluous organ present right side ...'

Jamie shuddered as Rago's eye, magnified to monstrous

proportions by the visor, bored relentlessly into his own.

'Simple brain circuitry ...' Rago continued tonelessly, 'signs of recent rapid learning ... little intellectual development.' At last Rago straightened up and took off the visor. 'Assessment: possible marginal utility for elementary labour tasks,' he concluded.

'Shall I prepare the second specimen for scrutiny?' Toba asked eagerly.

Rago considered the Doctor for a moment. 'Negative. They will be identical. Conserve power,' he decided.

The Quark disconnected its probes, the apparatus withdrew and the panel tilted back to the vertical. Jamie hung beside the Doctor pale and drained, his stomach cramped with nausea from the effects of the body scanner.

Toba turned expectantly to his superior. 'Since these specimens are of inferior quality we can destroy them,' he proposed.

'Negative. They will perform in a labour force.'

'We have the Quarks for such functions,' Toba objected.

'I repeat, Toba: the Quarks' power must be conserved.' Rago turned abruptly away and stood staring into the Doctor's mild brown eyes. The Doctor stared unflinchingly back, the faintest of smiles flickering around his mouth.

'Set up a Neuro-Initiative Test on this specimen,' Rago suddenly ordered, pointing at the Doctor.

The Doctor's smile vanished at once and he swallowed apprehensively. 'Oh dear me,' he muttered miserably, 'not a NIT.'

In the survey module, Teel struggled to maintain visual contact with the Capitol, but the image of Director Senex oscillated fitfully and finally broke up into a storm of static. However, the Director's imperturbable voice continued to filter faintly through:

'Your image is fading, Educator Balan ... I regret that it is not possible to evaluate your ...'

'Oh never mind the picture, Father,' Kully butted in irritably, 'just tell us what you're going to do.'

The audio circuit hissed and squealed, and Senex became

33

only just distinguishable. 'I cannot understand you, Balan ... Send Kully and the strangers to the Capitol immediately ... I will question them here ...'

Kully shouldered his way between Balan and Teel: 'Father, listen to me ...' he shouted into the receiver, 'Father, there's no time ...'

Teel shook his head. 'I am sorry, Kully, but they have terminated reception.'

Kully thumped himself on the forehead. 'Typical Dulcian behaviour,' he exclaimed in despair. 'Something unusual happens, something you don't understand, and you just switch off. Up here.'

Kando glanced round from the transporter unit. 'The capsule is priming now, Balan,' she reported.

Kully wandered gloomily over to Zoe, who had been trying not to get in the way. 'Ever travelled in a capsule before?' he enquired.

'No. How do they work?'

Kully shrugged. 'No idea. Hate the things myself.' He turned suddenly to Balan. 'You see? The girl asked a question, therefore she can't possibly be a Dulcian. She must have an enquiring mind,' he said with a facetious grin.

Balan was unimpressed. 'Your father will decide,' he replied humourlessly. Then he turned courteously to Zoe. 'As soon as your two friends return they will follow in the second capsule,' he explained.

Zoe looked apprehensive. 'Wouldn't it be simpler to wait and all go together?' she suggested with a nervous little laugh.

'Travel capsules carry only two persons,' Kando informed her. 'Capsule one is primed, Balan.'

Balan squeezed Zoe's arm encouragingly. 'There is nothing to fear,' he told her gently.

Zoe giggled. 'Oh I'm not afraid. I'm looking forward to it,' she lied.

'Well, *I'm* not,' Kully murmured grumpily, leading the way over to a section of transparent tube set into the wall. Inside the tube was a long bullet-shaped vehicle, with a sliding canopy which opened to reveal two small seats, set one in front of the other. Zoe noted the absence of visible controls, apart from a digital display and a few touch-buttons in the front panel.

'Come on, then, let's try to stir up a bit of action in the Capitol,' Kully said, reluctantly squeezing his chubby frame into the cramped front seat.

After a momentary hesitation, Zoe climbed in behind him.

Balan leaned in and touched a sequence of buttons. 'I will programme for the Capitol if you will allow me,' he said firmly.

'Afraid I might get lost?' Kully chuckled, watching Balan operate the route lock button.

With a swish the transparent canopy and the hatch in the launch tube both slid shut.

'I hope you know how to fly this contraption,' Kully joked, as the capsule suddenly accelerated away along the tube and then abruptly tilted at a steep angle upwards.

Seconds later they were climbing at tremendous speed through dense white clouds, and the capsule was vibrating and gyrating sickeningly. Pale and silent, Zoe gritted her teeth and clung to her seat, convinced that she had left her stomach far behind her.

'Selectors are a bit worn,' Kully remarked casually over his shoulder, 'but you just sit back and relax. It'll be all right as soon as we level off.'

After a while the capsule stopped vibrating and gradually levelled off. 'Does this thing land automatically as well?' Zoe enquired in a faint voice.

'Usually,' Kully chuckled. 'In the old days everything had to be done manually, of course. Must have led to a great feeling of pride and achievement.'

'And an awful lot of accidents!' Zoe added ruefully.

'Yes, but at least people exercised their individual skills and judgement. Now all that's gone.'

Zoe gripped her seat even more firmly. 'You ... you mean you can't control this thing *at all*?'

Kully shrugged. 'There are some switches here for emergencies ... but I can't remember how to use them.'

The capsule suddenly dived sharply and then came level again.

'Very comforting!' Zoe muttered, clutching her tummy.

'Don't worry,' Kully cried gaily. 'Nothing will go wrong. Not on Dulkis. Father wouldn't allow it.'

'Why don't you get on with your father?' Zoe asked.

'Oh, he's all right, I suppose,' Kully admitted. 'He's just gone a little too far. He got rid of aggression and all that, but now curiosity's gone as well. There's no desire for adventure ...'

Kully's words were swallowed up by a piercing whine as the capsule pitched abruptly into a steep nosedive. Zoe could not help screaming as it accelerated faster and faster towards the vertical and the clouds merged into a dizzy blur outside the canopy ...

The Doctor and Jamie were rapidly growing weaker and weaker from the effects of the molecular adhesion pinning them firmly to the wall of the control centre. Helplessly they watched Rago and Toba setting up an elaborate testing apparatus on the central dais.

'For optimum slave personnel we shall require strength and obedience, but only sufficient intelligence to make them efficient and not dangerous ...' Rago was saying.

Jamie grimaced. 'So they want to know how clever we are,' he whispered feebly out of the corner of his mouth.

'Or how stupid we are ...' the Doctor muttered hoarsely. 'That might be more to our advantage, Jamie.' He squinted at the device through half-closed eyes. It resembled a game board perforated with differently shaped holes and with a pair of earphones wired to a network of circuitry beneath it. Along one edge of the board was fitted a vertical plate containing two fist-sized apertures side by side. Along the opposite edge ran a tray filled with an assortment of small solid shapes rather like model building-blocks.

'You have to fit the shapes into the correct holes,' the Doctor explained under his breath.

'But a wee bairn could do that,' Jamie croaked, 'it's simple.'

The Doctor nodded. 'That's what worries me, Jamie. It's too simple.'

Jamie's dulled eyes suddenly brightened. 'Doctor ... you

nodded,' he gasped. 'You moved.'

'Dear me, Jamie, so I did,' the Doctor muttered cautiously. He twitched his finger, clenched his hand, raised his arm and finally eased his body away from the wall. 'I'm free!' he breathed. 'How about you?'

Scarcely daring to try, Jamie eventually prised himself a few centimetres away from the panel. 'Aye, me too.'

The Doctor glanced covertly across the huge chamber towards the elevator system which had brought them up from ground level earlier. The Dominators were engrossed in their apparatus. A reckless idea flashed into the Doctor's mind ...

But at the same instant, one of the Quarks' antennae sparked and the robot marched menacingly towards the prisoners. 'Adhesion expired. Are the specimens to be refused?' it bleated shrilly.

'Negative!' Rago snapped, turning sharply. 'Commence the test.'

Prodded by the Quark, the Doctor shuffled wearily across to the dais. 'What are you going to do to us?' he asked submissively.

Toba clamped the earphones to the Doctor's temples and thrust the Doctor's hands through the circular openings in the vertical plate. 'Quark!' Toba ordered.

The nearest robot connected its probes into the circuits at the base of the board and its antennae glowed blood-red. The Doctor immediately contorted in agony, struggling to free his hands so that he could tear the screaming phones from his ears, but his hands were paralysed. After a few seconds the Quark's antennae stopped glowing and the Doctor sagged limply to his knees.

Toba's face was a waxen mask of cruel enjoyment. 'The goad will be repeated regularly until the puzzle is reassembled,' he rasped malevolently. 'Begin!'

Powerless to intervene, Jamie could only look on as the Doctor fumbled clumsily with the perspex shapes, trying to force them into completely unsuitable holes in the board.

'Come on, Doctor, the square hole ... no, the *square* hole,' Jamie cried as the Quark's antennae glowed and the Doctor dropped the shapes and twisted pitifully.

The Quark switched off the goad and the Doctor struggled to pick up the shapes in his horribly clenched hands again.

'Och ye canna be sae daft ... the *triangle* ...' Jamie pleaded. 'Whatever's the matter wi' ye?'

But the Doctor kept fumbling and dropping the pieces. A third time the goad was switched on and the Doctor sprang back, arched like a bow, with his swollen tongue trapped between gnashing teeth and his eyes crossing and bulging horribly in his lolling head. Frozen into silence, Jamie gaped in futile desperation at his tortured friend.

'Quark, terminate!' Rago ordered.

Toba wrenched the earphones from the Doctor's head, dragged his gnarled hands through the plate and shook him back to consciousness. Meanwhile Rago was staring intently at the specimen, almost as if he suspected that all was not as it seemed.

Boiling with rage, Jamie hurried over and supported the Doctor while he found his feet again. 'Are you all right, Doctor?' he murmured, peering anxiously into the flushed, contorted face.

'Yes, yes, I'm in the pink, Jamie. Just a little dazed though.'

'What are you up to? That puzzle was easy,' Jamie whispered.

The Doctor gave a sly wink. 'A stupid enemy is far less of a threat than an intelligent one,' he whispered, grinning mischievously. 'Just act stupid, Jamie. Can you manage that?'

'Aye, it's easy ...' Jamie caught the Doctor's eye and realised he was being sent up. 'Och you're in the pink all right,' he mumbled shamefacedly.

They fell silent as they became aware of Rago's unwavering gaze on them. Nudging Jamie to follow suit, the Doctor meekly shuffled to the edge of the dais and sat with his legs dangling and a vacant expression on his face.

Suddenly Toba rapped out an order and the Quarks marched forward and connected their probes into the edge of the circular platform. 'Power,' Toba snapped. The two sets of antennae sparked in unison.

Rago watched the Doctor carefully as he looked around, nodding and grinning and patting Jamie's knee reassuringly.

'Now stand up!' Toba boomed.

The Doctor obediently lowered his feet to the deck and immediately jumped back up onto the dais as a vivid blue flash exploded under his shoes.

'Stand up!' Toba repeated in an almost maniacal tone.

Gingerly Jamie edged forward and again there was a vicious crack as his sturdy hobnailed boots touched the deck, causing him to jerk his legs into the air as he rolled on his back on the dais.

'Get down!' Toba shrieked.

'Let's try over there,' the Doctor suggested in a ponderous voice, as if he were solving some fantastically complex problem.

'You are surrounded,' Toba snarled contemptuously.

The Doctor and Jamie stared at each other and then shook their heads, lifting their feet and pointing hopelessly at their smoking boots like a pair of vaudeville clowns.

'These specimens are utterly useless,' Toba hissed, turning to Rago. 'That is my assessment.'

The Navigator's waxen nostrils flared and the red rims of his eyes brightened. 'Their behaviour is at variance with information we already possess,' he said ominously. 'Those weapons we examined in the ruin could not have been devised by such apparent simpletons as these.' Rago turned to a Quark. 'Report to Fleet Leader. Fleet Refuel Project proceeds to plan. However, status of indigenous species is not yet determined.'

The Quark marched across to a communications panel and plugged itself in.

Rago surveyed his two prisoners cowering on the dais. 'Follow,' he ordered, turning abruptly towards the elevator.

'But we can't get off without ... without ...' the Doctor's plea trailed pathetically into silence.

'Jump!' Rago retorted.

Warily the two captives got to their feet and stood gazing down at the deck as though it were a yawning chasm below them. Then the Doctor clasped Jamie by the hand, shut his eyes and they both jumped safely off the dais.

'A simple electrical circuit, completed by your bodies when

you attempted to stand up,' Rago explained to the amazed pair. 'Evidently you know nothing of electricity.'

The Doctor frowned. 'Electricity? What is that?'

The Navigator strode over to the Doctor. 'Are you such a fool? You have intelligent eyes,' he rasped.

For a moment Jamie thought the Doctor was going to abandon his pretence, but he simply stared up at the huge Dominator with wide, innocent eyes. There was a spine-chilling pause.

'One final test ...' Rago announced, striding over to the elevator. 'Bring them ...'

4

Heads in the Sand

On the Dulcian mainland the Capitol basked in the warm
clear light from Dulkis's modest yellow sun, its thousands of
silver terraces gleaming and its endless windows reflecting
the golden sky. Long cool galleries filled with lush green
vegetation stretched in all directions and every few metres
small fountains cast fine shimmering sprays of purified water
in myriad colours. The atmosphere was relaxed and hushed.
Everywhere, the tall inhabitants moved about calmly in their
loose light togas, conversing in quiet unhurried voices.

In the Council Chamber, high in the domed summit of the
vast city, half a dozen elderly Dulcians were lounging in
padded reclining chairs, each fitted with its own small vision
screen and its individual refreshment rack laden with exotic
fruits and colourful iced drinks. The Councillors had high
foreheads and swept-back hair and the skin of their long
sensitive faces was lined but blooming. Around them, subtle
combinations of pastel colours endlessly mingled on the
curved opalescent walls and softly soothing sounds floated
continuously through the scented air.

Deputy Director Bovem arranged his flowing white robe
and settled back into the cushions. 'Very well. It is agreed,
subject naturally to the approval of Director Senex, that the
area in question be developed for exclusively leisure and
holiday activity,' he announced in a musical voice.

'But have the Councillors given all due consideration to the
submissions of the Industrial Committee?' asked a florid
member, sipping from a tall slim glass.

Bovem raised an elegant hand. 'Really Councillors, I do
not wish to hurry you, but we have been debating this matter

for several lunars and I feel sure ...'

He was interrupted by a series of bell-like tones and then a quiet voice filled the Chamber: 'Citizen Kully has arrived accompanied by a stranger. They wait in the Antechamber.'

Bovem touched a button in the arm of his couch. 'Let them remain there until Director Senex has been informed,' he instructed.

Without warning, a section of the wall dissolved and Kully came bursting in followed by Zoe, both of them out of breath. The wall automatically re-formed itself behind them.

Kully stomped straight over to Bovem, scattering sand and wiping his shining face with the hem of his skirt. 'If you think we're going to kick our heels while you gossip away for hours on end you're mistaken,' he shouted.

Bovem rose to his feet with strained dignity. 'Inform the Director that his son is here,' he ordered. Then he gathered his robe in a classically authoritative pose. 'This is an outrageous abuse of the Council's dignity.' he protested.

'Who cares about that?' Kully retorted. 'I've got vitally important news.'

The Deputy Director permitted himself a faintly ironic smile. 'What fairy tale have you concocted this time?' he demanded. 'And who is this young lady?'

Kully ushered Zoe forward. She looked pale and shaken after the hair-raising flight in the capsule.

'This is Zoe. Her friends will be arriving soon. I met them all on the Island.'

Balan frowned. 'Doubtless none of you possessed the necessary permits.'

'Don't be stupid!' Kully shouted exasperatedly. 'How could they have permits? They come from another planet.'

There was a startled pause. Then a murmur of disbelief rippled round the Chamber.

A gaunt, hook-nosed Councillor waved a languid arm. 'Nonsense. The existence of extra-Dulcian life has been conclusively disproved by the Scientific Committee.'

A younger Councillor shook his head. 'Not conclusively. It is possible that life in some form does exist elswhere,' he argued.

42

Kully grabbed an orange fruit from the nearest rack. 'Listen, there's no time for the usual three-lunar debate,' he snapped, biting hungrily and sending a stream of juice in all directions. 'Can't you understand what's happened? A spacecraft has landed on the Island with aliens and robots, and they've killed Wahed, Tolata and Etnin!'

The atmosphere in the Council Chamber abruptly changed. Bovem walked slowly up to Zoe and stared searchingly into her face. 'Aliens?' he murmured gravely. 'Murder?'

Zoe squirmed uncomfortably and said nothing.

'Kully!' called a thin, cultured voice. At once everyone looked round in surprise. A very tall figure with fine silver hair and a pointed beard was standing by the wall. His robe was edged with a narrow green band.

'Director Senex ... we were not aware ... ' Bovem faltered.

The Director raised his pale hand. 'Quite.' He gazed impassively at Zoe for a moment with keen blue eyes. Then he moved elegantly across to his chair. 'I shall speak with Kully and the stranger alone,' he announced.

The Councillors immediately rose and Bovem led them out in respectful silence. Zoe watched in uneasy bewilderment as Senex slowly took his seat. His face seemed filled with peace, wisdom and intelligence.

'Do you enjoy being treated as a clown, Kully?' he enquired at last.

Kully stared sulkily at his father and said nothing.

Senex turned to Zoe. 'What were you doing on the Island?' he said gently, glancing at her unfamiliar clothing.

Zoe shrugged. 'Nothing really. Just looking around.'

Senex glared at his son. 'How could you expose foolish innocent citizens to such danger?' he demanded severely.

'But I didn't take Zoe ...' Kully started to protest.

Senex waved his hand impatiently. 'We know all about your irresponsible escapades.'

Kully looked genuinely shocked. 'You knew? Then why didn't you prosecute me?'

Senex frowned. 'Prosecution would simply have flattered your reckless ego and it would have reflected badly upon myself.'

Kully clutched his head in his podgy hands: 'Why can't I be treated as an individual instead of always as "the son of our distinguished Director"?' he groaned despairingly.

The Director ignored this and turned back to Zoe. 'Please tell me exactly what happened,' he requested courteously.

Zoe took a deep breath. 'Well, your ... your worship ... the Doctor and Jamie and I had just landed on the Island in the TARDIS ...'

'The TARDIS?'

'Oh, a Time And Relative Dimensions In Space machine,' Zoe explained.

'Transcends Time and Space Field Parameters ...' added Kully helpfully.

Senex rose angrily to his feet. 'This game has gone quite far enough, Kully,' he warned.

'Oh, but it's true,' Zoe insisted, 'ask the Doctor and Jamie. They'll be arriving soon.'

Senex's noble face clouded ominously. 'What do you hope to achieve by this elaborate play-acting, Kully?' he demanded in an outraged undertone.

Kully could stand it no longer. He seized the loose folds of his father's robe and almost shook him off his feet. 'I told you the truth on the vision link,' he shouted. 'A spacecraft has landed. Three people have been killed. Radioactivity has disappeared and there are robots destroying everything in sight. Now please *do* something before it's too late.'

The Director was virtually trapped face to face with his raging son. 'And no doubt Zoe will confirm all this?' he murmured.

Zoe glanced uncertainly at Kully. 'Well ... I haven't actually *seen* the spacecraft and the robots ...' she mumbled apprehensively, 'but Jamie and the Doctor ...'

With unexpected force, Senex freed himself from Kully's tenacious grasp. 'So. We have only *your* word Kully,' he breathed. 'And bitter experience has taught us all just how reliable *that* is.'

Inside the ruined museum the tension was becoming

44

unbearable as Jamie and the Doctor stood facing one another a few metres apart, each guarded by a Quark with its probes extended and primed. Rago had handed the Doctor the laser gun from the showcase.

'What is it?' the Dominator demanded.

The Doctor peered at the weapon short-sightedly. 'It's a sort of a gun ...'

'Explain its function.'

The Doctor hesitated. 'Well, I ... it kills people ...'

'Fire it!' Rago commanded.

Jamie's heart leapt into his throat as the Doctor pointed the laser vaguely in his direction while pretending to work out its mechanism, but he gritted his teeth and kept quiet. For a few awful seconds the incessant chattering of the Quarks' circuits was the only sound.

Then Rago snatched the weapon and handed it to Jamie. 'You fire it!' he rapped.

Jamie frowned. 'Ah dinna ken how ta werk it,' he mumbled, pointing the barrel at Toba.

There was a violent bleating and flashing from the two robots and Jamie immediately swung the laser towards the Doctor.

'Obey!' Toba bellowed.

Suddenly the weapon emitted a shrill whirring and the Doctor ducked out of range with a genuine gasp of fright. Jamie continued to fumble and the gun repeated the whirring several times but did not discharge.

The Doctor was trembling and sweating but he pulled himself together and managed to grin simple-mindedly at the Dominators. 'We don't really understand such devices on Dulkis,' he blustered. 'You see, we haven't used them for decades ...'

Rago took the laser from Jamie and aimed it point-blank at the Doctor's head. 'So you do not understand this weapon?' he said quietly.

The Doctor shook his head, licking his dry lips. All at once the laser whirred and then fired. The Doctor had no time to even flinch. Jamie screamed in horror and covered his face.

'Neutral mode,' Rago explained, smiling cruelly at the

Doctor's sweat-soaked face, 'for testing only.'

Jamie was almost crying with relief and for a while the Doctor was unable to speak.

'Ah yes, the Clever Ones,' he eventually muttered. 'They invented the weapons, but they stopped us using them ...'

Rago's interest was aroused. 'Clever Ones? Then there are two distinct species on this planet?' he suggested.

The Doctor nodded resentfully. 'Not many Clever Ones left now. We don't like them. They tell us what to do.'

Tossing the gun aside, Rago grunted with satisfaction. 'There appears to be no danger from these primitives and the others are pacifists,' he brusquely informed Toba.

The Probationer raised his huge grasping gloves. 'These primitives are useless to us. They should be destroyed.'

Rago turned on him. 'Negative. They can perform menial tasks for us in due course.' The Navigator swung round to the cowering and inanely grinning Doctor. 'Keep away from us and from the Quarks until you are required,' he commanded. Then he strode out followed by Toba and the two robots.

When they had gone, Jamie and the Doctor hugged each other in sheer relief.

'Well done, Jamie,' cried the Doctor, dabbing at his face with a large spotted handkerchief, 'but perhaps you were just a trifle too convincing when they ordered you to shoot me!'

'Bloodthirsty lot,' Jamie said with a shudder. 'But what are they after, Doctor?'

'Judging by that message they sent to their Fleet Leader, I'd guess it's fuel of some kind.'

'But why do they want slaves? They've got those Quark beasties.'

The Doctor folded his handkerchief thoughtfully into smaller and smaller squares. 'I wish I knew, Jamie ...' he muttered. 'One thing is obvious: the Dulcians are in great danger.' He listened for a moment, then motioned Jamie to follow. 'They've gone. Come on, we must get back to that survey module.'

In the module, Balan and Kando were watching Teel complete a complex graph on a computer screen, their faces registering increasing concern and incomprehension.

Eventually Teel turned to them. 'It is not logical, but that is the statistical result. There has been a steady decrease in the radiation levels for the past 172 annos … until now.'

They stared at the display. 'Now it has suddenly vanished,' Kando murmured. 'It is not possible.'

Balan shrugged unhappily. 'It has happened, therefore it is a fact,' he informed the two young students. 'We have discovered that the radiation effects from an atomic detonation endure for 172 annos.'

Teel's fine, intelligent features puckered with doubt. 'But what is the explanation?' he demanded.

Educator Balan raised his hands, palms upwards, in a typical Dulcian gesture of resignation. 'No doubt our experts will explain,' he replied complacently. 'It is fruitless for us to seek reasons to prove facts. Facts are truth.'

Teel's jaw jutted defiantly. 'I submit that the survey unit must investigate this phenomenon,' he insisted, springing to his feet. 'The spacecraft that Kully reported …'

Angrily Balan cut his pupil short. 'There is no such craft, Teel. Nor are there any robots.'

'Oh I wouldn't bet on that if I were you!'

The three Dulcians spun round to see the Doctor and Jamie just emerging from the airlock.

'Kully was right,' the Doctor continued. 'There is certainly an alien spacecraft and most definitely there are robots.'

'And you're all in great danger,' Jamie added earnestly.

Balan ignored these revelations. 'Your friend Zoe is already at the Capitol and Director Senex will be awaiting your own arrival,' he informed them. 'Do not delay.'

The Doctor had caught sight of the graph still glowing on the computer screen. His eyebrows shot up in astonishment. 'There you are!' he cried excitedly. 'Just look at that. You can't ignore that!'

Swiftly Balan turned and cancelled the display. 'Please, Doctor, do not waste any more time in this foolishness,' he pleaded.

The Doctor stared furiously at Balan for several seconds. 'Quite!' he suddenly snapped. 'Come along, Jamie, perhaps

47

Director Senex will listen to us.'

Teel and Kando hurried across to prime the second capsule for launching, while Balan escorted the Doctor and Jamie to the launch tube and programmed the destination panel as they clambered aboard.

'Capsule primed,' Teel called out.

'This will deliver you direct to the Capitol,' Balan explained, 'and the Director will see you at his convenience.'

'The Director will see me *at once*,' the Doctor retorted as the canopy and access panel zipped shut.

With a hollow screaming noise the capsule shot out of sight along the tube.

Teel and Kando had been eagerly whispering together and they turned as Balan came back into the laboratory section.

'Now perhaps we can continue with our proper work,' the Educator sighed.

'Willingly,' Kando agreed, glancing covertly at Teel. 'Permission to commence soil-core sampling?'

'Granted,' Balan replied.

Grabbing their equipment, the students almost rushed for the airlock.

'Wait!' Balan cried sharply. 'I shall accompany you, to ensure that nothing distracts you from your tasks ...'

Zoe had been wandering impatiently round and round the Council Chamber, now and then glancing hopefully at the wall through which Director Senex had disappeared seemingly hours previously. Kully was lying in his father's chair, his grubby and bruised legs thrown casually over the arm, idly watching a thin trickle of sand running out of the side of his battered sandals.

'Oh, why are they taking so long?' Zoe cried exasperatedly after a long silence.

Kully yawned. 'Everything takes time on Dulkis. Nothing's ever rushed. Not any more,'he mumbled.

Zoe clasped and unclasped her hands in frustration. 'If what you told them about the robots is true ...'

'So even you don't really believe me,' Kully said disconsolately.

48

Zoe tousled her neat black hair. 'I don't know. I'm really worried. Jamie and the Doctor should have got here ages ago.'

'Perhaps my imaginary robots have gobbled them both up!' Kully chuckled.

Zoe gave a little sigh of apprehension.

'Sorry,' Kully said gloomily. 'You don't believe me. The Council don't believe me. It's my own fault, I suppose.' He stared at the little heaps of sand on the floor by the chair. Then he suddenly leaped out of the Director's seat and grasped Zoe by the shoulders. 'Would you come back to the Island with me?' he asked earnestly.

Perplexed and miserable, Zoe gazed listlessly at his grimy bulbous features. 'Why, what are you going to do?'

'Bring back some evidence. Make them believe me before it's too late. Will you come, Zoe?'

Zoe thought for a moment. 'What kind of evidence? Anyway, how could we get past your father and the Council out there?' she objected.

Kully seized her hand and headed straight towards the blank wall of the Chamber. It dissolved in front of them and before she could resist, Kully dragged Zoe through. 'We'll go through my father's private apartments,' he explained. 'Then we'll have to steal a capsule somehow ...'

Suddenly Kully stopped. 'Your clothes, Zoe ... not exactly Dulcian, are they?' he said with a frown.

Zoe glanced down at her tee-shirt and slacks and then at Kully's shapeless, pleated tunic. 'No, I'm glad to say they're not,' she retorted indignantly.

'They'll give us away. We'll never get past the Transport Monitors ...' Then Kully's face brightened. 'You can borrow something from Zanta! She's away in the Antipodes.'

'Zanta?' Zoe echoed doubtfully.

'My younger sister,' Kully explained. 'You're about the same size,' he grinned. 'Come on.'

Five minutes later, as arranged, Zoe met Kully in the curved shimmering corridor outside Senex's apartments.

Kully whistled approvingly. 'At least you look more like a girl now.'

Zoe grimaced at her chunky pleats and rather loose sandals.

'This clobber isn't very practical, is it?' she complained.

'Never mind, you look 90 per cent Dulcian,' Kully chuckled 'Your friends won't recognise you.'

Zoe looked worried. 'We'll probably pass them going in the opposite direction.'

Kully led the way rapidly along the smooth deserted corridor. 'Luckily I discovered some travel permits in Father's pockets,' he whispered, flourishing some small plastic tokens. 'All I have to do is forge his signature.'

'Kully, you're a shameless villain ...' Zoe giggled admiringly.

'And you are an alien imposter,' Kully grinned, seizing her hand and breaking into a trot ...

Their huge figures lit by a lurid multicoloured glow, the Dominators were studying a large seismological map of the Island displayed in fluorescent graphics on a panel in their control centre. Five red stars forming a regular pattern pulsated rhythmically, and complex clusters of symbols and figures flashed up in ever-changing sequences over the map. Beside the display, two Quarks were operating a large computer terminal.

'Depth of fourth bore revised in accordance with latest seismological data,' Toba reported in a voice hushed with concentration.

Rago nodded, his leathery face a livid red in the glare from the screen and his green eyes piercingly intent. 'Link with trajectory angles and collate detonation limits,' he ordered quietly.

'Command accepted. Computing now.'

The figures and symbols danced and flickered madly.

'There must be no error,' Rago warned in a menacing whisper. 'There will be no second chance.'

At that moment, one of the Quarks sparked and chattered into action. 'Alien specimens approaching!' it bleated.

'Not now!' Rago breathed venomously. 'I warned them ... Visual!' he ordered, turning to the Quark.

The display blacked out and a view of the area around the saucer flashed up in its place. Three white-suited but helmetless figures could be seen descending the slope of the dunes and approaching the Dominators' craft.

'Shall we destroy?' Toba suggested eagerly, trembling with excitement.

'Negative,' Rago retorted. 'These are new specimens.' He leaned forward in anticipation. 'They may be from the superior species. Investigate.'

Balan, Kando and Teel stood underneath the saucer, gazing in wonder at the sleek monster towering over them.

'So Kully was telling the truth,' Teel murmured, awestruck.

'Was he?' Balan said sharply. 'Then where are the robots?'

Kando glanced down at the maze of parallel tracks leading from the open hatchway at the bottom of the central shaft. 'Perhaps ... perhaps they are inside,' she suggested nervously.

Balan shook his head dismissively. 'Why seek unlikely answers to simple problems? This is probably some form of experimental craft being tested by the Technological Committee.'

'But why is it here on the Island?' Teel persisted stubbornly.

'No doubt it is highly secret,' Balan warned, turning to leave. 'Come, we have work to do.'

Kando and Teel stood their ground. 'Perhaps there has been an accident ... a forced landing!' Kando burst out.

'Yes, it is our duty to investigate,' Teel agreed, starting towards the hatchway.

'There has been no reference to any accident in the Bulletins,' Balan objected, 'and I forbid you to interfere.'

'If it is secret the Bulletins will not refer to it,' Teel answered triumphantly.

Kando joined him, her beautiful eyes alive with excitement. 'We must investigate,' she urged.

Warily the two students stepped into the cylindrical chamber. Speechless with rage Balan came hurrying after them. No sooner had he entered than the hatch slid shut with a slick whirr and the floor immediately heaved under their

51

feet as the elevator bore them rapidly up into the saucer.

The three Dulcians stared around them open-mouthed as they stepped out into the deserted control centre, echoing and dark.

'This is not the technology of Dulkis ...' Teel murmured almost reverently, gesturing at the crystal mosaic sphere glittering on the central control column.

Still struck dumb with amazement, Balan walked slowly over to the dais and grasped the slim rail surrounding it for support. From the shadows came a shrill giggling. Something glowed red and a nauseating throbbing burst out. Balan went chalk white and tried to let go of the rail. 'I ... I cannot move ...' he stuttered, gaping in utter terror at his shocked pupils.

The throbbing was repeated and Teel was flung across the chamber and pinned helplessly to the wall. Kando screamed in panic as two whirring, chattering machines with flashing antennae marched out of the gloom towards her. Slowly she backed away.

'Stand still!' croaked a hollow alien voice and Toba strode into the chamber hunched in his carapace of armoured plates.

Then Rago entered, his suit creaking menacingly as he loomed over Balan. The terrified Educator's mouth moved but no words emerged, only strange incoherent sounds. His eyes were bloodshot and popping out of his head.

'You ... you are not Dulcians,' Teel gasped, his slim body crumpled against the panel.

'Quark!' Toba barked.

The wall panel swung Teel like a dummy and suspended him horizontally while the globular apparatus descended over him. Then the Quark connected its probes into the bottom edge of the pallet.

'Activate!' Toba ordered.

Teel was bathed in the bluish aura as Rago fitted the visor over his head and strode over to examine the new specimen.

'As I anticipated, this one is different,' Rago reported with a grunt of satisfaction. 'Greater brain capacity ... Two hearts ... No superfluous internal organs ... Limited potential for physical activity ...' After a few minutes he straightened up and took off the visor. 'Affirmative. There are two species.

Neither presents any threat to us.'

Toba was staring at Kando's cowering figure beside the other Quark. 'Then we shall be able to assemble a labour force?'

'Affirmative. Of limited performance, but adequate,' Rago decided. 'We shall require the oscillation area around the central bore target to be cleared of debris. Search the Island. Round up all specimens.'

'Command accepted,' Toba acknowledged eagerly.

When Toba had left, Rago resumed his investigation of the semi-conscious Teel.

'I do not understand ...' Balan wailed, still helplessly stuck to the rail of the dais by molecular adhesion. 'Why should they wish to harm us?'

Dazed with shock, Kando shook her head. Then she began to whimper with terror as Rago turned his attention to her, his huge green eye swollen like that of some monstrous Cyclops by the lenses of the visor.

'Muscular development is relatively retarded,' the creaking giant rasped, stooping over her. 'However, endurance can be tested. It should prove a most informative experiment ...'

5

Slavery

After the capsule had screamed to a shuddering halt inside the terminal tube in the survey module, Kully gallantly offered to help Zoe disembark, but the independent young human jumped lightly out, none the worse for her second turbulent trip. They looked around the deserted module with a mounting sense of foreboding.

'Where is everybody?' murmured Zoe. 'What do you think can have happened?'

Kully glanced over the quietly humming systems monitors and shrugged. 'We'd better take a look outside.'

Just then Zoe glimpsed something through the small porthole nearest her. 'What on earth is that?' she exclaimed, leaning forward. Then she caught sight of a similar object through the neighbouring porthole. She ran from porthole to porthole and then turned slowly to face Kully as hot and cold pins and needles prickled the back of her neck. 'We seem ... we seem to be completely surrounded ...' she gasped.

As Kully scrambled to see for himself, a chorus of unearthly noises briefly penetrated the hull of the module. An instant later, the whole structure shuddered and several equipment panels burst into showers of sparks. Momentarily frozen with terror, Kully stared at the encircling Quarks inexorably closing in on them with throbbing probes and threshing antennae. Then he dived towards the airlock, yelling at Zoe to follow. Frantically he pressed and twisted and thumped the switches, but the door remained shut. Dense clouds of black smoke began to billow out of the shattered panels.

Again the module shuddered, this time tipping over at an

alarming angle before settling back in a series of violent rocking movements.

'We're trapped ... we're trapped ...' Kully shrieked, before being racked by a fit of retching and coughing.

A third time the module shook and then it rolled over and over several times like a barrel, flinging Zoe and Kully around like rag dolls. The din was appalling as they alternately screamed and choked in the deadly fumes, while the structure rapidly started to collapse around them.

When the module finally came to rest, the two prisoners felt blindly about in the poisonous darkness, their ears numbed by the prodigious reverberations of the battered hull.

Eventually they found each other. 'Maybe you'll believe in my robots now ...' Kully gasped, clasping Zoe round the waist with one arm and feeling with his free hand for the airlock controls.

'What about the capsule thing?' Zoe panted through her handkerchief.

'Can't navigate ... even if it still works ... we'd end up back in the Capitol,' spluttered Kully, jiggling the switches in vain.

'Better than being cooked in here.'

Desperately Kully levered with his fingernails around the tightly sealed edge of the airlock, but it was impossible to budge it.

Zoe sank to her knees, her lungs burning. 'I ...I just can't breathe ...' she croaked piteously, doubled in agony.

A few seconds later, Kully collapsed against the airlock panel.

Outside, standing hunched on the dunes like a huge rearing turtle, Toba ordered the circle of Quarks to recharge their probes. A tremor of pleasure ran through his massive frame as the robots bleated and sparked in unison around the scorched hulk of the module.

'And now complete destruction!' he commanded, in a frenzy of hatred and power.

'Negative. Command negated!' Rago thundered, striding up behind his unwitting Probationer.

The Quarks clattered and buzzed in confusion and then fell

56

silent.

Toba swung violently round. 'Intention was to prevent escape of any specimens,' he blustered feebly.

'Your obsession with destruction has seriously depleted Quark power reserves,' hissed Rago. 'Did you examine the craft?'

'All data has been recorded,' Toba claimed. 'The craft was empty.'

Rago stared briefly at the blistered wreck. 'Bring any further specimens to me intact at once,' he ordered. 'And Toba – I do not expect to have to correct you again.'

The Probationer glared at his superior from beneath lowered eyelids. 'Command accepted,' he whispered hoarsely.

Rago nodded curtly and strode away.

Toba had just started organising the squad of robots to continue the search of the Island when he suddenly noticed that the outer airlock door had opened in the hull of the module, releasing a huge pall of acrid black smoke. Then, to his astonishment, two dazed figures crawled slowly out and lay panting feverishly in the sand.

When at last they managed to raise their heads, Zoe and Kully found themselves staring at a semicircle of Quarks with Toba's towering frame in the centre relentlessly bearing down on them. With a gigantic effort Kully turned to Zoe. '*Now* perhaps you will believe me ...' he whispered.

Bovem met the Doctor and Jamie at the capsule terminal in the Capitol. As he hurried them along endless gleaming corridors to the Council Chamber, they tried to find out what had happened to Zoe but without success. Bovem seemed very evasive.

'Director Senex will explain, should he consider it fitting,' Bovem told them soothingly as he ushered them into the Antechamber. 'I shall announce your arrival.'

As they waited for what seemed like ages to be admitted, Jamie paced restlessly up and down. 'Where d'ye think the wee lassie can be, Doctor?' he asked anxiously. 'D'ye think they're holding her hostage or something?'

The Doctor roused himself from his reverie. 'Oh I'm sure

57

the Dulcians wouldn't harm her, Jamie.'

The tough young Scot gritted his teeth. 'They'd better not!' he muttered grimly.

Eventually they were summoned. They found themselves standing in the Council Chamber surrounded by a dozen elderly dignitaries. The Doctor looked impatient and uncomfortable under the steady gaze of Director Senex and made a feeble attempt to smooth his dusty, rumpled clothes and hair. Jamie simply stared around him with barely disguised contempt.

At last Senex spoke. 'As far as the Council is aware, your friend has left the Capitol in the company of my son Kully,' he blandly informed them. 'Presumably they returned to the Island.'

'Why did ye no tell us before?' Jamie shouted indignantly. 'Come on, Doctor ...' Jamie looked for a doorway in vain.

'That would not be advisable,' Senex warned quietly.

Jamie's blue eyes blazed defiantly. 'Ye mean we're prisoners?'

A murmur of protest ran round the noble assembly.

'There are no prisoners here,' Senex replied calmly.

The Doctor quickly intervened. 'There's no need, Jamie,' he explained tactfully. 'Dulcian society is totally pacifist.'

Jamie grimaced. 'Then how are they going to fight those Dominators and their Quarks?' he demanded.

The Director sat upright in his luxurious chair. 'It would seem to be true that you come from another planet,' he announced.

'So do the Dominators,' said the Doctor earnestly. 'We have seen them. We were taken inside their craft. They are utterly callous and they are here on Dulkis for some sinister purpose.'

The Councillors began stirring uneasily in their reclining seats. Senex called for order and was instantly obeyed. He turned and courteously addressed the Doctor. 'We should be grateful if you would inform us what has occured on the Island,' he declared.

'Och not again,' Jamie exploded. 'We're hanging aboot blethering and Zoe's in danger ...'

With phenomenal patience the Doctor briefly recounted events since the TARDIS had materialised on the Island.

'... and once the physiological tests were completed ... well, they let us go,' he concluded at last.

Senex appeared to be convinced. 'Did you discover the purpose of these tests, Doctor?' he asked.

'To see if we were clever enough to be useful,' Jamie spelt out with painstaking rudeness.

'Evidently you were not!' Deputy Bovem retorted.

Before the quick-tempered Highlander could bite the bait, the Doctor again intervened. 'With respect, Director Senex, I know that it is the Dulcian custom to deliberate and discuss at leisure, but the situation is urgent. Send someone to the Island to confirm our story,' he pleaded.

'Aye, and we'll be organising a way to defeat these Dominators,' Jamie added with relish.

The Director raised his hands, palms upward. 'The Dominators let you go free, so why should we fear them?' he demanded simply.

The Doctor adopted a menacing air. 'Don't expect them to think and act as you do,' he murmured, leaning very close to Senex. 'They are aliens. From another world.'

Senex smiled. 'So are you, Doctor.'

Disconcerted, the Doctor blinked and retreated a little.

Senex inclined his head kindly, as though he were talking to a small child. 'What could such aliens possibly want from Dulkis?'

The Doctor frowned. 'Well, they talked about refuelling their fleet ...'

The Director laughed: 'We have no suitable minerals here. The aliens are welcome to whatever they can use,' he said, to murmurs of agreement from the Councillors.

The Doctor shook his head thoughtfully. 'There is the puzzle about the disappearance of radiation from the Island,' he mused. 'Perhaps that is what they came for ...'

Senex shrugged. 'That is no cause for alarm, Doctor. Why seek menace where there may be none?'

The Doctor bit his lip for a moment, restraining his growing frustration. 'I am only guessing,' he went on. 'And there is the possibility that they are slavers – recruiting for some vast project.'

'You can't just sit here and do nothing!' Jamie shouted.

'Better do nothing than do the wrong thing,' remarked an aged member in a wavering croak.

Senex held up his hand. 'What do you suggest we do?' he asked the irate young Scot.

'First send an armed force to rescue Zoe and Kully ...' Jamie began eagerly.

'An *armed* force?' Bovem echoed in astonishment. 'Impossible.'

Outraged voices broke out all around the Chamber.

'For decades we have lived in peace,' Senex calmly replied. 'We have proved that universal restraint eliminates aggression.'

'Och, just try telling the Dominators that!' retorted Jamie scornfully.

The Doctor stirred himself into action. 'Jamie's right. I suggest you contact Balan on the Island – at least he might have some more news by now,' he proposed earnestly.

After a pause, Senex touched a button on his video panel. Amidst a snowstorm of interference, the interior of the survey module flickered unsteadily onto the miniature screen. There was a gasp of horror as the Councillors stared at their individual monitors. The images showed a total ruin, a blackened pile of wreckage.

Senex panned the scanner calling agitatedly for Balan over the audio link. There was no reply, only a rush of static. The remains of the module seemed deserted.

Sadly the Doctor hung his head. 'I'm afraid it's too late. I did try to warn you.'

'What ... what is that?' Bovem suddenly cried, pointing at his monitor.

Through the open airlock, a squat mechanical figure was entering the module, its antennae flashing and its probes twitching eagerly.

'That's a Quark! One of the robots,' the Doctor exclaimed.

'A Quark ... and you let Zoe go back there!' Jamie yelled at the dumbstruck Council. He grabbed the Doctor's arm and started to drag him away. 'We must go back, Doctor! We canna waste any more time!'

The Doctor held back a moment, staring intently at the screens. They all watched fascinated as the Quark suddenly seemed to notice the scanner. Its antennae sparked even more ferociously and its manic bleating rose to a frenzied climax as it approached, growing larger and larger on the screens. Its glowing probes reached out towards the speechless watchers. Then the screens fizzled and went blank.

The Doctor glanced around the stunned and silent assembly. 'Now will you believe us?' he whispered hoarsely. Then he and Jamie dashed out of the Chamber.

Jamie was soon sitting glumly in the rear seat of a transit capsule while in front the Doctor desperately tried to remember how to operate the machine.

'I suppose you know what you're doing,' Jamie muttered apprehensively.

'Oh yes. It's just a matter of the correct sequence of switches,' the Doctor reassured him.

Jamie leaned forward. 'No, no. I mean this contraption's heading back to the survey ship, right?'

'Well, I certainly hope it is Jamie. Why?'

'Och nothing,' Jamie shrugged. 'Just that there's an angry Quark waiting there to meet us ...'

'Oh dear,' the Doctor muttered. 'So there is.'

Toba and the Quarks had escorted Zoe and Kully across the sweltering dunes to the ruined museum. Ragged and exhausted, the two prisoners now stood in the blistering heat of the Dulcian noon, awaiting their fate with as much courage as they could muster. For some time Zoe had been stealing glances at their Quark guardians.

'Any idea how they're powered?' she whispered to Kully. 'If we knew, we might be able to sabotage them.'

'Wouldn't stand a chance,' Kully muttered, 'they're deadly.'

'They're only robots,' Zoe murmured, suddenly remembering the laser gun and the other weapons inside the ruin.

'Kully, I think we stand a chance ...' she breathed hopefully.

The nearest Quark emitted a threatening buzz.

'Attack them? Are you out of your mind, Zoe?' Kully retorted through clenched teeth.

At that moment, Rago and Toba came striding over the sandhills followed by Teel, Kando and Balan with a Quark escort. The prisoners were all herded together and the Dominators surveyed the small band of slaves.

'Work potential and stamina to be recorded for analysis,' Rago commanded.

'Affirmative,' Toba responded eagerly. 'But if any try to escape ...'

'No action. Report to me,' Rago insisted.

The prisoners watched as the two huge figures faced each other breathing heavily, manoeuvring for supremacy.

'Toba!'

'Command accepted,' Toba conceded after a long pause.

Rago threw him a cold emerald glare and then marched off, followed by all but two of the Quarks.

Toba slowly circled round the huddled captives, a hideous smile warping his leathern face. Then he addressed them in a hushed voice almost choked with excitement. 'If the tests prove favourable, you may be chosen to serve the Dominators,' he breathed.

'Dominators? Who on earth are they?' piped up Zoe innocently.

Toba swung round and bore down on her. 'Do not ever interrupt me again,' he whispered hoarsely, his warm acid breath making Zoe flinch in disgust. Toba resumed his circling. 'We are the Masters of the Ten Galaxies.'

'And we're the Dulcians,' Kully blurted out, 'and we don't serve anybody.'

The huge creaking figure towered over the plump little Dulcian. 'You will clear and prepare this site for drilling,' Toba rasped, gesturing at the rubble-strewn ground surrounding the star-shaped target.

'And if we don't?' Zoe challenged.

'You will be destroyed,' Toba hissed with obvious delight. 'So remember – you are working for your lives.'

'Well, I'm certainly not working for you,' Zoe snapped defiantly.

'Quarks!' Toba screamed. A shiver whipped up Zoe's spine as she heard the demented giggling and saw the ominous sparking emitted by the two robots as they stomped forward. Toba watched with a sadistic smile as the Quarks drove the five prisoners towards the scattered debris and forced them to form a short chain-gang.

Exhausted and cowed, Balan reluctantly stooped, picked up a small lump of concrete and passed it along the chain. At the other end, Teel heaved the block as far as he could away into the sand. Then the futile action was repeated, over and over again. For a while Toba gloated over their struggles with heavy slabs and twisted girders, and then marched away towards the distant saucer.

As they sweated and strained in the heat and the soft shifting sand, under the impassive, unblinking gaze of the Quarks, Zoe desperately tried to think. 'There are only two of these tin soldiers, but there are five of us,' she eventually murmured to the others. 'We've got to get away.'

'Where would we go?' Kando asked. 'We cannot leave the Island.'

'Perhaps the Capitol will send help,' Teel suggested.

Kully staggered under an awkwardly twisted beam. 'What ... what can they do?' he panted. 'We've got to get ourselves out of this mess.'

'Exactly what I intend to do,' Zoe agreed. 'How fast can these clockwork soldiers move, Kully?'

Balan stopped work and leaned on Zoe's shoulder. 'I cannot allow you to incite my students to rebellion,' he protested weakly, 'it will only lead to violence.'

'And submission will only lead to slavery,' Zoe retorted. 'What do you say, Kully?'

Kully nodded eagerly and turned to Kando.

'No, Balan is right,' gasped the tall Dulcian girl, trying to lift the slab Balan had just dropped. 'Violence breeds violence.'

Kully turned earnestly to Teel who was struggling to pull a thick steel rod out of the sand. Teel paused, glancing

63

uncomfortably at Balan and Kando. 'I understand your arguments ... but meek submission is humiliating,' he muttered resolutely. 'I am with Zoe and Kully.'

A spectacular discharge of sparks burst among the Quarks' antennae and they lumbered nearer, bleating suspiciously ...

As the Capsule hurtled through the Dulcian sky, Jamie craned over the Doctor's shoulder, his face frozen with horror. The Doctor had removed the instrument panel in front of him and was poking about in the tangle of wires.

'Have ye gone daft or something?' Jamie shouted above the harsh whining and buffeting of the craft.

'No, no, Jamie, all I've got to do is to ... oh dear ...' cried the Doctor in dismay, swapping a few connections over.

'But ye canna just take this contraption ta bits in mid air,' Jamie protested.

The Doctor pressed a switch, then another and shook his head. 'But we don't want to land in the middle of all those Quark things as you yourself pointed out,' he shouted, changing the wires over again. 'Don't worry Jamie, all I have to do is over-ride the autopilot.'

At that moment the capsule started looping in a terrifying corkscrew pattern. Jamie held on to his stomach and closed his eyes. 'But ... are there no any ordinary controls?' he yelled in anguish as they spiralled round and round.

The Doctor handed Jamie a spaghetti-like bundle of wires over his shoulder. 'Here, hold this, there's a good chap,' he cried.

Jamie grabbed the tangle and the Doctor immediately dived off his seat and began wriggling his way forward into the nose-cone. At once the capsule started bucking and rearing like a fairground machine. Jamie felt decidedly sick as he watched the Doctor's legs waving around every time the craft took a sudden dizzy plunge. 'What are ye doing in there?' he shouted anxiously.

There was an incomprehensible series of muffled comments as the Doctor twisted this way and that. 'Think I've got it!' he eventually declared, shuffling backwards into the cockpit clutching several printed circuits and even more tangles of wire. 'Anyway there won't be time for a second try,' he cried cheerfully manoeuvring himself back into his seat. 'Now I'm going to attempt to steer this thing.'

The Doctor fiddled with the circuits for a few seconds. All at once the capsule gave a bone-numbing lurch and then steadied itself again.

'We'll be down in no time at all, Jamie.'

'Aye, but in one piece?'

'Hang on!' the Doctor yelled as the craft tipped almost vertically and accelerated downwards at a phenomenal rate. 'We'll soon find out.'

The capsule fell for what seemed an eternity. Then very gradually the nose came up and it levelled out. Soon they were skidding along in the sand with a deafening roaring and scraping.

'Yippee!' cried the Doctor, still fiddling with the circuitry.

Finally the capsule crunched to a halt underneath the cliffs. Opening the canopy, the Doctor leaped out nimbly. 'Look, no Quarks!' he cried triumphantly. 'I think we've done rather well so far.' He sniffed the air a few times. 'This way, I think,' he declared, starting to scramble up the face of the cliff.

After an arduous, sticky climb they followed the crumbling ridge for a few hundred metres and then suddenly found themselves looking down on the ruined museum. The Doctor drew a bent and battered telescope out of his pocket and peered through it.

'What can ye see?' Jamie demanded impatiently, snatching the instrument. 'It's Zoe and Kully and the others!' he exclaimed, overjoyed. 'Let's go, Doctor.'

'Wait!' the Doctor commanded sternly, taking the telescope and quickly scanning the area. 'We'll split up and work our way round separately from behind them, just in case. I'll follow the ridge for a bit first. You go down that way ...'

Under the cliff, the five prisoners had resumed their task. Although Balan and Kando could hardly manage to shift anything at all, Zoe Kully and Teel put on a convincing show while secretly whispering among themselves.

'Have you got any ideas?' Kully asked. 'We must be quick or the others will be too exhausted to move.'

'There's a laser gun in that museum place. We've got to get hold of it somehow,' Zoe murmured.

Teel bent down beside them. 'There is only one Quark now,' he said.

Cautiously they looked up. One of the robots had moved over to the drilling target to take soundings and measurements.

With a muffled gasp, Balan suddenly fell to his knees. 'I am ... I am sorry,' he panted pitifully.

Their Quark sentry tramped over to examine the fallen Dulcian. 'Is this specimen broken?' it bleated harshly. 'Move it aside and resume working.'

Zoe winked significantly at Kully and Teel, then she and Kando helped Balan over to the shadowed area by the remains of the museum entrance and propped him up against the wall.

Meanwhile the Quark transmitted a terse report to its masters. 'Initial assessment: one specimen broken. Three others showing signs of unserviceability. Only one still performing at high efficiency,' it screeched.

'That will be one of the males,' Rago's voice observed through the Quark's audio circuit.

'Correction. A female,' retorted the robot.

'The name's Zoe ...' Zoe muttered to herself as she knelt beside Balan, keeping her eyes glued on the chattering Quark.

'Work the specimens to exhaustion,' Rago ordered brutally. 'Record the times of collapse.'

Kully had been watching Zoe's movements like a hawk. Now he positioned himself so that he blocked the Quark's view of the museum entrance. Nearby, Teel redoubled his efforts dislodging the steel rods to distract the machine's attention.

Very slowly Zoe stood up and started to back into the gaping doorway. The Quark was still preoccupied observing Teel's valiant struggles ... a few more backward steps and she would be within reach of the laser gun.

Suddenly Kully realised that he could only see one Quark,

the one he was blocking. He glanced fearfully round; the Quark by the target had disappeared. He tried to call out a warning to Zoe, but his throat felt like sandpaper and no sound came.

Zoe took three more paces and then her heart froze as she heard an unearthly giggling and sparking behind her. She stopped dead. A scream flew to her lips but was never uttered. Without looking round, she began to walk slowly forward again into the open, with the robot's mechanical footsteps shaking the floor beneath her as it followed. At every step she expected the Quark's glowing probes to discharge their murderous ultrasonic quanta and to smash her body to fragments.

6

Fighting Back

In the cool Capitol the Councillors were locked in dispute with their Director. Senex seemed to be reconciling himself to the need for action, whereas Bovem led a majority in favour of doing nothing.

'We must hope that the Doctor will succeed in devising an effective course of action,' Senex stated firmly.

'With respect, I am reluctant to rely upon the assistance of an alien,' Deputy Bovem objected. 'We should support the recommendations of the Emergency Committee.'

'Chairman Tensa is able,' Senex agreed, 'but can he deal with this unprecedented crisis?'

Bovem looked shocked. 'Tensa has proved his competence dealing with floods, droughts, earthquakes ...' he protested.

The Director smiled indulgently. 'All *natural* disasters, Bovem, not the result of aggressive intelligences.'

At that moment the wall parted and a surprisingly robust young Dulcian entered with an air of determined ability. A grateful sigh of relief rose from the troubled Councillors, as though all their problems were solved at last. They sat up expectantly.

Tensa looked at them gravely. 'We have three alternatives,' he announced abruptly. 'If these aliens are indeed hostile – which has not been proved beyond question – we can fight, we can flee or we can submit.'

There was a doomed silece. The Councillors waited, as if hoping for more, for some magical solution. Tensa remained silent.

Senex rose slowly to his feet. 'We cannot fight, we are not able. We cannot flee, there is no refuge. We can submit, but to what?'

'Who knows?' Tensa replied curtly.

The assembly stared aghast at Chairman Tensa, as though all their trust and expectations had been betrayed.

Eventually the Director sank back into his luxurious chair. 'So we can only wait ...' he concluded.

Fortunately for Zoe, Kando had fainted and fallen on her face in the burning sand, and her collapse had distracted the Quark from Zoe's suspicious behaviour. Having revived Kando and laid her next to Balan by the museum entrance, the others carried on the struggle to clear the drilling site, though Teel was getting rapidly weaker from the un-accustomed physical exertion. Determined as ever, Kully and Zoe had soon devised another escape plan.

'So all we need now is somewhere we can hide ...' Kully whispered.

'The bomb shelter,' Teel suddenly muttered. 'I am sure they built one ... part of the atom tests.'

Kully glanced surreptitiously at the Quarks. 'Where is it?' he asked, passing Teel a jagged sheet of metal.

Teel shrugged apologetically and shook his head.

'Fat lot of use!' snapped Zoe irritably. 'Listen Kully, once you're inside, give me time to get the Quarks into your line of fire.'

'Don't forget to duck,' Kully joked under his breath, heaving a slab onto his shoulder and bending at the knees. 'Wish me luck.'

'Don't forget to point the gun the right way,' Zoe muttered anxiously.

Kully staggered a few paces with his burden, then he groaned dramatically, stumbled and fell.

Immediately the two Quarks stomped over to him. 'Specimen has failed,' one bleated.

'Join the other failed specimens!' screeched the second.

With grossly exaggerated effort, Kully dragged himself painfully across to the entrance and lay down in the shade beside Balan and Kando. Meanwhile, closely watched by the Quarks, Zoe picked up the slab Kully had dropped and struggled on.

Balan clutched feebly at Kully's sleeve. 'This is mere foolishness. You cannot possibly succeed,' he croaked.

But the plucky little Dulcian chose his moment and then crawled swiftly into the ruin. Once inside, he heaved the splintered remains of the door shut as best he could and then scuttled among the showcases, feverishly searching in the semi-darkness for the laser gun Zoe had described. At last he found it where Rago had thrown it down earlier. Holding the unfamiliar device out in front of him with his face averted, Kully cautiously approached the crumbling window, racking his brains to remember the detailed instructions Zoe had given him.

Outside, Zoe staggered along under the concrete slab, followed at a short distance by the two Quarks monitoring her progress. As she gradually drew level with the window, she glimpsed Kully out of the corner of her eye levelling the laser gun through the ragged hole in the wall. As arranged, she stumbled a few more paces and then sank to her knees with a moan.

'One more specimen has failed,' screeched a Quark.

'Fire, Kully, fire ...' Zoe muttered between her teeth, anxiously awaiting the whirr and slam of the laser.

Sweat streamed into Kully's eyes and his hands shook violently as he forced himself to operate the primer and poised his finger on the trigger, fighting to steady himself to fire.

Sensing that something was wrong, Teel let out a shuddering cry and crumpled to the ground.

'All specimens have failed,' the Quarks trumpeted. 'All specimens stand up!'

'Why don't you fire?' Zoe groaned, her eyes tightly closed and the hair on her neck prickling with suspense as she defied the Quarks' command as long as she dared. Still nothing happened.

Propped against the window frame, Kully had taken aim at the Quark nearest to Zoe's slumped figure. Just as he was

71

about to press the trigger button, a brawny hand reached over his shoulder and yanked the weapon savagely aside.

'What d'ye think ye're doing ... Zoe's oot there!' a shocked voice blasted into his ear.

Spinning round, Kully came face to face with Jamie. 'I know that, you fool, I was aiming at the Quarks!' he hissed. Turning back, Kully hurriedly took aim again.

Outside, Balan, Kando, Teel and Zoe had all obediently got to their feet and were now directly in the line of fire.

'It's no good. I've lost my chance,' Kully fumed resentfully.

Jamie looked ashamed. 'Sorry,' he mumbled.

The Quarks had herded their captives together. 'Specimens will be returned to Dominator Rago,' one of them screeched in a voice like a knife-blade on glass.

Suddenly the other Quark sparked and giggled madly. 'One specimen is missing ... the specimen Kully,' it shrieked, stomping frantically round and round the pathetic huddle.

'Now Balan's in the way,' Kully muttered, still squinting hopelessly through the sights.

Jamie put a restraining hand on his arm. 'Aye, well maybe it's no such a guid idea,' he said doubtfully. 'I think we should wait till the Doctor gets here.'

'He'd better be quick,' Kully snapped testily, 'because those Quarks will be after me any second now.'

At that moment the Doctor was very close, keeping a sharp look-out for Jamie as he darted along the base of the cliffs towards the ruin and stopping every few metres to spy out the land. Suddenly he saw a straggling group of Dulcians approaching, escorted by two Quarks. Among them he recognised Zoe, looking dazed and unhappy in her borrowed attire. The Doctor shrank into a hollow and tried to think, but almost at once a familiar tramping sound behind him sent his spirits plunging even further. Before he could move, a sizzling bang brought down part of the sandstone overhang around him so that he was buried up to his waist and immobilised.

'You were ordered to keep away from our operations,'

Toba snarled, striding up followed by several Quarks.

The Doctor twisted awkwardly round and grinned sheepishly. 'I do try to, but everywhere I go I bump into Quarks and things, all over the Island. Where can I go?' he whined pathetically, cowering before the mighty Dominator.

Toba's green eyes bore fiercely into him for several seconds and the Doctor began to fear that his pretence was about to be exposed. Just then the group from the drilling site stumbled up the slope on its way to the saucer. Zoe stared at the half-buried Doctor with a mixture of horror and relief, but she dared not call out or break rank. For his part, the Doctor was relieved to see that Jamie was not among the party, but Zoe's plight filled him with anxiety.

All at once Toba ordered the procession to stop. 'One of the specimens is missing,' he hissed.

'Specimen Kully has escaped,' bleated one of the Quarks.

To the Doctor's surprise, a smile of satisfaction cracked its way across Toba's waxen features. The Dominator jabbed a creaking glove towards him. 'Take this cretin with the other specimens to Dominator Rago,' he commanded.

In vain the Doctor attempted to heave himself out of the mound of sand. Leaning forward, Toba grasped his coat by the lapels and dragged him effortlessly clear. Meekly the Doctor scurried over and, with a crafty wink at Zoe, joined the procession. The two Quarks immediately whirred into motion again, driving their captives away across the dunes.

Ordering his squad of Quarks to follow, Toba set off eagerly down the slope towards the ruin.

Inside the museum, Jamie and Kully waited in gloomy silence – Jamie sprawling morosely on a fallen beam and Kully wandering aimlessly about lamenting his humiliating failure with the laser gun.

Eventually Kully could bear the suspense no more. 'We daren't wait any longer. Something must have happened to the Doctor,' he murmured.

Before Jamie could reply they heard a movement outside the ruin.

Kully turned expectantly to the window and was about to

call out 'Doctor' when the sturdy Scot leaped on him, clamped a hand over his mouth and they both hit the floor like a couple of sandbags.

'Kully ... I know you are there!' Toba's voice thundered, making the showcases rattle around them.

They lay listening to the crazed giggling of the Quarks' circuitry, their hearts pounding fit to burst.

'Do ... do you think he saw me ...?' asked Kully weakly.

'Ah telt ye ta keep away frae the windy,' Jamie muttered savagely. 'Gimme that thing ...' and he snatched the laser gun from the trembling Dulcian.

Outside the ruin, flanked by his Quarks, Toba's enormous frame was twitching with excitement. 'Now you will learn the consequences when a Dominator is disobeyed,' he screamed. 'Quarks! Destroy!'

There was a sickening slamming noise and the doorway completely disintegrated leaving a gaping hole in the wall. Kully clutched Jamie's arm, wide-eyed with terror.

Shaking free, Jamie scrambled to his knees, crawled swiftly across to the window and leaped to his feet, flattening himself beside the edge of the frame. With deft, rapid movements he primed the laser, aimed and fired several short sharp bursts.

The Quark nearest to Toba exploded in a shower of molten components and clouds of treacly smoke.

For a moment Toba was paralysed with astonishment and rage. Then he hunched behind the semicircle of Quarks and rapped out a string of hysterical orders: 'All units. Total destruction. Utter annihilation. Death! Death! Death!'

Ear-splitting whines rent the air and then the Quarks' deadly ultrasonic bolts began streaming relentlessly into the ruined building. Taking terrible risks, Jamie dodged around the window frame desperately trying to get another shot at the screaming Dominator and his sizzling robots. But the air was soon filled with choking dust and smoke and murderously sharp fragments of stone and metal whizzing in all directions.

'If only I could *see* them ...' Jamie yelled in frustration, firing the laser at random in the hope of hitting something.

All at once there was a terrible crash behind him and he whipped round to see that Kully had been pinned underneath a huge beam as a section of the roof had collapsed. Dropping the gun, Jamie scrambled over and vainly tried to shift the huge concrete rafter. Then he had a brainwave. Grabbing the laser, he carefully aimed it at the beam close to Kully's quaking body. As the helpless Dulcian stared at him in abject terror, Jamie fired the laser with just enough blast to shatter the rafter in two. Then he threw all his weight against the lighter section and it slid off, setting Kully free. Miraculously he had not been crushed, only dazed.

'Let's get out of here,' Jamie yelled above the colossal din of the Quarks' barrage and the collapsing building.

Suddenly Kully grabbed his arm. 'This way!' he shouted, dragging the protesting Highlander under a tangle of criss-crossed beams just at the same instant as the whole front wall of the museum caved inwards and the remains of the roof hurtled downwards. Seconds later there was a titanic explosion and the wreckage of the museum blew apart in a searing hail of fire and debris.

When the smoke and the dust had cleared, the museum no longer existed. Nothing moved in the devastation spread around on the sand.

'Destruction completed,' Toba breathed, his voice hushed with malicious satisfaction. Then, followed by the surviving Quarks, he turned abruptly and strode away.

After an exhausting trek from the drilling site, the Doctor and Zoe together with Balan, Kando and Teel, were herded into the control centre in the saucer. As soon as the Quarks had delivered their reports to Rago, the atmosphere became electric as Probationer Toba faced his superior defiantly.

'You deliberately disobeyed my instructions,' Rago fumed. 'You wasted power destroying the structure and the specimen Kully.'

'And possibly my young friend Jamie!' the Doctor shouted, his face contorted with rage and sorrow.

Zoe gazed at the Doctor in horror.

Toba's eyes clouded with cunning. 'My life was threatened and a Quark was destroyed.'

'The result of your own negligence,' Rago retorted.

Toba smiled a nightmare smile. 'Does the Navigator suggest that I should have allowed the specimen to escape?'

'This is an Island. The specimens cannot escape,' Rago sneered. He turned to the Quark escort. 'Take the specimens to the central bore and prepare the target for drilling. The inferior specimens will remain here,' he added, indicating Zoe and the Doctor.

The dusty haggard figures of Balan, Kando and Teel were driven roughly out of the control centre by the two Quarks. Zoe and the Doctor lingered apprehensively under the glinting gaze of another robot. Zoe was almost frantic with concern for Jamie, but as soon as she tried to question the Doctor he put his finger to his lips and nodded warningly towards Rago and Toba.

The two Dominators had moved across the chamber to the Quark control unit on the far side. A vivid red symbol representing the robot destroyed by Jamie was pulsing among row upon row of green symbols denoting serviceable Quarks.

'Probationer Toba, I begin to question whether you possess the qualities of intelligence and detachment vital in a Dominator,' Rago rapped out with exaggerated disdain. 'You have repeatedly destroyed the creatures and installations of this planet, and squandered vital Quark resources to no useful purpose, merely to gratify your lust for destruction.'

Toba gestured defiantly at the huge navigation charts glowing on the panels behind them. 'Was it by weakness and indecision that the Dominators mastered the Ten Galaxies?' he demanded.

Rago stiffened. 'It was by rational ruthlessness,' he retorted, his eyes ablaze with fanatical certainty. 'What threatens us, we destroy. What can serve us, we exploit. Everything else, we ignore.'

'Well, at least we're honest,' murmured the Doctor wryly, listening intently.

'But the primitives have disobeyed us. They have attacked us and we do not know what the superior aliens may be planning elsewhere on the planet,' Toba protested.

'I alone am competent to assess such matters,' Rago thundered. 'I shall report your conduct to Fleet Leader.'

76

'And I shall protest at yours,' Toba shouted. 'You have jeopardised our mission by weakness. You have humiliated me before inferior creatures ...'

Rago thrust his creaking, leathery face close to Toba's. 'It is not unknown for mutinous subordinates to be executed,' he hissed.

'Nor is it unknown for an incompetent superior to be replaced,' Toba ranted unflinchingly.

'Quark!' Rago rasped. 'Place Probationer Toba under restraint.'

The Quark guarding the Doctor and Zoe advanced on Toba, its probes whirring ominously.

'Quark!' Toba countered, his malevolent eyes fixed on Rago. 'Secure the prisoners.'

The robot lurched to a halt. Its antennae glowed and its probes stabbed the air as its legs jerked it round to face the Doctor and Zoe, and then back round to face Toba again. The two captives watched from the shadows, fascinated by the robot's paralysing confusion.

'Quark, I am the Senior Dominator. You obey me,' Rago thundered.

The Quark emitted an agonised bleating and then tramped resolutely towards Toba. The Probationer licked his mean lips and backed away a few paces.

'Will you submit or shall I order molecular adhesion?' Rago demanded coldly.

Toba lowered his huge head and his body slumped in defeat. 'I submit ...' he whispered hoarsely.

Rago watched as the Quark continued to advance on Toba with inexorable purpose. Then, when the humiliated Probationer looked up in naked terror and let out a macabre whimper, Rago smiled and casually instructed the robot to return to the prisoners. 'You are fortunate that Fleet still requires your services, Toba,' he sneered. 'You will now return to supervise final drilling operations. And allow nothing to distract you.'

Again Toba bowed his head. 'Command accepted,' he whispered and marched out.

Rago strode across to the Doctor and Zoe. 'I require

information about your planet,' he rapped, looming over them.

'What plan ...' Zoe began.

The Doctor silenced her with a sharp nudge and a pantomime cough. Then he gazed innocently up at Rago, nodding and smilingly meekly.

'Your responses had better be satisfactory,' Rago hissed, 'for your own sakes.'

7

Buried Alive

Balan, Kando and Teel were appalled to see the devastation
from the Quark attack on the museum. Wreckage was strewn
all over the drilling site which they had sweated so hard to
clear earlier. The Quarks forced them back to work with
brutal shoves and harsh metallic threats. After only a few
minutes, Balan began to gasp and tremble with the strain
while Teel and Kando struggled bravely among the
smouldering debris.

'Kully must be dead. No one could have survived in
there ...' Kando murmured.

'The attempt was sheer madness,' Balan whispered faintly.
'It is useless to resist.'

Teel blinked the stinging sweat out of his eyes and stared
hard at a tangle of beams heaped in the centre of the ruin. For
a fleeting moment he thought he saw something moving. He
tried to attract Kando's attention, but a Quark whirred
warningly behind him and he reluctantly resumed his back-
breaking task.

Only thirty metres away, the tip of a slim metal shaft was
twisting and turning under the beams trying to force its way
upwards, but the heavy girders held it fast. Time after time
the shaft was withdrawn a few centimetres and then thrust
sharply upwards again only to become fouled in the tangled
wreckage.

Teel strained to see out of the corner of his eye but
eventually gave up, blaming the heat and his exhaustion for
deceiving his senses.

At the other end of the vertical shaft, several metres beneath the specially reinforced floor of the ruin, Jamie and Kully were struggling in the stuffy and dusty gloom to force the periscope up into the open. But try as they would, the shaft only moved so far and then jammed solid.

The atomic shelter was a featureless, boxlike room containing four bunks, an air-filtering unit and two dimly glowing fluorescent lighting strips. A steel ladder led up one wall to a square hatchway in the ceiling. The hatch was tightly shut.

Finally, worn out with their frantic efforts, Jamie and Kully collapsed onto the bunks.

'It's no good. The whole building must be piled on top of it,' Jamie panted.

'We'll just have to wait until someone digs us out,' Kully shrugged.

Jamie snorted and attempted to take a few deep breaths in the close, stale atmosphere. 'Meantime we'd better stop breathing,' he muttered sarcastically.

Kully glanced at the ventilator unit. 'The batteries are too low to run that thing,' he said hopelessly. 'They won't power the lights much longer either.'

Wearily Jamie hauled himself to his feet. 'Look, Kully, we've got to get that trap door open again,' he insisted. He dragged himself up the ladder and started heaving against the unyielding steel hatch with his shoulder.

Kully glanced with grudging admiration at the brawny Highlander's bulging calves as he strained upwards. 'Even if you get it open you'll probably find the Quarks waiting for you,' he objected gloomily.

'That's a risk we'll have to take,' snapped Jamie, resting for a few seconds and swallowing great gulps of stale air.

Kully frowned. 'Don't you see, Jamie? It's suicide either way. The harder we work the sooner we use up the air.'

'Sitting there moaning's no better,' Jamie retorted angrily, puzzled that all the fight seemed to have gone out of Kully suddenly.

'The Dulcians believe it is undignified to struggle against one's fate,' Kully said staring vacantly into space, as if talking to himself.

Jamie twisted round and glared contemptuously down at the forlorn little figure. 'Och come on, Kully ... I thought ye were different. Ye sound like those auld fossils in the Council. I thought ye'd fight!' he taunted, putting his shoulder to the immovable hatch again.

'I always wanted adventure ...' Kully agreed, sniffing glumly. Then his plumpish face brightened a little. 'I enjoyed exploding that Quark. That was tremendous fun!' he cried, more cheerfully.

Shaking the sweat out of his eyes, Jamie rested again. 'If we can get out of here, maybe we can explode some more,' he suggested temptingly, 'so get your fat carcass up here and push, will ye?'

Reluctantly Kully clambered up and squeezed himself breathlessly next to Jamie. Nose to nose they each clung to the rungs with one hand and shoved against the steel hatch with their opposite shoulder.

'Now ... heave!' Jamie commanded.

Time and again they heaved, pausing briefly to gulp a few breaths of sour, dusty air. The blood hammered in their ears like gunfire and their tight, aching chests were crushed in an invisible vice.

But the hatch did not budge a millimetre ...

Outside, so near and yet so far away, Balan, Kando and Teel were on the brink of total collapse. For the second time they had almost cleared the area immediately surrounding the drilling target. Two Quarks were now positoned face to face over the star-shaped marking and Dominator Toba had arrived with the drilling rig itself.

With a sadistic smile, Toba ordered Balan to carry the heavy awkward device over to the target. The rig consisted of a bulky cylindrical head, with fluted vanes running vertically around the side and a tapering barrel projecting downwards. A tripod support, slightly longer than the barrel, splayed out from the lower rim of the cylinder.

Balan tottered over the undulating sand and dumped the rig between the waiting Quarks' extended probes. Choking with the effort, he managed to lever it upright.

'Centre it!' Toba rasped, cuffing him viciously.

Staggering feebly in the shifting sand, Balan threw all his weight against the drill and eventually managed to manoeuvre the mouth of the barrel exactly over the centre of the star. Then he stumbled back, out of the way.

Toba ordered the Quarks to engage power. With eager whinnyings, they inserted their probes into sockets in the cylindrical head of the rig, while their antennae glowed blood-red.

Teel and Kando had cautiously approached and now supported Balan's sagging body between them, while staring in apprehensive fascination at the drilling operation.

'Angular bore parameters locked,' Toba rapped out.

'Affirmative,' chorused the Quarks.

'Initial depth parameter locked.'

'Affirmative.'

'First stage: commence.'

At first nothing happened. Then the ground shook as a low whining noise rose from the rig, steadily increasing to a higher and higher pitch. All at once an intense beam of light shot from the tip of the barrel a few centimetres above the target. After a few seconds, a clean black hole about ten centimetres across appeared in the centre of the star as the sand parted, melted and then fused around the energy beam.

The three Dulcians reeled backwards, averting their faces from the searing glare and covering their ears against the unbearably rapid throbbing of the machine. However, Toba seemed totally unaffected – his green, red-rimmed eyes resembled two miniature lasers as they reflected the massively concentrated power of the drill.

After a while the incandescent beam vanished, the sickening noise subsided, and the red glow faded from the Quarks' antennae. Toba peered into the crackling bore-hole and nodded approvingly, almost savouring the oily smoke which curled up into his face.

Shivering in his pupils' arms, Balan opened his eyes wide with terror and confusion. 'What do they want here?' he gasped faintly. 'What are they doing to our planet?'

Toba stepped back. 'Second stage,' he rapped. 'Commence.'

Under Rago's intensive interrogation, the Doctor had been trying to discover more about the Dominators' intentions while giving away as little as he could, but his persistent hesitations had finally exasperated the looming Navigator.

'Senex, your leader ... he is in the Capitol?' Rago repeated, at the end of his patience.

The Doctor scratched his head, coughed, shrugged, blew his nose and then frowned. 'Well, that's difficult to say ... I'm not absolutely sure,' he blustered.

Rago swung round on Zoe. 'Quark. Molecular adhesion!' he snapped.

Chattering eagerly, the robot swung out its probes and sent the terrified girl reeling against the wall where she hung limp and staring, like a severed puppet.

Rago turned back to the inanely grinning Time Lord. 'I asked you a question,' he hissed.

'Indeed you did,' the Doctor nodded, smiling despite Zoe's anguished moans behind him. 'Yes, Senex is most likely at the Capitol,' he conceded at last.

'How can I travel there?'

The Doctor looked sad. 'I'm afraid you can't, the capsule terminal at the survey module was destroyed. By Dominator Toba, I believe.'

Rago's face darkened with fury. Then he turned and ordered the Quark to prepare the saucer for flight.

The Doctor glimpsed Zoe's frightened, pleading face. 'Well, I do happen to know of a capsule not far from here,' he mumbled.

Rago fixed him with a searching glare.

The Doctor babbled on nervously. 'I didn't mention it before because I'm not sure it still works, but I'm sure you could get it going,' he smiled flatteringly.

'How large is this machine? Will it transport a Quark?'

The Doctor thought quickly. 'Oh dear no, I don't think so,' he muttered apologetically.

Rago waved his creaking gloves impatiently. 'We shall take our own craft,' he announced, striding across to the central dais.

Coughing and sniffing, the Doctor scurried diffidently

after him. 'Actually, if you remove the seats I think a Quark will just fit in,' he suggested.

The Doctor flinched as the Dominator abruptly rounded on him. Watching anxiously, Zoe feared that her friend had finally gone too far. To her relief, Rago nodded.

'You will show me the capsule immediately,' he ordered. Then he strode away to give instructions to the Quark, cancelling flight preparations.

The Doctor shuffled across to Zoe. 'Don't worry, my dear, you'll be right as rain once the effects wear off,' he murmured encouragingly.

'Why did you ... tell that monster ... about the capsule?' Zoe asked, fighting bravely against the paralysing effect of molecular adhesion.

'So we might have a chance to investigate the saucer's propulsion system,' the Doctor murmured, 'then we could discover what these Dominators are looking for here on Dulkis.'

Zoe did not look entirely convinced.

'Besides,' the Doctor added, 'if they take us off to the Capitol we won't be able to find out about Jamie ...'

Zoe looked even more anguished. 'If only they managed to find the shelter,' she whispered to herself.

The Doctor had been trying to eavesdrop on the Quark's complex coded transmission to the Fleet Leader at the communications unit, but he swiftly adopted his cretinous manner as Rago approached.

'Instruct Probationer Toba to rendezvous with me,' Rago concluded. 'Release the female.'

The Quark trained its probes on Zoe and, with a brief pulse of ultrasonic energy, set her free.

'And now you wil lead us to the capsule,' Rago commanded.

The Doctor bowed. 'Kindly come this way ...'

Rago stared suspiciously at the capsule, lying slightly on its side in deep sand under the cliff, a jumble of wires bristling out of the nose-cone. Then he glared at the Doctor, who tapped the battered hull and signalled the thumbs-up sign, while nodding and grunting encouragingly. Zoe lingered nearby, still stiff and dazed after her ordeal in the saucer, and watched the Doctor's pantomime with uneasy scepticism.

'A primitive machine, but functional,' the Dominator declared at last. 'Repairs can be effected quite easily.'

'Oh, certainly,' the Doctor agreed eagerly.

'It is well that you appreciate the futility of deception,' Rago added, completing his inspection.

The Doctor nodded vigorously, like some silent-movie comic, and Zoe had to suppress a sudden urge to giggle.

At that moment, Toba arrived.

'I intend to travel to meet the alien leader,' Rago informed his subordinate. 'You will remain and complete drilling operations.'

'Command accepted,' Toba readily acknowledged. He stared at the capsule in amazement. 'You intend to use this crude device?'

'Affirmative.'

Toba's malevolent eyes narrowed craftily. 'Is that wise? It could prove hazardous,' he rasped.

'I shall take a Quark as escort,' Rago retorted. 'You, Toba, will command in my absence.'

A spasm of excitement jerked through the Probationer's giant frame. 'Command accepted!' he rapped.

'However,' Rago continued with deliberate emphasis, 'I do not expect to find further destruction on my return.'

While the two Dominators and the Quark were busy preparing the capsule for flight, Zoe and the Doctor managed to confer quietly.

'...but why didn't you tell me about the shelter before?' the Doctor grumbled resentfully. 'I've been worried to death about Jamie.'

'I've hardly had much of a chance,' Zoe replied hotly.

The Doctor pondered silently, keeping a close watch on the group huddled round the capsule. 'I suppose it's just possible they found the shelter,' he sighed eventually. 'But if they didn't ...'

Zoe clutched at his sleeve. 'Couldn't we just creep away now back to the ruin ... and at least try to find them?' she pleaded, her eyes prickling with tears.

Gently the Doctor put his arm round her shoulder, but before he could reply Toba came striding over to them.

'You will follow me!' he commanded.

Zoe opened her mouth to resist, but the Doctor firmly propelled her forward, following Toba back in the direction of the saucer.

As they departed, the Doctor glanced back at the capsule where Rago and the Quark were busy making final adjustments. 'Happy landings,' he murmured.

In the atomic shelter, the plight of Jamie and Kully was now desperate. They clung to the ladder under the trap door, gasping for breath, their skins burning and their throats dry as ashes. In vain they listened, straining to detect the faintest hint of rescue. Some time earlier, the vibration of the drilling rig had provided a short-lived burst of euphoria and hope. But since it had stopped there had been total silence: nothing.

'It's no good, it's the end,' Kully whimpered. 'They've abandoned us. We'll never get out now.'

Jamie sagged against the cold steel rungs of the ladder, sweat pouring down his face and dripping off his chin. 'Doctor, where are ye?' he gasped, 'Where are ye?'

Then slowly Jamie roused himself. With an almost superhuman effort he balanced his body and placed both hands against the hatch. Then he straightened his legs and pushed his head up against his hands. Kully stared at him as if he were mad. Jamie's face went beetroot, he let out a blood-curdling yell and roared: '*MacCrimmons for ever ...*'

Kully stared speechless at the extraordinary totem-like figure with its squashed crimson face performing an almost magical rite in front of him.

Suddenly there was a faint grating sound, a trickle of dust and then a brief waft of cool air. Jamie bent his knees, lowered his arms and seized Kully in a wild embrace.

'It ... it moved ... it moved ...' screamed Jamie.

Kully looked doubtfully up at the heavy trap door: 'You must have imagined it ...'

'Come on, man, heave!' Jamie shrieked, almost knocking

himself out as he thrust frenziedly upwards again with head and hands.

Sceptically Kully did the same. The hatch stirred and rose a few millimetres and cool, fresh air rushed through the gap.

'We did it, we did it!' Kully yelled, drinking the air greedily. 'What did I tell you, Jamie?'

After a few seconds they were obliged to lower the trap and rest.

'Aren't you the wee ray of sunshine,' Jamie panted ironically. 'But we're no free yet.'

'Oh don't be such a defeatist,' Kully scolded him, 'it's no good giving up now.'

'Who's giving up?' Jamie demanded, throwing himself at the hatch again.

'Well, *I'm* not,' Kully cried, adding his considerable weight.

Gratefully they gulped great lungfuls of air as the trap rose several centimetres.

'Even if we canna get oot, at least the air can get in,' Jamie observed while they rested once again.

'No good wasting time,' Kully panted, heaving away with all his might yet again.

Shaking his head in wry astonishment at Kully's miraculous new lease of life, Jamie straightened his legs and pushed. Suddenly the hatch gave way so abruptly that they all but toppled off the ladder. Jamie just managed to reach through and grab a piece of metal piping to prop the trap partly open. After another brief rest they moved a rung or two further up the ladder. Then, with a final heave they opened the hatch completely.

Jamie scrambled through and sat thankfully on the ledge, his head and shoulders partially hidden among the debris. 'Well, come on up. No use hiding down there,' he urged.

Cautiously Kully hauled himself up through the square opening. They had only a brief opportunity to luxuriate in the fresh air before a feared and familiar noise made Kully start so violently that he almost tumbled back into the shelter.

'Quarks,' Jamie exclaimed, peering intently through the wreckage. He could just make out Teel and Kando working at the drilling site surrounded by several robots. 'These Dominators aren't much good without their Quarks, are they?' he mused.

Kully squinted uneasily through the debris. 'So?'

'So, we destroyed one. Why not others?'

Kully looked incredulous. 'Attack the Quarks?' he whispered. 'But we had the laser thing before. Now it's buried somewhere under this lot.'

Jamie squeezed his fleshy arm encouragingly. 'Och, we MacCrimmons never had such things – but we did for the Redcoats right enough,' he muttered dramatically.

The Dulcian scratched his balding head in bewilderment: 'MacCrimmons? Redcoats?' he echoed blankly.

'Never mind, ye wee Sassenach,' Jamie murmured impatiently. 'Listen, we'll rescue Teel and Kando. Are ye with me?' he demanded, wrenching free the length of pipe with which he had propped open the hatch, and brandishing it confidently.

Steeling himself, Kully swallowed nervously and then nodded.

With the light of battle in his eyes, Jamie led the way. They wriggled cautiously through the maze of debris and into a gully behind the ruin which led up the cliffs and was not visible from the drilling site. After a strenuous climb, they were soon edging their way along the meandering clifftop, spying on the scattered groups of Quarks at work among the dunes stretching below them. Eventually they came upon one of the perimeter targets, where Balan and two Quarks were operating a rig.

They threw themselves down in the sand and shielded their eyes as the drill reached maximum power and the whole area lit up like a magnesium flare.

'They seem to be drilling in five places ... in a kind of pattern,' Jamie shouted into Kully's ear above the whining throb of the rig.

'But what for?'

'I dinna ken,' Jamie shouted, 'but I ken what we're going to do right enough.' Using his piece of pipe as a lever, Jamie quickly dislodged a small but heavy boulder from the brittle sandstone. Then grasping it in both hands, he leaped to his feet and hurled it with every ounce of his strength over the cliff edge.

Narrowly missing Balan, the missile struck one of the Quarks squarely on its vertical antenna. Instantly, both Quarks disconnected themselves from the rig and swung round, scanning the dunes in a frenzy of bleating. Balan flung himself headlong in a panic, and lay still.

Chuckling with delight, Kully dug furiously with his fingers and prised up another rock. 'Do it again ... do it again ...' he begged, passing it to the crouching Jamie.

Jumping up, Jamie repeated the attack. 'Take that ye wee porridge pot!' he yelled as the second stone crashed onto the domed head of the same Quark.

The other Quark jerked round and fired its probes. A fountain of molten sand flew up into Jamie's face as he threw himself flat. Suddenly the cliff started to disintegrate around them as the two Quarks fired simultaneously, carving deep gouges out of the soft ridge.

'Time to go!' cried Jamie, scrambling up. But at that same moment there was a mighty roar and the whole cliff collapsed, hurling him helplessly down onto the dunes and leaving Kully scrabbling desperately halfway up the crumbling face in an avalanche of sand.

Picking himself up, Jamie raced towards a steep V-shaped gorge dividing the cliff at right angles nearby. Sizzling spouts of sand soared all around him as he fled up the sloping cleft with both Quarks tramping rapidly in pursuit.

Meanwhile Kully had managed to scramble back to the clifftop, tripping, as he went, over the length of pipe. Seizing it, he stooped low and scampered towards some large spherical boulders precariously perched on the edge of the gorge. Reaching them, he saw Jamie below him, running for his life as the gorge exploded around him. Kneeling behind the biggest stone, Kully inserted the pipe at an angle and heaved. To his delight, the boulder stirred and settled back again. Tingling with excitement, Kully waited until the two Quarks were almost exactly beneath him and then threw all his weight against the pipe.

Gradually the huge stone moved forward. Then it tipped over the lip of the gorge and rolled faster and faster, bouncing down the steep slope in gigantic arching leaps. Recklessly Kully stood silhouetted against the sky yelling in triumph as the boulder flattened one Quark completely and knocked the other on its side in a cascade of sparks.

'Mac ... Crimming's for ever. Death to the Redcoats!' Kully's victorious cry changed abruptly into a squawk of terror as the edge of the gorge gave way under him and he plunged over and over in a flailing of arms and legs, finally coming to rest next to the astounded Jamie in a hollow.

'Well...' he spluttered, spitting sand out of his mouth and blinking his watering eyes. 'Well, I'm with you now all right!'

A little way down the gorge, the damaged Quark was already whirring back into action. Levering itself upright again, it swung its glowing antennae wildly about like a bundle of fluorescent blades, seeking out its prey trapped in the dead-end of the valley.

8

Clues

The Council had been in session for hours. Director Senex
reclined in his chair, silent and pensive, only half listening to
the interminable drone of the Councillors' deliberations. The
violent memory of the Quark attack in the survey module was
burnt indelibly in their minds and they had still not recovered
from the shock and disappointment of Chairman Tensa's
advice.

There was a long silence. Suddenly the Director's face
betrayed the deep and impotent anger surging through his
being. 'It is our tragedy to do nothing. We are the prisoners of
our own negative philosophy,' he declared. 'Little wonder
that some of our youth – like my own son – are determined to
rebel.'

'But why should the aliens intend us harm?' asked Deputy
Bovem for the thousandth time. 'No intelligent race would
indulge in irrational purposeless violence ...'

Scarcely were the words out of his mouth than the wall of
the chamber parted to admit the huge lumbering figure of
Rago, closely followed by his Quark escort. There was an
awed and appalled silence while the Dominator flashed his
emerald glare around the assembly.

'Who is in control here?' Rago rasped.

Senex cleared his throat. 'I am the Director,' he replied
calmly.

'If you would care to make an appointment ...' Bovem
began.

Rago turned on the Deputy, his boots and gloves creaking
eerily. 'Listen and obey,' he commanded. 'I require
information.'

Chairman Tensa strode forward. 'I must protest. Such discourtesy to the Council is intolerable!' he cried.

Rago stared at him incredulously. 'Protest?' he hissed. 'You defy me? You defy a Dominator?'

Tensa stood his ground. 'Our Director's rank demands respect,' he retorted.

'Demands ... respect?' Rago echoed, his harsh voice brittle with mockery. 'Your leader is nothing to me. I respect only superior force.' He swung back to loom over Senex who had risen with great dignity. 'I command you to supply ...'

'Sir, you would do better to request rather than command,' Tensa interrupted, forcing his way between Senex and the massive alien.

'After all, your visit is not even on the Council Agenda,' objected an aged Councillor.

Tensa opened his mouth to continue.

'Quark!' Rago rapped, stepping quickly back and pointing at Tensa's outraged face. 'Destroy.'

A ghost of a smile, chased by a look of sheer uncomprehending horror, flitted across Tensa's fine features. Before he could speak, the robot bleated its warning and then discharged a brief, devastating bolt of energy. Tensa's robe fluttered to the floor around the pulverised remains of his body. The Councillors recoiled and fell back in their chairs in stunned silence.

Rago towered over Senex. 'I have no desire to repeat such action,' he stated tonelessly. 'Let it demonstrate that we Dominators are to be obeyed without question.'

Senex stared back at the alien, his eyes dulled with shock.

'You will place at our disposal the strongest of your species,' Rago instructed him.

After a long pause, Senex recovered his voice. 'You ... you seek our assistance?' he said in a dreamlike monotone.

Rago smiled a bleak, humourless smile. 'Assistance? I require slaves. Nothing more, nothing less,' he retorted.

Somehow Senex managed to talk through his numbed lips. 'Had you come to Dulkis in peace we should have done all in our power to assist you, but we cannot bow to ...'

'What we require, we take,' Rago thundered dismissively.

'We control ten galaxies. Our mission is to colonise certain others. For this task our Quarks are needed, therefore we must replace their functions on our home planets.'

'With slaves,' Senex added flatly.

'Exactly. Those selected from your population will be fortunate. They will be saved.'

'Saved?' croaked Bovem. 'Saved from what?'

'Only the strongest are suitable,' Rago hissed, striding towards the wall and rounding on the cowering assembly. 'You will co-operate or perish. The choice is yours.'

The wall opened and the alien and his robot disappeared. After a long time some of the Councillors ventured forward and knelt by the broken body in their midst.

'Can we not punish them?' the aged Councillor cried in a choking voice, wringing his gnarled hands incessantly.

Bovem glanced round at each member in turn. 'What did the alien mean ... some of us would be saved?' he breathed. 'Saved from what?'

Sinking back into his chair, Senex shook his head and sighed. 'Perhaps from ourselves,' he murmured hopelessly. 'Perhaps from ourselves ...'

When the Doctor and Zoe arrived back at the saucer with Toba, the control centre was humming with activity. Quarks marched about, plugging themselves into computer terminals and systems displays as they performed the complex sequences of the drilling operation. Toba began to stride up and down, bloated with self-importance and revelling in his temporary role of commander.

'Report progress to Fleet Leader,' he instructed a Quark. 'All perimeter bores completed. Central bore approaching optima ...'

The Doctor stood in the shadows with Zoe, his hands plunged deep in his pockets, long furrows stretching each side of his nose. 'We must find out what they're drilling for,' he exclaimed.

'Fat chance with all these Quarks everywhere,' Zoe grimaced.

'Hmm. If only we could distract them somehow,' mused

the Doctor, peering vainly about for inspiration.

At that moment, two symbols started flashing on the Quark control unit. Toba rushed over and thumped the panel with his giant fist. One of the symbols stopped flashing and remained glowing.

'Another Quark has been destroyed and a third has been damaged,' Toba raged.

'This could be just what we need,' the Doctor muttered, pulling Zoe further into the shadows. They watched the frenetic alien intently.

'Quarks follow!' screamed Toba.

Immediately the robots disconnected themselves and followed Toba out of the control centre in a sparking, chattering line. Soon Zoe and the Doctor were left quite alone.

'Who would destroy a Quark?' Zoe wondered.

The Doctor grinned broadly. 'I think I can guess!' he cried, rubbing his hands together gleefully.

'Jamie!' Zoe exclaimed after a momentary pause. 'So they did escape after all.'

'Alive and kicking by the sound of things,' the Doctor agreed. 'Good lads! We must make the most of our opportunity.' He scurried off round the huge circular chamber, peering closely at print-outs, displays, inspection panels and crystal switches, and muttering furiously to himself the whole time.

Zoe did her best to keep up with him. 'What exactly are we looking for?' she asked breathlessly.

'I want to find out what they feed this thing on,' replied the Doctor, darting into an elaborate assembly of flickering tubes.

Zoe trailed after him. 'Well, the Quarks seem to use ultrasonics, so presumably it's a fuel capable of producing random amplified fields and accelerated phases,' she suggested.

'Hmm, it must be quite powerful too,' added the Doctor, poking thoughtfully among the coloured fluorescent columns.

'Well, that's what I just said ...' Zoe stopped and blushed, realising too late that she had been sent up. 'Look, if you don't

94

want my help, Doctor ...'

'Oh but I do, Zoe,' the Doctor assured her, backing carefully out of the mass of tubes and standing upright again. 'Now, my dear, where do you think the essential power source is lurking?'

Zoe walked around for a few seconds frowning with concentration. 'Well, if they use ultrasonics ...'

'No, no, no ...' cried the Doctor, 'more likely to be some form of particle acceleration.' He dropped to his knees and started to crawl round and round the central control dais, his nose to the deck like a bloodhound. Eventually he stopped, sniffed, crawled backwards a few metres, stopped, sniffed, crawled forwards a metre and finally stopped. Then he tapped a small panel in the side of the dais.

'Here we are!' he cried. 'Just as I expected.' He tapped again and then listened. 'Or is it?' he demanded, kneeling up and staring enquiringly at Zoe.

She shrugged impatiently.

'Well, there's only one way to find out.' Taking a small penknife from his pocket, the Doctor began prising at the edge of the access panel, still muttering away. Suddenly the panel sprang free. Carefully the Doctor removed it and peered inside. He cocked his head and listened. Then he sniffed a few times and to Zoe's astonishment, licked his finger and poked it into the opening for several seconds. 'Oh dear ...' he sighed. 'Oh dear, oh dear, oh dear ...' He clicked his tongue and shook his head.

'Whatever's the matter Doctor?'

Instead of answering, the Doctor pulled out a compact, tubular instrument, shook it, blew on it and then tied it to a long piece of string. Cautiously he lowered the gadget into the opening, paying out the string as it went.

Suddenly a series of sharp clicks emerged from the gadget. The Doctor frowned and nodded energetically. 'I thought so...' he murmured, paying out more string. The clicking increased dramatically as the Geiger counter registered radition.

'Atomic reactor?' Zoe asked, craning over the Doctor's shoulder.

95

The Doctor stared down at the clusters of spherical vessels filling the entire area under the dais. 'No, my dear, nothing as crude as that,' he replied at last. He hauled the Geiger counter out of the trap and thoughtfully wrapped the string tightly round it. 'No. This is almost certainly a form of negative mass flux absorption system.'

Zoe's eyebrows shot up. 'A what?'

'A sort of radiation vacuum cleaner,' the Doctor explained. 'It would account for the sudden disappearance of radio-activity from the Island.'

'You mean this thing sucked it all up?'

'In a manner of speaking, Zoe, yes.'

Zoe pondered a moment. 'Then what on earth are they drilling all those holes out there for?'

The Doctor tapped his nose with the cocoon of string. 'I wish I knew, my dear ... I wish I knew ...' he mumbled vacantly.

When Toba and his cohort of Quarks reached the fourth perimeter target near the gorge, Balan was still lying dazed by the rig. Toba yanked him to his feet.

'A Quark has been destroyed, another damaged. Who was responsible?' he hissed.

The frail Dulcian whimpered helplessly. Toba shook his victim like a bundle of sticks. Balan stared like a terrified animal. 'I did not see ... I was working ... I was almost hit ...' he pleaded.

The Quarks had formed a circle round the rig and were scanning the area with wickedly slicing antennae. 'Evidence of alien assault,' one of them squawked.

Toba gripped Balan's stick-like arms mercilessly. 'Is there a resistant force on this Island?' he demanded hopefully.

'There is no force on Dulkis,' Balan answered feebly.

The Dominator flung the old man aside and gazed around, his green, red-rimmed eyes alight with malice. 'Quarks, search the Island. Destroy any alien specimens not accounted for. Total destruction!' he raved, his huge nostrils flaring hideously. Having ordered a Quark to escort Balan back to the saucer, he marched away to the central bore target by the ruined museum.

There, Kando and Teel still laboured to clear the remaining debris under the relentless surveillance of a pair of Quarks.

'Perimeter four has been attacked and a Quark eliminated,' Toba spat, stamping up to them.

Kando turned excitedly to Teel. 'Kully must have ...'Too late she bit her lip and blushed.

Toba seized her by the hair and twisted viciously. The willowy girl folded like a wounded gull. 'What do you know about this?' Toba screamed.

'Leave her ...' Teel blurted out, wielding a metal strip.

Dropping Kando, Toba turned on the youth. 'Do you dare to defy a Dominator?' he challenged in an awesome whisper.

Suddenly Teel hurled himself forward, flailing uselessly at the enormous armoured figure standing over the pale, quaking girl.

Toba did not move, but merely gloated with creaking grunts of pleasure as Teel battered vainly against his plated chest. Eventually, the Dominator tired of the game as his assailant's slim arms quickly weakened.

'Quark. Restrain!' he commanded.

One of the robots advanced on Teel, opening its probes like a pincer.

'No!' Kando gasped, scrambling up.

Toba seized her wrists and shook her like a dish cloth. 'No one ever questions a Dominator,' he rapped.

The Quark caught Teel round the waist and lifted him effortlessly off the ground. Then it tightened its grip and Teel almost folded in half.

'Stop. Please stop!' Kando cried, hanging limp from Toba's gloves.

'Power!' Toba ordered.

There was a dull cracking sound and Teel uttered a long hollow moan of agony.

'Stop. I'll tell you ...' Kando shrieked.

'Release!' commanded Toba.

The Quark immediately opened its probes and Teel dropped to the sand, writhing silently.

'Who attacked my Quarks?' Toba demanded, thrusting his face into Kando's as he raised her level with him.

'It ... it must have been Kully.'

'The specimen Kully is destroyed,' retorted Toba, twisting Kando's slender wrists in opposite directions. She struggled to speak, but the excruciating pain paralysed her throat.

Then the Dominator's emerald eyes shrank into tiny brilliant points. 'The other boy ... the stupid one. He must be responsible ...' he hissed. 'Where is he?'

Kando shook her head and then closed her eyes, waiting for the end. But her tormentor suddenly released her and she slumped at his feet, huddled and trembling.

Toba loomed over his two victims, as if he were about to crush them out of existence. 'One of you must know where the stupid one is,' he breathed at last. 'And you will tell me ...'

The Doctor only just had time to replace the inspection panel in the dais when the Quark drove Balan into the control centre. While the robot went over to monitor the bore-project display, the Doctor and Zoe managed a furtive conversation with the exhausted Educator. Zoe was overjoyed to hear that Jamie had probably destroyed another Quark and damaged a third. Despite Balan's condition, the Doctor plied him with whispered questions in an attempt to solve the mystery of the drilling operations.

'Balan, when the Dulcian scientists exploded the atomic device on the Island all those years ago ... where did they obtain the fission material?'

Balan cast his clouded mind back as best he could. 'I believe that their requirements came from somewhere in the northern hemisphere ...'

'The other side of the planet. Then why are the Dominators drilling here?'

Balan shrugged wearily. 'Perhaps because the planet's crust is very thin just here.'

The Doctor slapped himself on the forehead. 'The magma!' he gasped, turning to Zoe. 'The molten planetary core ...' He turned back to Balan. 'Could the magma be radioactive?'

The Educator looked uncertain. 'The minor eruptions which occur here from time to time have never registered such radiation, Doctor.'

'But are we sure these Dominators are drilling for fuel?' Zoe interjected.

The Doctor gestured at the schematic display in front of the Quark. 'It's the pattern that intrigues me, Zoe,' he murmured. 'Four drill holes arranged in a square, with a fifth hole where the diagonals cross in the centre ... fascinating ...'

Zoe squinted across the chamber at the project display. 'I think that fifth hole is the one by the ruin, Doctor.'

The Doctor nodded. 'The bull's-eye ...' he murmured.

At that moment Probationer Toba burst in followed by the Quark with Kando and Teel. The latter was stumbling, doubled over with both arms clutched across his chest.

'Quarks, assemble the specimens,' ordered Toba.

The two robots herded Kando and Teel next to the Doctor, Zoe and Balan. Zoe tried to help Kando support the injured Teel, but they were brutally shoved apart.

Toba walked slowly round the frightened huddle. 'The other simpleton – the boy – is missing,' he rasped. 'He has defied the Dominators and attacked the Quarks. Where is he?'

There was a long silence. Zoe glanced anxiously at the Doctor. Balan gazed in horror at Kando and the semi-conscious Teel.

Toba walked round them again, his vast hands clenching and unclenching with an ominous squeaking. 'You will die, one by one, until you inform me ...' he tormented them.

Still there was silence. Toba stopped and jabbed his creaking glove at Balan. 'You were a witness. Speak.'

The Educator stared mesmerised into Toba's glittering eyes.

The Dominator stepped back. 'Quark, destroy!'

One of the robots whirred expectantly. Kando cried out and clung convulsively to Teel. A sizzling bolt tore through the air and Balan's protective suit collapsed in a heap, empty.

Striding over it with savage indifference, Toba towered over the Doctor. 'You know the simpleton boy. Where is he?

Answer or die.'

The Doctor hesitated, fiddling nervously with his tie and blinking meekly. Then his eyes narrowed and he curled his lip in disgust and contempt. But he remained silent.

Zoe held her breath, watching the Doctor's struggle to contain his outrage with anxious admiration.

'Answer!' hissed Toba.

The Doctor compressed his lips and set his jaw. Something in his eyes seemed to disconcert the Dominator, something he had not anticipated.

After a brief duel of wills, Toba turned abruptly and lumbered away a few paces. 'Quark!' he rapped.

The nearest Quark jerked its probes round towards the Doctor and waited, its antennae glowing red and its circuits clattering in growing excitement.

Zoe thrust her fist into her mouth and shut her eyes ...

9

Last Chances

Jamie and Kully had managed to escape from the gorge by the skin of their teeth after the damaged Quark, hard on their heels, had suddenly ground to a smoking halt half-way up the slope, its traction mechanism finally burnt out, but its probes still firing intermittently. As they dragged themselves dazed but unharmed onto the plateau above, they found their escape cut off. A huge crescent of Quarks was advancing towards them, driving them relentlessly back into the gorge.

'Where did all yon tin Sassenachs spring from?' Jamie exclaimed, pulling Kully down into a hollow just in time to avoid the vicious crossfire of ultrasonic pulses which suddenly shredded the air above them.

A stinging torrent of sand erupted a few metres away and fell on them, almost completely burying them. Jamie wriggled furiously to and fro, working his way in a kind of trench towards the steep cliff edge.

'Come away, Kully!' Jamie yelled above the sizzling din. 'Let's get to the shelter and lie doggo till things cool down a wee bit.'

'Doggo?' Kully echoed, spitting the sand out of his mouth and trying to imitate Jamie's example.

With a series of deafening roars, several more huge columns of sand shot into the air and scattered around them. Jamie turned himself round and grabbed Kully's flailing hands, and hauled the squirming Dulcian towards the steep drop.

'Come on, they're far too close for comfort!' Jamie panted, heaving Kully's sweating bulk through the trench.

When the exhausted Dulcian reached the precipitous edge,

he went rigid with terror. Without thinking, Jamie rolled himself over the cliff and dragged Kully after him ...

Half rolling and half sliding down the brittle sandstone face, they soon reached the dunes below. Then, after a hair-raising skirmish with a Quark patrol advancing from the direction of the saucer, they eventually reached the deserted ruin.

Bundling Kully through the hatch into the atomic shelter, Jamie searched frantically around in the wreckage until he located the tip of the periscope mechanism. After a brief struggle, he managed to clear away the obstruction that was preventing it extending properly. Nearby, he came across the blocked inlet for the ventilator system and soon dislodged enough sand to allow at least some air through into the shelter below. Then he took cover.

Squeezing himself through the hatch, Jamie carefully lowered it shut after making sure that no loose debris could jam it again. He found Kully lying on one of the bunks.

'That was marvellous fun,' Kully panted, 'especially the avalanche.'

'Aye, we fair stirred them up,' Jamie chuckled, getting his breath back. 'We'll lie low a wee while and keep 'em guessing. Then we'll oot and bag another Quark or two.' Just then his stomach rumbled noisily. 'Och, I'm fair starving,' he grinned.

Kully patted his own ample belly. 'Fighting is hungry work,' he agreed cheerfully. Levering himself off the bunk, he began to rummage in a small locker unit underneath it. With a whoop of triumph he stood up brandishing a slim bar wrapped in foil. Tearing off the wrapper, he broke the bar in half and handed Jamie a piece of a grey waxy substance.

Jamie sniffed at it unenthusiastically. 'What's this stuff?'

'Basic nutrients,' Kully explained, cramming his portion into his mouth and chewing greedily. 'Proteins, vitamins, carbohydrates. You can survive on it for annos.' He swallowed and licked his lips.

Jamie bit off a tiny piece and chewed tentatively. 'I hope I'll no need to do that: it tastes like old candles,' he grimaced, tossing the remainder to Kully.

Rousing himself, Jamie went across to the periscope,

grasped the handles and pushed upwards. It slid quite freely, despite emitting a nasty scraping sound. 'Let's see how the land lies ...' he muttered, peering into the binocular viewer. For a while he was silent , twisting the tube slowly from side to side, then he turned.

Kully stopped chewing and stared at him.

'We've got visitors ...' Jamie said. 'Lots of them.'

'Quark, order cancelled. Toba, what is the meaning of this?'

Zoe cried out in gratitude and relief as Rago's powerful voice suddenly rang around the control centre.

Hissing with frustration, Toba spun round to face his leader as he emerged from the elevator followed by his escort.

Rago stared down at Balan's suit, at the cowering figures of Kando and Teel, and finally turned to his sullen subordinate. 'Explain, Probationer Toba,' he snapped.

The Doctor mopped his glistening face and squeezed Zoe's cold hand gratefully. 'That was a trifle near the mark ...' he whispered wryly.

Toba brazened things out as best he could. 'We were attacked, Navigator Rago. A Quark was destroyed, another damaged. In the emergency I decided to ...'

'Emergency? Rago sneered. 'A handful of primitives manage to incapacitate a Quark and you interrupt vital projects to waste time and valuable power chasing them all over the Island?'

Toba creaked forward a few paces: 'I decided to hold an inquiry, Navigator ...'

Rago turned impatiently and frowned dangerously at the bore-project display. 'Is drilling complete?'

'All four perimeter bores are completed,' said Toba hurriedly.

'And the centre target?'

Toba hesitated uncomfortably. 'A minor delay ... caused by strata deviations.'

Rago leaned closer. 'The only deviations have occurred in your behaviour, Toba. Quark power reserves approach minimal levels and drilling is incomplete, yet you fritter precious resources in fruitless chases and in killing insignificant aliens.'

Toba was aware of the Doctor's contemptuous stare boring into his back. 'I considered it my duty ...' he protested.

'Your duty is to complete the project according to schedule,' Rago thundered. 'Have the rockets been installed at the perimeter targets?'

The Doctor's face lit up with profound interest and anticipation and he edged surreptitiously closer to gain a better view of the project display across the vast chamber .

'Not yet,' Toba admitted after an embarrassed pause.

'Do it at once,' Rago ordered. 'Is the seeding trigger approaching criticality?'

'There has not been sufficient time to determine.'

'Time?' Rago boomed, the rims of his eyes burning like red-hot rings. 'Toba, if you have jeopardised this most vital stage of our mission by your obsessive irresponsibility, then you will remain here on Dulkis and perish with the weaker primitives.'

The Doctor observed intently as Toba hurried across to the central dais and opened a heavily armoured circular panel near the one he and Zoe had examined earlier. A soft pink glow spread over Toba's body as he withdrew a large opaque object resembling an ostrich egg, encased within a kind of glass shell with short blunt spikes protruding in all directions. The Probationer peered at each protrusion in turn, the glow transforming his features into a caricature carnival mask.

'Report!' Rago rapped impatiently.

'The seeding trigger approaches criticality minus gamma.' Toba carefully replaced the device and closed the thick panel.

Zoe glanced at the Doctor. He was muttering silently to himself and nodding knowingly as he watched Toba's every move.

'Minus gamma. Then there is not a moment to lose, Toba,' Rago warned urgently. 'The centre bore must be completed and projectiles will be inserted in the perimeter targets immediately. Understood?'

'Command accepted,' Toba promptly acknowledged.

Rago strode across to the Quark control unit and passed his enormous hand over a sequence of coloured keys. 'The search is cancelled. All Quarks to position at drilling stations and conserve power until further instructions,' he ordered. Then he turned back to his subordinate. 'I shall communicate with Fleet Leader regarding the exploitation potential of the primitives. Meanwhile, keep them under constant supervision.'

Ordering the two Quarks to follow with the four surviving prisoners, Toba strode towards the elevator.

'Toba.'

The Probationer stopped and waited.

'This is your final chance. Do not waste it.'

As the captives were prodded into motion by the Quarks, the Doctor glanced sideways at Zoe. 'Speaking of chances,' he muttered, 'from now on we must be sure not to waste any of ours.'

For some time the assembled Quarks had remained motionless and silent outside the ruin, like a plantation of dwarf mechanical trees waiting for some unwary bird to light among them. Jamie peered apprehensively at them through the periscope, while Kully lay on a bunk, nervously devouring the emergency rations out of the locker. The tension was almost tangible, like the closeness in the air before a thunderstorm.

Suddenly Jamie whooped with delight. 'More visitors, Kully!' he exclaimed, as the Doctor, Zoe, Kando and Teel trudged into view.

Kully elbowed him aside. 'Balan isn't with them,' he muttered anxiously, panning the periscope. Then he groaned.

'More Quarks?' Jamie eagerly seized the viewer again, but he too groaned as he watched Toba arrive and start supervising some of the Quarks around the rig. 'We've got to get them in here with us. We canna just leave them up there ...,' he said, focusing on the Doctor and Zoe.

'Here we go again,' Kully sighed, clutching his head in despair.

The young Highlander grinned mischievously and glanced quickly round the bleak concrete shelter. His eyes lit on the plastic sheeting covering the bunks. He whipped a gleaming dirk out of its sheath inside his sock and rapidly slit the sheeting free from one of the mattresses. Kully watched in baffled silence as he cut a long narrow strip from one side.

'Now listen carefully, Kully,' Jamie said firmly, 'this is what we'll do ...'

Guarded by a single Quark and huddled some distance from the drilling apparatus, the Doctor and the others covered their ears and averted their faces as the rig began to whine and throb and an intense beam of light flashed down the barrel into the target hole. As the ground vibrated and the whole area shimmered in the hot searing glare, the Doctor attempted to squint under his thick dark eyebrows to observe the awesome procedure.

Zoe put her mouth close to his ear. 'Any idea what they're looking for?' she shouted.

The Doctor forced his blinking watering eyes to stay at least partially open for a few more seconds. Then he turned to her. 'Oh, I don't think they intend to take anything *out* of the hole, Zoe,' he yelled back. 'More likely they're going to drop something *in*.'

'But what?'

Before the Doctor could reply, he caught a glimpse of someone moving among the debris up by the ruin, behind their Quark sentry. 'Oh dear me ... oh no ...' he muttered, as Jamie emerged crouching low and dropped onto his stomach behind a low ridge of sand.

The attention of Toba and of the Quarks was totally absorbed in the screaming and throbbing drill, as Jamie started wriggling his way towards the unsuspecting robot. With his back to the rig, the Doctor was able to watch in anxious fascination as Jamie knelt up behind the Quark, reached into his shirt and unrolled the thin plastic strip. Reaching forward, Jamie carefully wound the strong material round and round the robot's thick, concertina legs, binding them tightly together.

The reckless lad froze as the Quark's antennae waggled and flickered and its domed head stirred suspiciously. Then the robot suddenly shifted slightly and its rectangular foot came down, trapping Jamie's hand underneath. Thrusting the end

106

of the plastic strip into his mouth, Jamie stifled his agony.

Promptly the Doctor stepped forward. 'Excuse me, sir!' he cried.

The sparking robot immediately unfolded its probes and went to advance on the Doctor, but as it tried to take a step it overbalanced and its bulky body pitched forward into the sand.

At that same moment, Kully scampered out from behind the ruin and enveloped the Quark's antennae in the plastic sheet, completely depriving it of its senses.

Blowing frantically on his throbbing hand, Jamie leaped up and, while Kully hurriedly shepherded the astonished prisoners safely into the ruin, he dragged a heavy beam from some nearby wreckage and heaved it on top of the struggling robot.

The disabled Quark started to emit a piercing distress signal which at first was inaudible against the howl of the drilling rig, but eventually Toba heard it.

Ordering operations to cease, Toba scanned the area in a frenzy. 'A Quark has been attacked and the specimens have escaped ...' he screamed as the glare and the noise of the apparatus subsided. Striding towards the ruin, Toba hurled the beam aside and ripped the sheet off the stricken Quark, which began rolling about on its back like a mechanical beetle.

'Quark, where are the specimens?' Toba demanded.

'Sensors temporarily inoperable. No data recorded,' bleated the robot pathetically.

Toba swung round hysterically. 'Quarks, search. Search and destroy ...' he shrieked, starting to clamber over the wreckage around the ruined museum, kicking and hurling debris in all directions.

'Command cancelled!' Rago's voice sliced like a blade through the hot muggy air.

Toba lurched to a halt, his huge limbs jerking spasmodically.

'Why has drilling been interrupted yet again?' Rago demanded icily, approaching between the assembled Quarks.

Toba mumbled an explanation.

Rago surveyed the silent rig. 'Probationer, if you cannot perform the tasks assigned to you here, you will never gain

107

full Dominator status,' he rasped. 'Complete the bore.'

With as much dignity as he could muster, Toba clambered back onto the sand and strode back to the rig.

'The primitives will not escape unpunished,' Rago added with condescending generosity, as Toba ordered the Quarks by the rig to reconnect power. 'Fleet Leader confirms that Dulcians are totally unsuitable for our projects. Therefore they will die with their planet.'

Toba's eyes flashed with malignant satisfaction. 'Then the sooner we complete operations the better.'

'Exactly. I shall now supervise the positioning of the projectiles at the perimeter targets. Inform me when the centre bore is prepared for the seeding trigger.' Rago commanded a detachment of Quarks to accompany him and then strode rapidly away across the dunes.

Jamie had only just had time to squeeze himself through the hatch before the frenzied Toba clambered onto the wreckage above the open trap-door. In the shelter below, the six fugitives had then waited in total silence, scarcely daring even to breathe until the two Dominators moved away. Then at last Jamie had carefully lowered the heavy trap and jumped down to join the others.

'That was extremely rash of you, Jamie,' the Doctor scolded him, smiling appreciatively, 'those Quarks can be appallingly dangerous.'

'Och, they're nae so terrible,' Jamie grinned, giving Zoe an affectionate hug.

Kully turned from the periscope. 'Where's Balan?' he asked.

Gently, Kando explained what had happened.

'You did all you could, Kully,' Teel murmured, nursing his bruised ribs. 'Thanks to you and Jamie, the rest of us are safe.'

'I'm not so sure about that,' Jamie told him. 'I just heard those Dominators saying that the Dulcians are no use to them.'

Kando smiled innocently. 'Then they will leave us in peace now.'

Jamie glanced at the Doctor and Zoe in embarrassment.

Then he turned to the three Dulcians. 'They said that you would all die ... with your planet,' he mumbled helplessly.

Kully peered back into the periscope. 'They can't destroy Dulkis ...' he protested indignantly.

Just then the shelter began to vibrate as Toba's unit resumed drilling outside.

The Doctor coughed and cleared his throat. 'I'm afraid they can. I believe they intend to use your planet as fuel for their fleet.'

There was a long, shocked silence. The Doctor shrugged, smiled bleakly and then examined his fingernails minutely. 'I'm most terribly sorry.'

Then Zoe stuck her chin out. 'But Doctor, you decided that their saucer uses atomic power,' she objected.

'There are no suitable radioactive minerals in this hemisphere,' Kando reminded him.

The Doctor waved his arms impatiently. 'No, no, no, there is no reactor in the saucer, only a radiation accumulator and converter system.'

Everyone looked blank.

'Negative mass flux absorption,' the Doctor cried, glancing triumphantly around him.

'What?' Jamie gasped.

'They suck up the radiation, store it and then convert it into propulsion?' Zoe speculated.

'The Doctor beamed at her. 'Precisely, Zoe.' He turned to the Dulcians. 'Remember how all the radioactivity disappeared from the Island as soon as the saucer arrived?'

Kando and Teel nodded and a glimmer of understanding flickered between them.

Jamie was speechless for a moment. 'So, why are they doing all that drilling out there?' he suddenly blurted out, in a burst of frustrated desperation.

'Can't imagine why no one's asked me that before!' the Doctor cried, fumbling in his pockets and unearthing a broken stick of chalk. Then he rushed over to the wall and started drawing feverishly. 'Four deep holes ...' he said, marking out the corners of a square with little crosses. 'Another deep hole – the one outside here –' he announced, putting a small star at the centre of the square.

The Doctor glanced over his shoulder at the semicircle of puzzled faces staring intently at his sketch. 'Now, a rocket is fired down each of the four corner holes which all meet at a point far below the surface ...' Turning back to the wall, the Doctor quickly drew a side view, showing the four angled shafts intersecting exactly below the fifth one. Once again the Doctor glanced round at his audience. 'My guess is that they intend to drop that seeding device – the thing we saw the saucer, Zoe – down the fifth hole ... Simple, really, isn't it!'

Jamie nodded. 'Aye,' he mumbled.

'Well, don't you see?' cried the Doctor. 'They're going to fire the rockets through the planet's crust – which is very thin just here on the Island – and into the magma.'

'But that could cause a volcano,' Zoe interrupted.

'Exactly, Zoe.'

'And if they explode the seed device in the middle of it ...'

'... then the planet will become a vast mass of molten radio-active material,' the Doctor concluded. 'If their calculations are correct, a vast fuel source at exactly the right particle density and energy flux.'

Turning back to the wall, the Doctor added the trajectories of the rockets and the seeding trigger and then with violent swirls of chalk drew a colossal explosion. He stared at his handiwork in silence for a moment. When he turned round again, the others were looking at him as if expecting some word of comfort or advice. He smiled bleakly, shrugged, sighed, and stared at his fingernails.

'Aye, well we'll just have to stop them, won't we?' Jamie said at last.

The Doctor agreed. There was another long silence, broken only by the sickening vibration caused by the throbbing rig outside. Zoe began to imagine she could almost feel the planet shuddering in horror at its approaching fate.

The Doctor realised that everyone was waiting for him. 'Yes, well, that's easier said than done, Jamie ...' he flustered. 'Perhaps if we could somehow get hold of that seeding trigger ...' He sat on a bunk and stared at his diagrams, hunched with concentration.

Suddenly Jamie jumped up. 'Hey, Doctor ...'

'Please, Jamie, I am trying to think.'

'Aye, but I think I know how ...'

'Jamie!' Zoe snapped irritably.

The impetuous young Scot grabbed Kully's arm. 'Listen, I know how we can get hold of this atomic seed thing.'

'Oh really, Jamie?' exclaimed Zoe with a sarcastic smile.

Jamie rounded on her. 'The Doctor said they were going to drop it down that hole outside ...'

'Indeed I did,' agreed the Doctor absently.

'Aye, well, it's simple. We dig a tunnel from here out to their shaft and catch the wee thing on its way down!'

Zoe turned eagerly to the Doctor. He remained staring silently into space, and still, like a Buddha.

'Och well, it was just a thought ...' Jamie trailed glumly into silence.

All at once the Doctor sprang to his feet. 'Just a thought. And so simple, Jamie, only you could have thought it!' He seized Jamie's hand and pumped it enthusiastically up and down.

Jamie grinned sheepishly, as if uncertain whether to regard this as a compliment.

'We could use the periscope,' Zoe suggested. 'Just line it up on the drill and that's the direction ...'

The Doctor held up his hand. 'There's one little snag. Our tunnel will have to be quite a few metres long and we haven't much time.'

'But the sandstone should be reasonably soft,' Zoe pointed out.

'And Kully and I can slow those Dominators down a wee bit,' Jamie laughed, flinging his arm round the Dulcian's shoulders.

Kully nodded eagerly. 'We are experts at sabotaging Quarks,' he reminded them.

The Doctor looked serious. 'You've both been very lucky so far,' he warned them. 'Now if we could only devise some kind of weapon for you ...'

'Weapon?' Kully echoed, glancing at Kando and Teel.

They smiled and nodded encouragement. 'There's nothing down here except out-of-date rations and medical kits.'

'Medical kits!' cried the Doctor. 'The very thing. It's surprising what one can achieve with a few simple chemicals. See what you can find, Kully.'

While Kully searched through the lockers beneath the bunks, the Doctor led Zoe and Jamie over to the periscope. 'We must establish the direction for our tunnel very accurately,' he advised, as Zoe raised the tube and peered into the smoked-glass binocular, sighting it as best she could on the incandescent glare of the flashing rig.

'That's the bearing ...' she said at last, blinking and massaging her watering eyes.

'Righto, Zoe.' The Doctor squinted at right angles to the alignment of the periscope's handles and then marked a point on the wall of the shelter with his chalk. 'We'll have to move this bunk first though.'

As soon as they had cleared the space, the Doctor carefully drew a large circle around his chalk mark. Jamie could hardly wait to start chipping away at the concrete with his dirk, but for all his enthusiasm, the sharp blade screeched and skidded uselessly across the hard surface.

'I think perhaps I had better start you off ...' the Doctor chuckled, groping in his pockets and finally producing a strange object like a slim torch with a bulbous end and with various switches along its casing.

Jamie snorted scornfully: 'Och, how are ye going to dig a tunnel wi'a screwdriver?' he demanded.

The Doctor looked indignant. 'This is not merely a sonic screwdriver, Jamie ...' he retorted, adjusting several switches and then pointing the device at the wall at arm's length. 'Now ... watch ...'

Everyone looked on in astonishment as the Doctor's gadget emitted a powerful warbling sound. All at once, in the centre of the chalk circle, the solid concrete seemed to soften and then melt and finally to evaporate before their eyes.

In no time at all the Doctor bored a large hole right through the shelter wall to the sandstone beyond. Then he left the others to take over the tunnelling and turned his attention to the contents of the medical kits which Kully had unearthed in the lockers.

While Jamie, Kully, Kando and even Teel worked like beavers digging into the softish ground, Zoe helped the Doctor to measure and mix various combinations of chemicals in a number of small phials. Some of the mixtures frothed violently, changed colour threateningly and gave off clouds of evil-smelling vapour. But the Doctor seemed oblivious of any hazards, hunched over his task and muttering to himself like some mediaeval alchemist in his den.

Eventually Jamie grew impatient. 'Doctor, I don't think we can wait any longer ...' he said, crawling backwards out of the growing hole and brushing the sand out of his hair.

'Hang on, Jamie,' the Doctor muttered, carefully pouring a little of each mixture into a test-tube. He shook the foul liquid until it suddenly went colourless, like water. 'If this works, you'll not only be able to distract the Quarks, you'll most likely blow them to smithereens. Let's try it out shall we?'

'In here?' Zoe exclaimed in alarm.

The Doctor grinned reassuringly. 'Just a tiny quantity.' He took a little silver pill from a bottle and held it poised over the mouth of the test-tube. 'Now, Jamie, just add one of these pills to the mixture before you throw it. Like this ...'

The Doctor popped the pill into the tube and stuck a small cork in the end. 'Don't forget Jamie, you must throw it before ten seconds have elapsed, otherwise ...'

'Six ... seven ... eight ... Doctor!' Zoe shrieked.

With a start the Doctor flung the phial over his shoulder. There was a blue flash and a brief roar as it exploded under one of the bunks behind them. The Doctor grinned as everybody jumped in fright.

'It works!' he cried, hugging Zoe ecstatically.

'Och, ye could have blown us all tae bits,' Jamie gasped, pale as milk.

The Doctor shook his head. 'That was nothing. With ten times as much in each tube you'll have quite an effective armoury ...'

All of a sudden there was total silence. Everybody listened. Then they all turned to the Doctor. He was looking suddenly haggard. The drilling had stopped.

It seemed that their last chance was to be denied them after all.

Desperate Remedies

Jamie and Kully were soon edging their way out of the back of the ruin and scrambling up the cliff between two bluffs which afforded some cover from the drilling site. Their mission to create a diversion had now become one of interception. They must prevent the seeding trigger from reaching the centre bore target.

Armed with the phials of colourless liquid and the box of tiny pills, they followed the meandering cliff-edge in the direction of the saucer until they reached one of the perimeter sites guarded by two silent and motionless Quarks below them. They crouched at the edge. Jamie held out a phial and nodded. Kully dropped in a silver pill and began counting while Jamie jammed in the cork. Then Jamie hurled the bomb as far as he could and they both flattened themselves and waited.

'Seven ... eight ... nine ...' Kully muttered.

There was a brilliant blue flash and a huge bang. They craned over the edge to see one of the robots marching spasmodically round and round in circles, jerking its probes and its antennae, while its distress signal blurted out in strangled metallic rasps.

Jamie frowned. 'Not quite enough.' He held out another phial, Kully popped in a pill, Jamie corked the tube and flung it.

There was another explosion. This time fragments of metal flew up in the air toegther with a fountain of sand. Again Kully and Jamie peered down. One Quark was scattered in pieces over the dunes. The other was wheeling crazily round on the spot, squeaking and grating with smoke pouring out of its head, its antennae hanging like rotten leaves.

'This is fun,' Jamie grinned.

'Let's do some more,' Kully agreed.

They scrambled up and followed the clifftop until they eventually reached another of the perimeter sites. As before, two silent Quarks were guarding it.

'This is just a wee bit too easy,' Jamie chuckled as they prepared another bomb.

Kully popped in the silver pill. 'As easy as one ... two ...'

Toba was making final depth-soundings on the centre bore when he suddenly heard distant explosions and then the Quarks' feeble distress signals. Spitting with fury, he was about to order the two Quarks to disconnect from the rig and to hunt down and destroy the alien attackers, when he remembered Rago's warning. Grinding his flinty teeth in frustration, he prepared to resume drilling.

At that moment, Rago appeared from the direction of the saucer. The expression on the Navigator's face sent a chilly spasm through Toba's massive frame.

'More Quarks have been destroyed or incapacitated,' stormed Rago accusingly.

Toba allowed himself an ironic smile. 'You should have permitted me to destroy the primitives.'

'Silence!' Rago thundered. 'We now have only eight operational Quarks. Power levels are minimal. Report reserve status,' he ordered, turning to the Quarks.

'Two units,' bleated one.

'Five units,' bleated the other.

Rago's jaw creaked as he grimaced with rage. 'Barely sufficient to complete drilling,' he rasped. 'The rockets are installed, Toba. Inform me as soon as your operations here are concluded.'

'Command accepted.'

As the Navigator strode away, the rig blazed into life again beginning the crucial final stage of the bore.

On the clifftop above, two figures knelt in the sand.

'They've started drilling again,' Jamie mouthed. 'We still

have a chance ...'

The sound of the drilling starting up again brought a profound sigh of relief from the Doctor as he grabbed the next plastic sheet filled with sand from Kando at the mouth of the tunnel and handed it to Zoe, who emptied it onto the huge pile growing ever larger in the middle of the shelter. At least the race to intercept the seeding trigger was not yet lost, but there was so little time left ...

'How much further have you got, Teel?' the Doctor called into the vibrating darkness of the tunnel.

'A little more than my own length ...' came the brave young Dulcian's muffled reply.

The Doctor did a quick mental calculation and turned to Zoe. 'Still a long, long way to go ...' he frowned. 'Teel, come out and rest now. Zoe's turn.'

When Teel's feet appeared, the Doctor and Kando reached into the hole and pulled him out. The exhausted Dulcian, covered in dirt and sweat, staggered to a bench and collapsed gratefully. Armed with Jamie's dirk gripped between her teeth, Zoe clambered into the tunnel and dragged herself into the hot, throbbing gloom by walking on her elbows and knees.

When she reached the face, she pulled the plastic sheet out of her belt and spread it out as best she could behind her. The vibration of the drilling rig caused a constant trickle of sand to run into her eyes as she dug desperately away at the crumbling sandstone ahead, scraping the loose sand past her body and onto the sheet so that the others could empty it periodically in the shelter. The task was agonisingly slow and awkward and it was horrifying to feel that the shuddering tunnel might collapse at any moment and trap her.

Eventually she stopped to rest her aching arms a moment. All at once the tunnel shook with a series of violent shocks. Zoe's heart almost froze as the tunnel started cracking all around her.

In the shelter, the Doctor had dived for the periscope. 'Jamie and Kully have attacked the rig!' he shouted, cheering as the two Quarks careered sideways and the rig itself toppled over, belching smoke and sparks. 'Zoe, the drilling's stopped!'

117

'So will the tunnelling if they're not careful ...' muttered Zoe, digging away again for all she was worth.

Peering through the eyepiece, the Doctor watched Rago rush into view escorted by three Quarks. Expertly he lip-read the hurried dialogue between the two Dominators.

'See what damage your "harmless" aliens are doing with their primitive explosives? Now we must surely destroy them,' Toba insisted.

Rago flung out his huge hand. 'Replace the rig and continue. I shall personally pursue and destroy these saboteurs,' he retorted.

Seeing his revenge denied him, Toba sullenly concurred. As Rago set off towards the gorge, accompanied by the three Quarks, Toba struggled to re-position the rig over the target.

The Doctor said nothing as he re-joined the others at the mouth of the tunnel, but his gentle face betrayed increasing anxiety about the fate of Jamie and the diminishing likelihood of thwarting the Dominators in their evil purpose.

Unaware of Rago's intentions, Jamie and Kully slid helter-skelter down into the canyon on their way back to the shelter. No sooner had they reached the bottom than they were dismayed to see Rago and his Quarks advancing inexorably along the floor of the canyon towards them. Whooping with delight, Kully started preparing a bomb, but Jamie grabbed his arm and yanked him roughly back up the slope. Their progress was painfully slow as the sand gave under them, forcing them to take three steps for every one gained in height.

Rago's eyes burned with contempt as he ordered his squad to attack. Three pairs of probes were trained in deadly concentration on the desperate fugitives crawling up the slope like wasps trying to escape from a jar of treacle. Huge scars were gouged in the slopes and bluffs as the Quarks fired simultaneously, but miraculously neither was hit.

'Recharge force units,' Rago commanded. 'Report failure.'

The robots whirred and sparked intermittently.

'Reserves below minima,' one of them announced.

Rago spat viciously. 'Toba is responsible for this entire

fiasco. Quarks, quantise aggregate pulses. Single discharge. Destroy them.'

Just as Jamie and Kully reached the top of the canyon, a savage tearing noise split the air around them. Kully gasped and choked and then uttered a terrible scream of agony. Jamie seized his wrist just in time to prevent him from rolling back into the gorge and hauled his dead weight up over the edge and onto the plateau.

'We're safe now, Kully ...' he panted. 'The Quarks can't climb up here.'

Kully's face had gone a ghastly yellow and his teeth were chattering with shock. 'Something's happened ... my arm ... leg's gone cold ... can't move arm now ... better leave me behind ...'

Jamie put his arm protectively round Kully's paralysed shoulder. 'Nonsense. Ye'll be right as ninepence in a wee while.'

Peering over the edge, Jamie realised that Rago had ordered his Quarks to scale the longer but gentler slope at the end of the canyon. Despite their depleted power reserves, they were making good progress. If they reached the plateau, he and the wounded Dulcian had no chance at all.

Jamie quickly counted the remaining phials of chemicals stuck around the top of his sock. There were four. 'One each ...' he muttered, setting the phials upright in the sand and prising the box of silver pills out of Kully's frozen hand. 'Hang on, Kully ...' he urged, dropping a pill in each phial and frantically jamming in the stoppers.

'Four ... five ... six ...' He picked the phials up. 'Seven ... eight ...' He leaped to his feet. 'Nine ...' He threw the four phials together like a brace of daggers. They flew into the canyon and landed in an arc at the feet of Rago and the Quarks.

There were four sharp thunderclaps. Jamie saw the robots scatter in all directions, reeling and tottering, their probes firing indiscriminately into the air and at each other, and their distress signals bleating feebly. Two of them blew each other up and the third almost hit Rago before bursting into flames.

'Ye'll no dominate Jamie MacCrimmon ...' the young

Highlander yelled down at the scorched and tattered figure lying amidst the wreckage of his Quarks.

As Rago clambered awkwardly to his feet, Jamie hoisted Kully onto his shoulders and set off across the plateau towards the clifftop that overhung the ruin.

If they met any Quarks now, they were done for ...

With Kando valiantly taking her turn in the tunnel, Zoe was manning the periscope while the Doctor and Teel emptied sheetful after sheetful of sand onto the heap which was now almost touching the ceiling.

'Toba's got the drill working again,' Zoe reported. 'We can't have much time left, Doctor.'

The Doctor glanced at the mound of excavated sand. 'We must be nearly through to their shaft by now,' he murmured hopefully.

'It feels very close ...' Kando reported faintly, as she pushed another load of sand towards the tunnel-opening with her feet.

'So near and yet so far ...' the Doctor mused, helping Teel with the sheet.

At that moment, the trap-door thudded open and Kully suddenly sprawled onto the mound and slid stiffly to the floor. Jamie jumped in after him and heaved the hatch shut before slithering down beside him. Briefly, Jamie explained what had happened since the intrepid pair had set out on their vital mission.

'Luckily for Kully, the Quarks' power-levels were low ...' he concluded.

Zoe and the Doctor had made the casualty as comfortable as possible in the sand.

'It's my left side ... it's paralysed ...' he moaned.

The Doctor gently took hold of Kully's left wrist. 'Can you move your fingers at all?' he asked.

Kully shut his eyes and screwed up his face with effort. His fingertips twitched a little, then his thumb stirred.

The Doctor smiled encouragingly. 'You *are* lucky. I think it's only temporary.'

Kully managed a plucky grin. 'Don't worry about me,

Doctor. What about the tunnel?' he murmured feebly.

'Thanks to you and Jamie we've almost finished it.'

Zoe gave a startled shout. 'Doctor, they've stopped drilling again!'

The Doctor rushed to the periscope just in time to see the battered figure of Rago limping up to Toba as the Quarks began dismantling the rig. Once again he deciphered their brief exchange, his own lips moving as he read theirs.

'The centre bore is completed, Navigator.'

'Good, I shall enjoy absorbing this miserable planet and its insignificant creatures, Toba. Bring the seeding trigger immediately. No more delays.'

There was just the faintest of smiles on Toba's grim visage as he glanced at his superior's undignified disarray before marching obediently away.

Jamie had already taken Kando's place at the tunnel face and he was soon sending out load after load of sand.

'Any sign of that bore shaft yet, Jamie?' the Doctor yelled anxiously as he returned to help the others.

'Och no. The roof keeps caving in though . . .' came the faint reply out of the foetid darkness.

They worked like beavers in the hot, stifling atmosphere of the cramped shelter, while Kully lay on the mound and kept up a brave repartee of encouragement. Hours seemed to pass, but everyone had lost all sense of time, endlessly repeating the same automatic movements over and over again. And very soon there would be no more space in the shelter to dump the eternal flow of sand . . .

Then all at once Zoe grabbed the periscope handles. 'The Dominators are coming back . . . they've got the device!' she cried.

The Doctor dropped the heavy plastic sheet he was carrying and peered into the binocular. He watched as Toba carefully handed the seeding trigger – still in its curious spiky glass shell – to Rago. The Dominators' faces were bathed in a lurid pink glow as they conferred over the centre bore target.

'Recall all operational Quarks. Prepare the craft for departure and rendezvous with Fleet. Inform Fleet Leader that refuelling orbit may commence on schedule.'

'Command accepted.'

Rago cradled the weirdly glowing device almost lovingly in his massive gloves. 'I shall insert the seeding trigger. You will return and synchronise the perimeter target projectiles immediately. Soon we shall see this planet and its species burst asunder.'

The Doctor's face clouded with indignation as he mouthed the Dominator's terrible words. He watched Toba stride purposefully away to prepare the rockets and then focused the periscope on Rago. The Navigator was pressing the tips of the bristling glass spikes in an apparently random sequence and with each movement the pink glow intensified. Eventually the glass shell came apart and Rago delicately withdrew the opalescent egg within.

'Criticality minus beta.'

Unable to watch any longer, the Doctor closed his eyes and leaned his forehead against the periscope. 'We're too late ...' he sighed dejectedly. 'We've failed ...'

'We're through, Doctor!'

Spinning round, the Doctor saw Jamie's dirt-streaked smile filling the tunnel mouth.

'Only a wee bit too far to the left,' Jamie cried as he clambered out. 'Not bad at all.'

The Doctor whipped back to the periscope. Rago was bending over the borehole, the seeding trigger poised in his outstretched hands.

In a single bound, the Doctor flung himself at the tunnel and vanished into the darkness.

Zoe flew to the periscope. She uttered a cry of despair. Rago's hands were empty. 'It's gone ... we missed it,' she said, stifling a sob of disappointment.

There was a long silence. Jamie, Zoe, Kando, Teel and Kully stared glumly at one another and then turned anxiously towards the tunnel.

After a while, they heard muffled mutterings and then a frantic scrambling. Gradually the Doctor emerged feet first from the narrow opening. He stood up and then turned to face the astonished group. He was holding the huge egg as though it were a bomb.

'You did it.' whispered Zoe.

'So, we are saved,' Kando burst out, with a brilliant smile.

'Not quite saved ...' murmured the Doctor, moving in slow motion as if the slightest shock would be disastrous. 'We still have to neutralise it.' With infinite care, he turned the glowing device over and over in his trembling hands. Then he looked at them, appalled. 'It's sealed ... completely sealed ...' he gasped. 'I can't open it.'

They all stared at him helplessly.

'Ye mean it was all for nothing?' Jamie exclaimed bitterly. 'Are we going to be blown to smithereens after all?'

The Doctor nodded. 'I'm afraid so, Jamie. Unless we can get it away from Dulkis immediately ...'

Teel and Kando were kneeling beside Kully. Their three faces were overcast with incredulity and anguish. Jamie and Zoe gazed at the Time Lord with barely concealed resentment.

Suddenly the Doctor grinned mischievously. 'Whatever's the matter with you all?' he demanded, weighing the lethal object almost nonchalantly in one hand, his eyes beginning to twinkle. 'Teel and Kando, you take Kully to the capsule near the saucer, get back to the Capitol and warn them that there might be a little earthquake and a volcano or two popping up here and there. Jamie and Zoe, you go straight back to the TARDIS and wait there for me ...'

He was interrupted by a chorus of protest.

'But why? What are you going to do?' Jamie demanded.

'No time to explain now,' the Doctor cried, pushing his way through them to the periscope. 'Ah good, coast's clear at last.' He scrambled up the mound of sand under the trap-door, clutching the seeding trigger under his arm like a rugby ball.

Kully tried to get up. 'But you must come with us to the Capitol. My father will want to see you ...'

'So sorry. Some other time. Got to dash ...' The Doctor planted his head against the hatch and pushed it open with a crash.

'On behalf of the Dulcian community ...' Teel began, standing up with shy solemnity.

123

'Apologies. Not now. Compliments and so on to the esteemed Council …' the Doctor waved.

A moment later he was gone.

There was a stunned silence.

'Where's he gone?' Zoe asked at last.

Jamie shrugged. 'Och, we'll just have to do as he says. I hope he's not up to anything too daft though …'

Inside the giant saucer, the Dominators were completing final preparations for firing the perimeter rockets and for immediate take-off from Dulkis. The control centre hummed and flickered with intense activity.

'Remaining Quarks about to board,' Toba reported.

'Particle flux?'

'Confirmed.'

'Good. Perimeter targets primed,' Rago checked.

'Seeding trigger *in situ*. Approaching criticality minus alpha,' Toba warned.

'Affirmative. Target projectile and take-off countdowns locked in sequence.'

At that moment, beneath the massive craft, a dapper figure was scurrying breathlessly up behind the last Quark as it entered the elevator at the foot of the central shaft. Just as the access panel began to close, the figure took something out of his coat and placed it carefully on the floor of the cubicle behind the robot.

'Just a little something for the journey …' he murmured, jumping back in the nick of time as the hatch clicked shut.

Then he turned and ran away across the dunes as fast as his short legs would carry him.

High up in the control centre, Toba was monitoring the flight displays. 'Propulsion flux at optimum,' he announced.

'Initiate take-off,' Rago ordered.

A colossal shudder ran through the saucer as it wobbled and then began to rise slowly from the sand.

'Target rockets fired. All maximum penetration …' Rago reported with satisfaction. 'Seeding trigger now at critical … at critical plus … plus …'

Toba glanced across at his superior in alarm. Rago was

staring in utter disbelief at the elevator cubicle which had just brought up the last of the Quarks.

'Toba ...' Rago gasped in a hoarse nightmarish croak, pointing at the floor of the cubicle. 'Toba ... abandon ...'

At that moment, the saucer tipped slightly and something rolled out of the cubicle and trundled noisily across the deck towards the dais. It was the seeding trigger, now glowing a deep crimson.

The Dominators gaped speechlessly at the giant egg as it zig-zagged around the gently gyrating deck, glowing brighter and hotter every second ...

The vast saucer had shrieked away into the Dulcian evening sky just as Jamie reached the TARDIS, after helping Teel and Kando to carry Kully to the capsule.

'Thank goodness you're safe!' cried Zoe, meeting him in the doorway. 'But there's no sign of the Doctor yet.'

'Och, I knew I should've gone with him ...' Jamie panted, shaking his head ruefully.

All at once there was a mighty roaring noise and a jet of flame erupted out of the sand nearby. They flung themselves face-down and covered their heads. After a few seconds the roaring ceased and the ground stopped shaking. A thick column of smoke and sand hung over the TARDIS. Badly shaken, they scrambled up. In the distance they could see three similar palls of smoke rising high in the air.

'They've just fired the rockets at the perimeter boreholes ...' yelled a familiar voice. The Doctor came stumbling over the dunes, dusty and out of breath. 'Quick, you two – into the TARDIS!' he shouted.

'But where's that big egg thing?' Jamie asked.

'Later ... later. Get inside ...' the Doctor gasped as he reached them.

Jamie pushed Zoe into the dilapidated police box and followed her. 'Yon Dominators got away ...' he muttered angrily.

Just as the Doctor was about to enter, a brilliant flash of incandescent white light burst over the darkening sky. He turned and paused in the doorway, a faint smile hovering over his grimy face. A few seconds later, there was a sharp crack which rumbled and echoed and re-echoed overhead for quite some time.

The Doctor winced. 'I think I prefer them poached myself ...' he chuckled.

Suddenly the ground started to tremble and the surrounding dunes began to undulate like waves on the sea, causing the TARDIS's ancient woodwork to protest vociferously.

'Doctor ... come on ... the whole planet's going to blow up!' Jamie yelled from inside.

The Doctor smiled with benign satisfaction. 'No, no, Jamie, the planet is quite safe now,' he called. 'This is only a local earthquake caused by the rockets. It'll only affect the Island, you know.'

There was a moment's delay and then Jamie appeared in the doorway next to him. 'Aye, maybe, Doctor. But we happen to be on the Island.'

At that moment, there was a terrifying tearing sound and a huge split started to open up in the dunes, belching orange sparks and sticky red lava and hissing clouds of gas and steam.

The Doctor's eyes widened as he watched the boiling, bubbling fissure rushing hungrily towards them.

'Oh dear,' he mumbled, rubbing the end of his nose with a crooked finger. 'Oh my goodness me ... out of the frying pan and into the fire ...'

Contents

1	A Candidate for Death	7
2	The Rescue	17
3	The Rebels	27
4	The Genius	39
5	The Companions	49
6	The Krotons Awake	57
7	The Militants	65
8	The Attack	75
9	The Second Attack	85
10	Battle Plans	93
11	Eelek's Bargain	101
12	Acid	113

1

A Candidate for Death

In the gloomy, cavernous underground Hall of
Learning, the assembled Gonds were waiting. They
stood in ranks before the huge, outward-curving silver
wall that formed the far end of the Hall. In the centre
of the wall, a ramp led up to a closed sliding door.

There was a hush of expectation in the shadowed
Hall. When the ceremony was concluded, one or two
privileged students, the brightest and best, would pass
through that door, achieving the greatest honour
known to the People of the Gonds.

They would become Companions of the Krotons —
and they would never be seen again.

Selris, Leader of the Council of the Gonds stood
waiting impassively by the message-place in the silver
wall, the gleaming breastplate of his office making him
stand out from his fellow Gonds in their drab one-
piece coveralls. His craggy, weathered face and steel-
grey hair showed him to be somewhere in his mid-
fifties. Yet for all his years, Selris stood as hard and
massive as one of the rock pillars that supported the
roof of the Hall. A mild man until roused to anger, he
was still perfectly prepared to defend his authority
with the stone fighting-axe that every adult male
Gond wore at his belt.

The little round door of the message-place opened, silently and mysteriously like a metal eye. Selris reached inside and removed the message-sheet and the round door closed.

Selris opened the scroll and studied it for a moment. Then his deep voice boomed out into the tense silence. 'Class three one nine six of the First Grade. The names of the two selected candidates are . . . Male: Abugond.'

A murmur arose from the crowd. Abu, a slender, serious faced young man looked down, modestly accepting the congratulations of his friends.

The low murmurings died away, as Selris spoke again. 'The second name is . . . Female: Vanagond.'

All eyes turned to Vana, a slender fair-haired young girl. Somehow, her outstanding beauty made it hard to believe that she was among the most gifted of her generation of students.

Vana looked delighted, astonished, and a little apprehensive all at the same time. But Thara, the tall, handsome young man standing beside her looked both horrified and afraid. 'No!' he murmured. 'No!'

Selris spoke again. 'Abugond and Vanagond, alone of your fellows you have been chosen to receive the highest honour that can befall a Gond. Soon, you will be Companions of the Krotons. If you will now step forward, you will be invested in your robes of honour.'

Selris turned to a dark, smooth-featured man at his side. 'Eelek . . . '

Eelek stepped forward, a silver cloak over his arm. He nodded towards Abu, who came out of the ranks of the Gonds and stood before him. With ceremonious care Eelek draped the silver cloak about Abu's shoulders. He took a crescent-shaped silver pendant and hung it about Abu's neck . . .

While this was going on, Thara and Vana were

8

arguing in low voices. It would be Vana's turn next for the investiture. She attempted to move away, but Thara was gripping her wrist.

She struggled to free herself. 'Please, Thara!'

'You can't go!' whispered Thara fiercely. 'I won't let you.'

'I must.'

'Look, Vana — we can run away. There's still time . . .'

'You know that's not possible. We must obey the Krotons.'

'Why?' demanded Thara fiercely. 'Why must we obey?'

A big hand clamped down on Thara's shoulder and his father's voice said, 'Because that is the Law of the Krotons.'

They turned. Selris was looming over them. Thara was about to speak, but Selris shook his head sternly, indicating the silver wall. There by the ramp Abu stood waiting, draped in the silver robe with the pendant about his neck.

The door slid silently upwards. Slowly Abu climbed the ramp, and went through the door into the darkness beyond. The door came down behind him.

Behind the City of the Gonds there stretched an area known as the Wasteland, a dead poisoned landscape of rocks and gravel, its monotony broken by the occasional withered plant or petrified tree. Evil-smelling vapours drifted across the bleak terrain.

Since nothing lived there, the area was usually silent, except for the melancholy sighing of the chill wind that haunted the Wastelands.

Suddenly that silence was broken by a strange, wheezing, groaning sound. The square blue shape of a London Police Box materialised at the foot of a steep,

9

rocky cliff.

The door opened and a man emerged. He was on the small side, with a thatch of untidy black hair and a gentle, rather humorous face. He wore baggy checked trousers, a vaguely disreputable-looking frock coat, a wide collared shirt and a scruffy bow tie.

All in all, he was an odd, rather clownish figure. But the little man, like the Police Box behind him, was considerably more impressive than he seemed to be. He was, in fact that wandering Time Lord known only as the Doctor, now in his second incarnation. The Police Box was the TARDIS, an extremely sophisticated space/time craft. Unfortunately, the behaviour of the TARDIS, like that of the Doctor himself, was often erratic in the extreme. Consequently, the Doctor frequently had very little idea as to where, or indeed when he was.

It was this matter that was preoccupying the Doctor's two companions as they followed him from the TARDIS. The first was a brawny youth in Highland dress, complete with kilt, who stood staring around him with his usual air of truculent disapproval.

James Robert McCrimmon, Jamie for short, was a young Scottish piper who had joined the Doctor during the Time Lord's visit to Earth at the time of the Jacobite Rebellion of 1746.

Jamie had been the Doctor's companion through many adventures, and could never make up his mind whether the Doctor was a magician, a madman, or something between the two. One thing Jamie was quite sure of was that the Doctor wasn't safe out on his own and needed someone sensible, such as Jamie himself, to keep him out of trouble.

The Doctor's second companion was also from Earth, though from a time many hundred years after the eighteenth century. A very small, very neat, very precise girl with short dark hair, Zoe Herriot had been a computer operator on a space station before stowing away on board the TARDIS. She wore the simple, functional clothes of her time, a short skirt, blouse, waistcoat and high boots, all in gleaming plasti-cloth.

Like Jamie, she was never quite sure what to make of the Doctor. Zoe was so intelligent and so highly trained that she was a sort of human computer in herself, and she consequently found the Doctor's erratic scatter-brained approach to life and its problems disconcerting in the extreme.

When the companions emerged from the TARDIS all three reacted in their own different ways. Gazing interestedly around him, the Doctor stretched and said happily, 'Lovely, lovely, lovely!', bestowing upon the bleak and hostile landscape the benign approval he accorded to almost everything in the cosmos.

Jamie glared about suspiciously, alert for enemies, and sniffed the drifting vapours. 'Bad eggs! Let's try somewhere else.'

Zoe looked thoughtfully about her, trying to gather evidence for some kind of rational decision. 'Just a minute, Jamie. Where *are* we, Doctor?'

'Och, you don't expect *him* to know, do you?'

'Let's explore, shall we?' said the Doctor happily, ignoring, as usual, the doubts of his companions. 'Just a moment.' He popped back inside the TARDIS and emerged carrying a rolled black object.

Jamie looked at it incredulously. 'Your umbrella?'

The Doctor closed the TARDIS door, opened the umbrella — and pointed skywards. 'Twin suns. Bound to be hot.'

Zoe looked up. Two fiery balls hung in the sky, doing their best to glow through the overcast clouds. The Doctor was right, thought Zoe. The climate was both dull and oppressive at the same time. The twin suns settled one thing — they weren't on Earth.

The Doctor set off apparently at random across the barren landscape. Resignedly, Jamie and Zoe followed.

'I don't think I like it here much,' said Zoe. 'It looks — dead.'

'Aye, and it smells dead too.'

'Sulphur, isn't it?' Zoe looked at the Doctor. 'Could be poisonous.'

'Nonsense. The TARDIS instruments would have warned us. It's just a mixture of ozone and sulphur. Very bracing.'

They trudged across the featureless landscape for some time. Looking round, Zoe saw that they were in a kind of enormous crater. The ground began to slope gently upwards as they neared the low rise that formed the crater's edge. Suddenly the Doctor stopped and picked up a gleaming shard from the ground at his feet.

'What's that?' asked Jamie.

'A most interesting mineral formation. Magnesium silicate.'

'He means mica,' explained Zoe.

Jamie grunted, none the wiser.

The Doctor scrambled to the top of the rise, and waved his umbrella triumphantly. 'Aha! All dead, is it?'

Zoe came to join him. Beyond the rise the ground sloped sharply downwards again into a kind of natural hollow. Inside the hollow, and filling it almost completely there was a city.

Perhaps city was too grand a word, thought Zoe as she studied it. It looked more like a village, a settlement or a colony. It consisted of a cluster of low stone buildings on either side of a broad shallow river, the banks of which were lined with luxurious vegetation. The largest building of all seemed to be built into the ridge on which they stood.

'Yes, fascinating architecture,' said the Doctor. 'It's more typical of a low-gravity planet, but as far as I can tell this is fairly close to Earth-normal.' He jumped up and down experimentally.

Zoe studied the city thoughtfully. 'An Inca-type culture, perhaps. That big building below could be a temple.'

'Yes, very possibly . . .'

They were interrupted by a shout from behind them. 'Hey, Doctor, down here. Come and see!'

The Doctor turned. 'Let's see what Jamie's found. Careful, Zoe.' Taking Zoe's arm, he helped her to scramble back down the slope.

They found Jamie a little below them and some way to their right, standing in front of a huge dully gleaming section that seemed to bulge out of the side of the ridge.

'What is it, Jamie?' asked Zoe.

Jamie shrugged. 'I dunno. Look, there's a kind of ramp.'

And indeed, before the gleaming section, the ground sloped upwards with unnatural smoothness.

'There's a door too,' said Zoe.

Set into the centre of the area was an oddly shaped door, a kind of diamond shape with the upper and lower points cut off by horizontal lines.

Studying its position, Zoe realised that it could well be some kind of back door to the temple-like building on the other side of the ridge. Though if that was the case and the building stretched clear *through* the ridge it must be enormous . . .

'Do you think it's some kind of wall, Doctor? Because if it is —'

'No, I hardly think so, Zoe. Not a wall, exactly.'

The Doctor walked up the ramp and peered at the dully gleaming surface.

Jamie sniffed, 'That bad egg smell's a lot stronger here.'

The Doctor was busily scratching at the surface with the ferrule of his umbrella and muttering to himself. 'Hmm, how very fascinating.'

Zoe followed him up the ramp and Jamie came to join them. 'This bit here — it's metal, isn't it?'

Zoe nodded. 'Covered in moss and lichen, though.' Which meant, thought Zoe, that it had been here for a very long time.

The Doctor was holding the flat of his palm against the dully, gleaming surface. 'Metal? Would you say so?' All at once he leaped back. 'I think we'd better go.'

By now Zoe's scientific curiousity was aroused. 'But why, Doctor?'

'Because this isn't a wall or a building. It's a machine!'

The door began gliding smoothly upwards. The Doctor grabbed his two companions and almost dragged them behind the shelter of a nearby boulder. They watched fascinated from their hiding place as the door slid fully open.

After a moment a young man emerged. He wore a silver cloak and a pendant, and his face was utterly, terrifyingly blank. He stood there for a moment staring vacantly, as the door came down behind him.

Jamie stared hard at the young man, puzzled by his odd manner. 'What's the matter with him?'

The Doctor too, was watching intently. 'Sssh!'

Circular hatches slid open in the wall on either side of the door and twin nozzles appeared. The Doctor was about to shout a warning, but already it was too

14

late.

Vapour hissed fiercely from the nozzles, forming a thick cloud engulfing the young man completely. There came one terrible scream — then silence.

The cloud dispersed, drifting away.

The silver-cloaked young man had disappeared and all that was left of him was the pendant that had hung around his neck.

The Doctor and his companions emerged from their hiding place. Everything was silent.

Before the Doctor could stop him, Jamie ran up the ramp and picked up the pendant. It crumbled to nothingness in his hands.

'Poor man,' said Zoe softly. There was nothing left of him, she thought. Nothing at all.

Jamie said wonderingly, 'What happened to him, Doctor? What is that thing?'

'I'm not sure,' said the Doctor grimly. 'But whatever it is, I think we'll do well to keep away from it.'

He led the way back up the ridge.

'Where are we going?' called Zoe.

'To that temple place. We shall try approaching this problem from the other side!'

In the Hall of Learning, Eelek was helping Vana into her robe. He hung the silver pendant about ner neck.

She moved forward, and stood waiting before the door.

2

The Rescue

As Vana stood by the door, waiting, like Abu and so
many others before, to become a Companion of the
Krotons, Thara was arguing furiously with his father
Selris.

'Father, please, give the order that she doesn't have
to go. You're our leader.'

Selris looked not unsympathetically at his son. Tall
and strong, jaw jutting determinedly, Thara was, in so
many ways, a younger version of himself. But Selris's
duty was quite clear. 'The Krotons have chosen Vana.
It is a great honour.' And that, Selris's manner
implied, was that. The matter was closed.

'The Krotons!' snarled Thara. 'Why do we obey
their orders? We don't even know if they exist!'

He sprang forward, placing himself between Vana
and the door.

Vana was shocked by such blasphemy. 'Thara! You
mustn't say things like that!'

Eelek tried to push Thara aside. 'Get out of the
way!'

But Thara was taller and stronger than Eelek. He
refused to budge. 'She is not going into that machine!'

'She has to,' said Eelek flatly. 'No-one defies the
Krotons.' Once again he tried to thrust Thara aside.

17

'All right!' said Thara grimly. Grabbing Vana's arm he swung her behind him, then drew the axe from his belt, glaring defiantly at Eelek. 'Come on, then!'

But Eelek was a politician, not a fighter. 'Don't be stupid,' he said wearily, and beckoned to the Learning Hall Guards.

'Stop, Thara!' shouted Selris, fearful that his son would be injured, perhaps even killed.

Eelek turned to the approaching guards. 'Disarm him!'

Thara brandished his axe. 'Keep back!'

The guards hesitated. Like his father, Thara was a skilled and powerful fighter. They would overcome him in time but some of them would die doing it.

At this precise moment, the Doctor, Jamie and Zoe appeared at the top of the broad stone steps leading down into the underground hall.

They had found the city itself deserted, naturally enough since most of the Gonds were packed into the Hall of Learning for the ceremony. The temple too had appeared to be deserted. Attracted by the sound of voices they had made their way to the steps that led down into the Hall of Learning. Only now did they find themselves discovered and opposed, as astonished guards moved in to surround them. The guards were armed with long savage-looking pikes with gleaming diamond shaped blades at the tip.

'What if they're not friendly?' asked Zoe worriedly.

'Just let me talk to them.' The Doctor stepped forward with a friendly smile. The guards raised their pikes and the Doctor stepped back hurriedly. 'We are friends!' The guards didn't seem impressed. 'Don't be afraid,' he said encouragingly. 'We're not going to hurt you.' Still no response.

'I think we're in for trouble, Doctor,' warned Jamie

18

cheerfully. He seemed to be looking forward to it.

At last one of the guards, a brown fierce-looking fellow and obviously some kind of leader, stepped forward and said, 'Who are you?'

'Never mind that,' said the Doctor impatiently. 'Tell your men to let us pass.'

'Answer me. Who are you and where are you from?'

The Doctor sighed. 'We haven't time for explanations now.'

'You're not Gonds,' said the guard captain accusingly, as if this in itself was a crime. 'Your clothes, the way you're dressed . . . '

'Look,' said the Doctor, 'I assure you that we're friendly.'

Jamie squared up to the guard captain. 'Are you going to let us by or not?'

Zoe meanwhile had been watching events at the far end of the crowded hall. 'Doctor, look!' she called.

At the other end of the hall another group of guards was closing in on Thara, who was standing protectively in front of Vana.

Thara glared at the nearest guard, his axe raised to strike. 'I'm warning you, one step nearer . . . '

Eelek turned to Selris. 'He's your son. Do something about him.'

'Eelek's enjoying this,' thought Selris bitterly. He had long been a rival for the leadership. He would do anything that could bring Selris and his family into disrepute.

'Thara, be reasonable,' shouted Selris. 'The Krotons have sent for Vana.'

'She's not going. Nobody ever comes back from there . . . ' Thara broke off. The slight distraction had enabled one of the guards to sidle closer. Suddenly the razor-sharp edge of a pike-blade was inches from Thara's throat.

He could dodge and kill this one pikeman, thought Thara, but the others . . .

He felt Vana struggling to pull free. 'Let me go, Thara,' she pleaded. 'I don't want them to hurt you.'

Realising that unless he surrendered he would be probably cut down before Vana's eyes, Thara released her and stepped back, returning the axe to his belt.

The Doctor and his companions were watching all this from the steps. 'What's happening to that girl?' asked Zoe.

Jamie said, 'She's wearing robes just like that man who we saw killed!'

Zoe turned to the Doctor in horror. 'Is she going to be sacrificed?'

'Oh, I hardly think so, Zoe. These people are too civilised for that.'

'Whatever it is, we ought to stop it,' muttered Jamie.

The Doctor raised his voice commandingly. 'Wait!' he called. 'Wait a minute.'

Scandalised, the guard captain ordered, 'Do not interrupt the ceremony!' He turned to his men. 'Take them!'

Jamie glared at him. 'You wouldn't talk so brave without your guards behind you. Why don't you have a go?'

The guard captain held up his hand to halt his men. 'Wait — get back!' He swung round on Jamie. 'I am Axus! I accept your challenge!'

'That's just fine with me,' said Jamie happily.

'Now, Jamie,' said the Doctor reprovingly, 'there's no need to be rash.'

'Don't worry, Doctor. I'll soon deal with this laddie.'

At a sign from Axus, one of the guards offered Jamie his axe. Scornfully, Jamie waved it away. 'I'll no' be needing that.' If he couldn't have his trusty claymore he preferred to trust his bare hands rather than risk using an unfamiliar weapon.

Arms outstretched like something between a boxer and a wrestler, Jamie squared up to his opponent. Axus lashed out with his axe. Quickly, Jamie ducked and stepped back.

'Look out Jamie!' called Zoe.

Axus sprang forward, his arm raised to strike, and Jamie stepped inside the upraised arm and grabbed Axus's wrist, holding the axe-arm high.

The two fighters were locked motionless for a moment, their strength almost perfectly matched. Then, slowly, very slowly, Jamie began forcing the captain's axe-arm downwards. With a final heave and thrust, Jamie wrenched the axe from Axus's hand and gave him a shove that sent him flying to the ground.

Seeing that the fight was over, and Jamie unhurt, Zoe looked back across the hall. 'Doctor, look!' she called. 'The girl . . . '

The door in the silver wall was sliding upwards. Vana gave Thara one last agonised look and then walked slowly up the ramp and disappeared into darkness. The door slid down behind her.

Pushing past the confused and distracted guards, the Doctor and his friends made their way to the other side of the Hall.

Eelek stared haughtily at them. 'Who are these people? What is going on?'

'The very question I was going to ask,' said the Doctor indignantly. 'What is happening here?'

The guard captain picked himself up, recovered his axe and came hurrying across the hall.

'They forced their way in here, Eelek.'

Selris was looking at the strangers in amazement. 'Who are you? Where do you come from?'

'Oh, I'll explain that later,' said the Doctor hurriedly.

Jamie said, 'Believe me, you wouldn't understand if we told you.'

'We come from another planet, another world,' said Zoe — and realised immediately from her listeners' reaction that Jamie had been right.

'That girl,' said the Doctor, 'Would you mind telling us where she's gone?'

'How can you be from another planet?' growled Selris.

Jamie said truculently, 'Look, we're wasting time! Where's that girl gone, that's what we want to know.'

'And what's behind that wall?' asked Zoe.

'They've sent her to join the Krotons,' said Thara despairingly.

Zoe stared at him. 'What are the Krotons?'

'You really don't know?' asked Selris.

Thara said impatiently, 'How could they — if they really are from another planet.' He turned to Zoe. 'The Krotons live in that machine — so we are told.'

Selris said patiently. 'Vana is joining the Krotons. It's a great honour for a Gond to become a Companion of the Krotons.'

'Honour!' said Thara scornfully. 'She didn't really want to go. No one ever wants to disappear into that thing.'

Eelek looked disparagingly at these oddly dressed newcomers. 'Who are you? Why are you asking all these questions?'

'Because,' said the Doctor, 'just a few minutes ago we saw a young man wearing a silver cloak like that girl — Vana, is it? Anyway, we saw him killed.'

'Abugond,' whispered Thara. 'It must have been Abugond.'

'Ridiculous,' sneered Eelek. 'How can these

22

strangers have seen Abugond?'

'Abugond is with the Krotons,' said Selris solemnly.

'Well, we saw *somebody* killed,' said Jamie bluntly. 'He left the machine and he was —' Jamie hesitated, at a loss to find words to describe what had happened.

'He was vaporised,' said Zoe.

Jamie nodded. 'Aye, that's right. Outside a door just like this one, only round at the other side of this thing.' He pointed. 'Out there!'

'You have been in the Wasteland?' whispered Selris.

'You are contaminated,' said Eelek. 'Nobody ever goes in the Wasteland.' He raised his voice. 'Stand back. They are contaminated.'

The effect was sudden and dramatic. The encircling Gonds stepped hurriedly back, and the Doctor and his friends found themselves isolated.

'Why does no-one go into the Wasteland?' asked Zoe.

'It is poisoned. Soon you will die.'

'Nonsense!' said the Doctor. 'It may have been poisoned at one time, but I assure you it's quite safe now.'

Jamie tugged at his sleeve. 'Doctor, that girl. If she comes out the other side in the same way . . . '

The Doctor nodded vigorously. 'Quite right, Jamie. We must try to save her. Come on.'

He hurried towards the steps and the others followed. No-one made any attempts to stop them, presumably through the fear of contamination.

Selris called after them, 'Where are you going?'

Zoe's voice came back. 'To the Wasteland.'

'But you can't. It is against the law of the Krotons!'

By now the Doctor and his friends were out of sight.

'I'm going with them,' said Thara suddenly, and hurried towards the stairs.

'Thara come back!' shouted Selris.

'If they can go to the Wasteland, so can I!'

'Come back, my son,' called Selris in anguish. 'You too will die!'

The Doctor, Jamie and Zoe slithered down the rocks and came panting to a halt outside the oddly-shaped door set into the ridge in the Wasteland.

'Well, there it is,' said Jamie grimly.

The Doctor nodded. 'Yes . . . I wonder how long we've got. I imagine there isn't much time.'

He strode up the ramp.

'What are you going to do, Doctor?' called Zoe.

'You two stay back there, out of the way . . . '

They heard a pounding of footsteps and the young man they'd seen protesting in the underground Hall came running to join them. 'Please, can I help you?'

The Doctor said, 'Not really I'm afraid, Mr er . . . ?'

'I am Thara.'

The Doctor was looking about him. 'Bring me a handful of loose stones, would you?'

Thara gave him an astonished look. 'What? What for?'

'You want to help, don't you?' snapped the Doctor.

'Yes . . . yes, of course.' Thara hurried to a bank of loose stones and came running back with a handful of small rocks and pebbles.

The Doctor selected two smallish, round ones and jammed them into the sockets from which the acid vapour had emerged. 'Right! Now, get out of the way all of you. Over there somewhere, behind those boulders.'

'Be careful, Doctor,' said Zoe. 'I think I can hear something. A kind of humming, a vibration.'

'I know, Zoe, so can I. I'm nearer than you, remember!'

The door slid slowly open and Vana stumbled out onto the ramp.

There was little resemblance to the attractive, intelligent girl they had glimpsed in the underground Hall. Her steps were shambling, her face empty and vacant. Thara stared at her in horror. 'Vana! What have they done to you?'

He jumped to his feet, but Jamie grabbed him and pulled him into cover. 'Keep down!'

As soon as Vana was clear of the doorway, the Doctor darted forward, grabbed her around the waist and began hustling her down the ramp. Already a muffled, hissing was coming from the blocked jets.

'Quickly, Doctor,' shouted Zoe. The hissing sound grew louder and the jamming rocks began to vibrate.

'Doctor, look out!' shouted Jamie. He jumped to his feet and ran forward. The pressure build-up forced the looser of the two rocks from its place. Corrosive vapour poured from the unblocked jet.

The Doctor moved with astonishing speed. With one hand he thrust Vana forward off the ramp and in the same moment, touched the spring that opened his umbrella, swinging it over his shoulder so that it acted as a shield.

Jamie grabbed Vana and pulled her clear. Seconds later, the Doctor too was safely out of range. The hissing of the jet stopped, as the corrosive spray died away.

Jamie lowered Vana gently to the ground and Thara knelt beside her. 'Vana? Vana, what's wrong?'

She opened her eyes and stared at him, with no sign of recognition.

'What's happened?' whispered Thara. 'What have they done to her?'

The Doctor was gazing indignantly at the tattered remains of his umbrella. The corrosive vapour had reduced it to a skeleton of warped metal struts and tattered silk. 'Vandals! Just look at that!'

'That could have been you, Doctor,' pointed out Zoe.

'My favourite umbrella!' The Doctor sadly tossed the twisted remains away.

Thara was almost frantic with worry. 'She doesn't know me, Doctor. She doesn't speak or anything.'

Jamie glared at the door. 'It must be something your Krotons have done to her.'

The Doctor was still testing Vana's reflexes. 'Hmm . . . almost catatonic! Dear me . . . '

'Isn't there anything you can do?' asked Zoe worriedly.

'I am not a doctor of medicine,' snapped the Doctor — a little unfairly, since he was in fact a doctor of almost everything. 'However, as long as there's no tissue damage . . . She needs rest and quiet. Is there somewhere we can take her, Thara?'

'My father Selris's house is quite near — on the edge of the community.'

'Good. We'll take her there, then. Give her a hand, will you?'

Thara helped Vana to her feet. Half-supporting, half-carrying her, he led her away.

Slowly the little party made its way across the Wasteland. As they moved Zoe gave one last glance over her shoulder at the mysterious door.

What happened inside there? What evil force turned bright, intelligent young people into stumbling mindless idiots, and then did its best to destroy them utterly?

What kind of monsters were hiding behind that door?

3

The Rebels

Zoe swigged gratefully at the liquid in the earthen-
ware mug. She wasn't quite sure what she was
drinking — it was fiery and fruity at the same time.
But together with the simple meal of cheese and fruit
provided by Selris, it had refreshed and revived her
after their ordeal in the Wastelands and the journey
back. Even Jamie had admitted that whatever the
drink was, it was, 'No' bad at all!'

Selris, newly returned from the Hall of Learning,
had been shocked by their story, and horrified by
Vana's condition. Even now he could scarcely take it
in. 'It's almost impossible to believe. The Krotons
have always been our friends — our benefactors.'

Zoe said, 'Well, you've only got to look at what
they've done to Vana.'

Selris nodded, looking across to the curtained
alcove on the far side of the simply furnished room,
where the Doctor was attending to Vana.

At that moment the curtain was drawn back and
Thara emerged. Jamie looked up, 'How is she?'

'Just the same.' Grim faced, Thara strode out of the
room without another word. Zoe looked worriedly
after him, wondering where he was going and what he
planned to do.

Jamie rose and looked inside the alcove where Vana lay stretched out on the bed, her eyes open and staring blankly at the ceiling.

The Doctor was leaning over her, in his shirt-sleeves, dangling his old-fashioned pocket watch on its gold chain in front of her eyes. The watch swung gently to and fro and Vana was following it with her eyes.

The Doctor was speaking in a low, soothing voice. 'Now you are resting . . . softly resting . . . your mind is empty . . . You are resting. You feel sleepy . . . so sleepy, Vana . . . very sleepy . . . '

Jamie looked on in astonishment. Suddenly he found his own eyelids heavy and his head beginning to nod. Hurriedly he turned away. Some more of the Doctor's magic, he thought. Perhaps he was saying a spell. He went back to join Zoe and Selris on the other side of the big room.

Selris was explaining things to Zoe. ' . . . and so, at the appointed times our best students enter the machine to join the Krotons. They can't all have been murdered, surely?'

'It's just possible, you know. If they had, you wouldn't know because that poison spray just . . . '

She shuddered at the memory.

'It dissolves everything,' said Jamie bluntly. 'And in any case, you people never go into the Wasteland.'

'But why have they done it? Why kill our best students?' asked Selris helplessly.

Zoe looked round the room. It was plainly and simply furnished with the basics of civilised living. There were chairs, tables, a bed, couches to sit on, scattered rugs on the floor. Basic comforts, but no really advanced technology. Perhaps the Krotons planned to limit the development of Gond civilisation by creaming off the best brains . . . 'What are they like, these Krotons?'

'No living person has ever seen them. They never come out of the machine.'

'Never?'

'Not for thousands of years. Not since the beginning'

Before Zoe could ask any more questions the Doctor came out of the alcove, shrugging into his coat.

Zoe looked up. 'How is she?'

'Asleep at last.'

'Will she be all right?'

'I hope so. It's difficult to say.'

'She was one of our most brilliant students,' said Selris sadly.

'The Doctor raised his eyebrows. 'Really? Competiton for you, Zoe!'

Zoe gave him a quelling look. 'Apparently no-one's ever seen these Krotons, Doctor.'

Jamie said, 'Aye, that's right. They never come out of that machine.'

They both looked expectantly at the Doctor as if expecting him to come up with a solution to the mystery on the spot. The Doctor however decided he needed more information. 'How did all this begin, Selris?'

'According to our legends, great silver men came out of the sky and built a house among us. The Gonds attacked them and the silver men caused a poisonous rain to fall, killing hundreds of our people and turning the ground black.'

Jamie grunted. 'That accounts for yon Wasteland.'

Selris nodded. 'Yes, that is so. It was afterwards said that anyone who set foot there died in terrible pain . . . '

In the Hall of Learning, the Custodian moved

reverently amongst the dark shapes of the Teaching Machines.

The Machines stood in long rows, half-concealed behind the pillars to one side of the stairs. The area was gloomy and shadowed, and the Custodian lit his way with a magic staff that was a gift of the Krotons. You touched a stud at one end and light appeared at the other. It was the badge of the Custodian's office and he carried it with immense pride.

He was a slight, balding man with a beaky nose and a bushy moustache. Not in fact a very imposing guardian, though this mattered little since his duties were purely nominal.

The Teaching Machines maintained themselves, and as for guarding them — well, who would dare to attack the Hall of Learning, the very centre of Kroton authority?

Absorbed in the routine of his task, the Custodian failed to notice shadowy figures flitting between the pillars in the darkened hall.

He checked the last Teaching Machine, turned away — and suddenly strong hands caught him and threw him to the ground. Someone snatched the torch from his hands and shone it on his face.

The Custodian struggled feebly, but he was held too strongly to move. He became aware of a handful of shapes looming over him.

'Who are you?' he quavered. 'What are you doing here? It is forbidden to enter the Learning Hall at this time. The Law of the Krotons clearly states . . . '

One of the dark shapes leaned forward menacingly. 'Ah, yes! The Krotons. You must know a lot about them?'

'What do you mean?'

'You're their servant aren't you?' accused another voice. 'You work for them.'

'I am only the Custodian of the Hall of Learning.'

The first voice said mockingly. 'Yes, of course. Then you can tell us all we want to know.'

'I am forbidden to discuss the secrets of the Krotons.'

'We just want to know how to get at them. We want to see these Krotons for ourselves.'

The Custodian was horrified. 'But no-one has ever seen the Krotons. Not for thousands of years.'

'You're sure they don't come out of that machine in the darkness when there's no-one here?'

'Come out? The Krotons? Never!'

'Then how do they give their commands? Answer me!'

'There are Messages, left in the appointed place. You must know that.'

'What else?'

'Sometimes there is a voice,' admitted the Custodian reluctantly.

'But you've never seen them? There's no way inside the Machine?'

'Only the Companions of the Krotons may enter.'

'Yes,' said the voice bitterly. 'And now we know what happens to them. But you can summon the Krotons — *can't you?* Answer!'

'It is not for me to summon the Krotons. I obey their commands.'

There was a moment of silence, then the Custodian heard his captors muttering amongst themselves.

The first voice said angrily. 'If we can't get inside the Machine, then we must fetch the Krotons out!'

'How can we do that?'

'By smashing their precious Teaching Machines.'

'Smash the Machines?' gasped the Custodian. 'You can't! The Krotons will destroy us all!'

He made a desperate attempt to escape, and

31

actually succeeded in breaking free for a moment, before the many hands of his attackers pulled him down again.

'Here, tie his hands,' ordered the leader. 'Careful, I don't want him hurt. You'd better gag him as well.'

As his arm and legs were bound with lengths of cord, and a piece of rag bound across his mouth, the Custodian realised with horror that the chief of his attackers was Thara, son of Selris, leader of the Council of the Gonds.

'Go on, Selris. What happened after this war with the Krotons?' asked Jamie.

'It was all so long ago. According to our legends, since then we have lived in peace. The Krotons never show themselves, but we learn from them, through the Teaching Machines.'

Zoe's interest was aroused. 'Teaching Machines?'

'They are in the Learning Hall, where you were today. They fill the mind with knowledge.'

The Doctor frowned. 'And does everyone use these Machines?'

'When they are young, yes. That is the Law.'

'Whose law, Selris?' demanded the Doctor.

'Ours. The Council of the Gonds.'

'But weren't your laws also given you by the Teaching Machines — by the Krotons, hmm?'

'Yes, that is true,' said Selris, almost as if realising the fact for the first time. 'Our laws, our science, our culture, everything we have has come from the Teaching Machines.'

'Yes . . . self perpetuating slavery,' muttered the Doctor. 'And at regular intervals, the Krotons choose your most promising students to be their Companions?'

Selris nodded, a look of dawning horror on his face.

'Doctor, do you . . . do you think they have all been killed?'

'Well, we *saw* one killed,' said Jamie bluntly.

Zoe turned to the Doctor. 'Why are the Krotons doing it, Doctor? What's their reason?'

'I don't know — yet. But it's time it was stopped. High time!'

'How shall I tell the people?' asked Selris helplessly. 'How can I explain?'

'Explain what?' exploded Jamie. 'Just tell them the truth.'

'That they've been tricked? That for thousands of years our best students have been murdered by the Krotons.'

'Why?' asked Zoe. 'What are you afraid of?'

'Another war between your people and the Krotons, I should imagine,' said the Doctor.

Selris nodded, the responsibilities of his leadership weighing heavily upon him. 'If I tell them, and if they attack the Krotons, there could be terrible bloodshed, as there was before. Another massacre. Another Wasteland here, instead of our community.'

'Selris!' A young Gond rushed into the room, taller and more slightly built than the rest they'd seen, with a thin, intellectual face.

Selris smiled. 'Ah, Beta, I thought you'd be along to meet our guests.' He turned to the others. 'Beta here is our Controller of Science, and also my son's good friend.'

'That's why I'm here,' gasped Beta. 'Because of Thara. He was at the Hall of Students, talking to the others. He and some of his friends, all the hot-headed ones, have gone out to the Hall of Learning. They're going to attack the Krotons — wreck the Teaching Machines if they have to, to fetch them out of hiding. You've got to stop them, Selris. I came as quickly as I could, but they'll be there by now.'

'Then it's too late.'

The Doctor jumped to his feet. 'Not if we cut across the Wasteland.'

Beta gave him a look of astonished horror. 'The Wasteland? But it's poisonous . . . '

'Nonsense. It may have been once, but any poison wore off long ago.'

'That's right,' said Jamie, pleased at the prospect of a little action. 'We've been through your Wasteland twice today and we're just fine. Come on!'

Talking about attacking the Teaching Machines was easy enough, but actually doing it was quite another. Thara's fellow students had a lifetime of conditioning to overcome and he had to whip up their courage all over again before they were ready to take action.

Axes in their hands, they stood around the bulky shape of the nearest Teaching Machine. All the Machines were exactly the same design — a console, a vision screen, a chair for the student, and a metal helmet suspended over the chair by a flexible arm.

'Well, come on!' shouted Thara at last. Raising his axe high, he brought it smashing down on the console. A crack appeared in the smooth gleaming surface. The others waited aghast, expecting some unimaginable terror — a bolt of lighting, perhaps even an angry Kroton. Nothing happened.

Emboldened, Thara raised his axe and struck again and again. The console began to splinter. With yells of triumph, the others ran to join him. Soon the console was shuddering under a rain of axe-blows.

Bound and gagged at the base of a pillar, the Custodian looked on in unbelieving horror.

The great Kroton Machine, the one built into the

Learning Hall, was alive.

Not perhaps in the way that a living, thinking being is alive. But it was so elaborately programmed to serve the interests of its unseen masters, so well-equipped with various means of information-gathering, evaluating, methods of attack and defence, that at times it could react with something very like intelligence.

It was doing so now.

In the control room at the heart of the Machine, instruments clicked and whirred, and spools revolved into life. A monitor screen lit up.

An observation servo-mechanism, in essence no more than a black box with a lens, slid forward on a long extensible rod and peered curiously into the monitor.

The Teaching Machine was a twisted pile of plastic and shattered circuitry. 'That should fetch them out!' yelled Thara.

By now the blood of the little band of rebellious students was up. 'Come on!' screamed one of them, hitherto the most timid. 'Let's wreck another!'

A voice boomed from out of the air. 'STOP!'

It was a loud, booming voice, with a harsh, throaty grating to it. Thara and his little band of rebels froze instantly.

'THIS IS A WARNING. LEAVE THE HALL. ALL GONDS LEAVE THE HALL NOW!'

'The Krotons,' muttered one of the students fearfully.

'LEAVE THE HALL. ALL GONDS LEAVE THE HALL NOW.'

The students began edging away, but Thara had gone too far to be frightened off now. 'That's just a voice,' he shouted. 'Don't be afraid!'

'THIS IS A WARNING.'

It was a warning Thara chose to ignore. 'Come out, you Krotons! Come out and fight!' He attacked the next Teaching Machine.

Thara's enthusiasm gave the others new courage. 'Murderers!' shrieked the timid student, now bold again. Together with the others he joined in the attack.

'Thara! Stop!'

Suddenly Selris was there, shoving Thara away from the Teaching Machine. At the same time the Doctor turned to the excited group of students and shooed them away like a flock of hens.

'Listen to me,' he shouted. 'This will do no good. No good at all. These Krotons must have enormous scientific powers. You can't defeat them with axes!'

He snatched the axe from Thara's hand and brandished it reprovingly at him.

The picture on the monitor showed the little group of students arguing amongst themselves. At the centre of the group stood one smaller and dressed differently from the rest. He was waving one of the primitive weapons.

With impeccable machine logic the servo-mechanism decided that this primitive was obviously the leader, inciting the rest to attack. Its data bank told it that when the leader was destroyed primitive attackers would usually flee.

Transferring the Doctor's image to its memory bank, the servo-mechanism moved away to take the necessary action.

Outside in the Learning Hall, the Doctor handed the axe back to Thara. 'Now, if this was an atomic laser it might be more use.'

'Atomic laser?' said Thara doubtfully. 'Is that better than an axe?'

'Look at the damage you've done,' growled Selris. 'Completely senseless.'

Thara was unrepentant. 'Look what they did to our friends!'

'Destroying the machines won't revenge Abu, or help Vana, will it?'

'We can't get in there,' muttered one of the students. 'If we attack their machines . . . '

'The Krotons will come out!' finished Thara.

There was a whirring sound and a round hatch beside the machine door slid open.

'I think *something's* coming out, right now,' said the Doctor worriedly.

And so it was. The 'something' was a gleaming, articulated metal snake, its whole head composed of a single glowing lens. The snake extruded from the hatchway and hovered, swaying in the air like a cobra looking for a victim.

'Doctor, what is it?' whispered Zoe fearfully.

'I don't know, Zoe, but whatever it is, we'd better keep well away from it.'

Suddenly the metal snake seemed to spot the little group and it streaked through the air towards them. They backed hurriedly away as it hovered in front of them, swaying to and fro hypnotically.

'What's it doing?' whispered Thara.

Zoe studied the strange object thoughtfully. 'Doctor, it seems to be *looking* at us.'

'How can it?' asked Jamie nervously. 'It's no' alive — is it?'

The lens transmitted the information back. The face of the primitive leader was the face before the lens. It had found its target. Relentlessly, the metal snake

37

homed in on the Doctor, singling him out from the others.

'Doctor, it's after *you!*' gasped Zoe.

The Doctor backed away still further. Tripping over a chunk of the broken Teaching Machine he fell over backwards . . .

The snake zoomed forwards aiming directly for his face. Helpless, flat on his back, the Doctor threw up his arms in a vain attempt to shield himself . . .

4

The Genius

All at once the metal snake started to waver, as if it had lost its sense of direction. It began weaving to and fro in the air, almost as if it had suddenly gone blind.

Still keeping his face covered, and peeping through his fingers the Doctor started to get up.

'Doctor, don't move,' called Zoe.

The Doctor got carefully to his feet. 'It's all right, Zoe. I'm quite safe!'

Jamie wasn't convinced. 'I wouldna be so sure.'

'Look,' said the Doctor happily.

He took his hands away from his face.

The metal snake, still sweeping to and fro, checked its swing and zoomed straight for the Doctor.

Calmly, the Doctor covered his face with his hands. Confused once more, the metal snake swung vaguely backwards and forwards, resuming its search.

Suddenly Zoe understood. 'Pattern recognition!'

'Exactly, Zoe,' said the Doctor from behind his hands. 'And the pattern is obviously my face!'

Selris stared at him. 'Then you mean that that thing was sent out to attack you — and only you?'

'So it seems. Flattering, isn't it?'

Zoe said slowly. 'Then the Krotons must know who you are — or know what you look like.'

'Yes, so they must, Zoe. Therefore they must have a scanner in the hull of the machine somewhere. If we can find it, we may be able to make contact with them and —'

In his excitement, the Doctor dropped his hands from his face. The metal snake spotted him at once and began zipping towards him. With a yell of alarm, the Doctor threw himself to one side.

The timid student suddenly saw his chance for real glory. As the snake waved about in quest of the Doctor, he leaped forward, swinging with his axe.

The metal snake froze, and hung poised for a moment, staring at him with its single glowing eye. Then a jet of corrosive vapour hissed out from a nozzle set just beneath the lens. The student gave one terrible scream . . .

When the vapour dispersed he had vanished. All that remained was the axe, flung to one side by his dying hand.

'Look, Doctor, it's going back,' shouted Jamie.

The metal snake was retracing, sliding back into the machine. It grew shorter and shorter until the lens went back through the circular opening, and the hatch slid closed.

Once again, the Doctor climbed to his feet. 'Yes . . . I'm afraid that poor fellow must have confused the attack mechanism.'

Jamie stared at him. 'Eh?'

'It was programmed to kill *once. One* person. *Me!* It must think it's succeeded — stupid machine!'

Thara picked up his dead friend's axe. 'There's your wonderful Krotons for you, father!' With a yell of rage he hurled the axe at the machine. 'Murderers!'

Selris grabbed his arm. 'Thara! Don't provoke them!'

'Is that all you care about — not provoking them?'

40

'What can we do against such weapons as theirs, my son?'

The grating metallic voice boomed out once more. 'THIS IS A WARNING. YOUR LEADER HAS BEEN DESTROYED. ALL GONDS LEAVE THE LEARNING HALL AT ONCE.'

'No!' shouted Thara. 'Stay and fight!' But the death of their fellow student had taken all the fight out of the rebels.

Selris shouted, 'All of you, leave the Learning Hall. Leave now!'

The Doctor too added his persuasions. 'I think we'd all better do as they say, you know!'

Thankfully the Gonds hurried to obey. For the moment at least, the rebellion was over.

The Doctor was sitting on the bed in the alcove examining Vana's eyes with a kind of primitive opthalmascope.

Switching the instrument off, he put it to one side and began feeling the unconscious girl's skull, probing gently with sensitive fingers.

Zoe picked up the instrument and studied it, switching it on and off. It was large and clumsy, but perfectly effective. 'Where did this come from, Doctor?'

'That? Oh, I borrowed it from their scientist chap — Beta.'

'I thought the Gonds didn't know about electricity?'

'Well, they don't really. That thing works from stored solar energy. You know, Zoe, the Gonds are quite advanced in some ways. Wish they had an ETC machine though . . . '

'There are strange gaps in their knowledge. I suppose it's because they only know what the machines teach them.'

41

The Doctor straightened up, and stood looking down at Vana, who seemed to be sleeping peacefully. 'Yes, precisely. And the machines are programmed by the Krotons. So those gaps must be very significant.'

Jamie and Selris came over to them.

Selris looked down at the girl. 'How is she, Doctor?'

'Slightly better, I think. It's difficult to be sure. Selris — do you think it would be safe to go back to the Learning Hall?'

Since the attack on the Teaching Machines, everything seemed quiet, though Selris had taken the precaution of putting the Hall under guard.

'I'm not sure, Doctor? Why do you ask?'

'Oh, Zoe and I want to have another look round, don't we, Zoe?'

'Do we?'

'Yes, of course we do. Hold your hand out, Jamie.'

Puzzled, Jamie held out his hand. The Doctor took out a little phial and shook three brownish pills into his palm.

'What's all this Doctor?'

'Just some pills I got from Beta.'

'I dinna need pills. There's nothing wrong with me.'

'They're for Vana. I want you to stay here and look after her.'

Jamie looked mutinously at him. 'Why can't I come with you?'

'Because I want you to see that she swallows these pills the moment she wakes up. It's very important, Jamie. I need someone I can rely on.'

'Och, well, all right,' said Jamie, mollified.

'I shall come with you, Doctor,' announced Selris.

'My dear fellow, that's quite unnecessary.'

'I am the leader of the Gond Council. I must know what is happening.'

'Oh, well come along then. Goodbye, Jamie.'

The Doctor bustled out of the room, followed by Selris.

Jamie put a hand on Zoe's arm. 'Watch him, Zoe. You know what he's like!'

Zoe smiled understandingly. 'Don't worry, Jamie, I won't let him do anything rash!'

She hurried after the others.

The Doctor hurried down the steps that led into the Learning Hall, and came to a sudden halt, staring down at his feet. 'Aha!'

Selris stopped too. 'What?'

The big flagstone beneath the Doctor's feet had a metal ring set into the centre. 'What's this?'

'It leads to the Underhall.'

'What's down there?'

Selris shrugged. 'Nothing. It's never used.'

The Doctor glanced over at the machine, then back down at the flagstone. 'Hmm, I wonder how far down . . . ' He looked hopefully up at Selris. 'Do you think we could just take a look?'

Puzzled but obliging, Selris knelt down and heaved at the heavy flagstone. Muscles bulging with the effort, he lifted it up and moved it aside, revealing an open space and the top of a steep flight of steps.

'You stay here, Zoe,' said the Doctor. 'We shan't be long.' He disappeared down the ladder, and Selris followed.

Left on her own, Zoe wandered over to the wrecked Teaching Machine. She studied its wrecked innards for a moment, trying to reconstruct its design and purpose.

She moved on to the next Machine and studied the controls. Then, unable to resist, she reached out and pressed what she judged to be the 'on' button. The screen lit up invitingly.

43

On a sudden impulse, Zoe slipped into the curved seat, reached up and pulled down the metal helmet, fitting it over her head. Immediately a sense of pleasurable anticipation flooded her mind. She felt keen and alert, eager to begin.

A circle of complex symbols appeared on the screen, revolving in a clockwise direction. Inside it was another circle, revolving counter clockwise.

Zoe studied the complicated display for a moment. Her fingers flickered over the keyboard, resolving the symbols into a logical mathematical equation. Immediately a tremendous sense of well-being flooded over her. It was like being given the most enormous pat on the back from a favourite teacher.

The equation vanished and an even more complicated display appeared. On the side of the machine there was a calibrated dial. Its needle began climbing . . .

The dial was reproduced in the control room inside the Kroton Machine. The servo-mechanism glided forward, registering the score . . .

The Doctor looked round the vast and gloomy Underhall. He saw three shining pillars, spreading out from the ceiling overhead and disappearing into the walls and floor.

He stared thoughtfully at them. They reminded him of something . . .

His face stern as he turned to Selris. 'All right, I've seen enough.'

As he followed the Doctor up the ladder, Selris said, 'I told you there was nothing down there, Doctor.'

'But there was, Selris — something rather curious.'

'Those pillars are just the foundation of the

44

Machine.'

The Doctor wasn't listening. 'Zoe!' he called. 'What do you think you're doing?'

He ran towards her, Selris close behind him.

Zoe was still sitting at the console of the Teaching Machine, hands flickering over the keys. There was a blissful smile on her face.

Selris pulled the cap from Zoe's head, and the Doctor heaved her bodily out of the chair. She smiled vaguely at him. 'You're soon back, Doctor. I was just trying the Teaching Machine.'

'You ought to know better than to do a thing like that,' scolded the Doctor.

'But it was all so easy, Doctor — and so pleasant. The Krotons were *very* pleased with me.'

'*Pleased* with you?'

'Well . . . I *felt* they were . . . '

The Doctor clapped his hands very hard in front of Zoe's face, so she blinked and jumped back.

'Zoe, whatever these Krotons are, they are not benign and friendly. We know that, don't we?'

'Yes . . . yes, of course,' said Zoe, remembering.

'They use these machines not only to teach but to programme — to plant impressions on the mind.' The Doctor turned to Selris. 'That's how they've enslaved your people all these years.'

Selris was staring at the console in astonishment. 'Just look at that score dial, Doctor.'

'What about it?'

'It's amazing. Even our very best students register less than half that score.'

'Well, Zoe *is* something of a genius, of course. It can be very irritating at times!'

Zoe smiled.

Jamie was almost dozing off when Vana began

twisting and muttering agitatedly.

She tried to sit up. Jamie forced her gently back on the pillows. 'Now then,' he said gruffly. 'Dinna' worry, you're all right now, Vana.'

Vana's face was flushed and her eyes were wild. 'The ball,' she muttered. 'The burning ball . . . It's over my head, swallowing me up . . . '

She flattened herself against the bed, staring above her in terror.

'No, Vana, there's nothing. There's nothing here . . . '

'I saw it!' she screamed. 'I saw it!' She sat up again, writhing in terror.

To Jamie's vast relief, Thara came hurrying over. He cradled Vana in his arms, soothing her. 'It's all right. There's nothing here, Vana. You're safe.'

Vana's face twisted in terror. 'It was flashing,' she babbled feverishly. 'All the lights . . . *burning my mind . . . the lights!*' She gave one final convulsive heave, and slumped back exhausted.

Thara stroked her hair, 'Vana, you're all right now. You're home.'

Her eyes widened and she looked vaguely at him. 'Thara, is that you?'

'She recognises me,' said Thara delightedly. 'Vana, listen, nothing can hurt you now. You're going to be all right.'

She clutched his hand. 'I went into the Machine, Thara . . . '

Jamie leaned forward. 'Did you see the Krotons?'

She stared blankly at him. 'Krotons? There was just the fiery ball, flashing, coming down on me.'

Her voice rose in panic, and Thara held her tight. 'It's all right, Vana. You're safe.'

Belatedly Jamie recollected his duty. 'Here, you'd better take these. Come on, it's medicine, swallow them down. Get her some water, Thara.'

Between them they managed to get her to take the pills and she soon sank back onto the pillow, her eyes closing in sleep.

Thara looked worriedly at her. 'A flashing ball, coming down on her, burning her mind . . . What did she mean? Is it another of the Kroton's weapons?'

Jamie shrugged, 'I canna' tell. You stay with her, Thara. I'm off to find the Doctor.'

The Doctor was scraping at the shining surface of the door of the Kroton Machine with an old Boy Scout jack-knife. A little way away, Zoe was doing the same thing with a nail-file. 'It's crystalline!'

The Doctor had come to the same conclusion. 'Very hard, but not brittle, I've never seen anything like it.'

Zoe nodded towards the flagstone. 'What was it like — down there?'

'Hmm? Ah yes, I saw what Selris calls the foundations. And do you know what, Zoe? It was like a *root structure*.'

'A root structure? But that would indicate . . . '

'Yes . . . That this so-called machine is organic in structure. Quite so.'

'Is that possible?'

'Why not? Some crystals do resemble simple virus forms. I wish I could get a fragment to analyse.'

'But if you're right Doctor,' said Zoe slowly, 'then this whole machine is a sort of living thing!'

'All life doesn't necessarily have feeling, you know,' began the Doctor.

He was interrupted by the boom of a gong. The Doctor winced. 'Great jumping gobstoppers, what's that?'

Selris came hurrying forward. 'It's the Krotons' signal. It means they have a message for me.'

47

He hurried to the circular hatch beside the door and waited. Seconds later the hatch slid open and Selris removed the inscribed plastic tablet, staring at it in amazement.

'Well,' said the Doctor impatiently, 'what does it say?'

Slowly Selris read aloud. 'Class three one nine seven . . . Selected: Female — Zoegond.'

'Zoegond?' The Doctor snatched the tablet from Selris and studied it. He looked up appalled. 'Zoe! They mean you!'

Selris looked gravely at Zoe. 'They have chosen you for a Companion of the Krotons.'

5

The Companions

The Doctor glared indignantly at Selris. 'A Companion of the Krotons? Yes, well, we all know what happens to them, don't we?'

'Oh, Doctor, what shall I do?' gasped Zoe.

'Well, Selris?' demanded the Doctor. 'She doesn't have to go — does she?'

Selris hesitated.

'Well? Does she or doesn't she?'

Reluctantly Selris said, 'I'm afraid she must, Doctor. Complete obedience is the First Law of the Krotons. If we fail to obey them, they have threatened —'

'To destroy you all, as they did before?'

Selris bowed his head. 'If you do not obey them, we shall die.'

Zoe sighed. 'Oh dear . . . '

'See what you've done?' snapped the Doctor. 'Fooling around with that ridiculous machine!'

'But I'm not a Gond!'

'Well, that stupid machine doesn't seem to know the difference. Oh well!'

The Doctor strode over to the Teaching Machine and Zoe hurried after him. 'What are you going to do?'

49

'Take the test of course. Can't let you go in alone. Now, what do I do?'

Zoe saw he was determined. 'First you sit down.' The Doctor sat. 'Then you put this on.' She fitted the helmet over his untidy mop of hair. 'Now, press the "on" button.'

The Doctor didn't move and Zoe realised that with the helmet covering his ears he couldn't hear her. 'Press the button!' she shouted.

'All right,' said the Doctor irritably. 'No need to shout! Now go away and don't fuss me — no, come back. What's this? It's all right, I know!'

Muttering crossly to himself, the Doctor settled himself before the console. 'Right, fire away. I'm ready.'

Nothing happened.

'The "on" button!' mouthed Zoe.

The Doctor glared at her and pressed the button.

The screen lit up. The Doctor stared indignantly at the circling symbols and began stabbing at the console. The symbols gave a final swirl, broke up and vanished.

'Doctor, you got it all wrong!' said Zoe. She glanced at the score dial, which was at its lowest reading.

'Oh dear, I was working in square roots,' grumbled the Doctor.

He leaned forward, addressing the screen. 'Can I have that again, please?'

'They don't give you a second shot,' said Zoe. 'Press the button again!'

The Doctor pressed the button and another even more complex circle of symbols appeared on the screen.

As the Doctor worked frenziedly at the console, Selris leaned forward and whispered, 'This is the most advanced Machine. Perhaps he can't answer the questions?'

'Of course he can,' said Zoe loyally. 'The Doctor'
almost as clever as I am.'

Selris looked doubtfully at the score dial. 'Is he?'

Zoe leaned forward to watch the Doctor's progress
just as his second equation broke up and disappeared
'Oh, Doctor,' she said reproachfully, 'You divided
instead of multiplying. You must concentrate.'

He gave her a distracted look. 'I am, Zoe, I am.'

Frowning ferociously, the Doctor stabbed at the
button once more. 'Ah, that's better.' He settled down
to work.

Inside the Machine the duplicate score dial began
climbing to the highest total yet achieved.

The Doctor sorted out the last and most complex
equation in record time, pulled off the helmet, and sa
back with a sigh of contented relief. He got out of the
chair, and looked at the dial. 'I rather think I've
beaten your score, Zoe.'

'You answered more questions. Anyway, it's not
supposed to be a competition.'

The Doctor rubbed his temples. 'Very clever the
way they make out you're pleasing them, isn't it?'

Zoe nodded. 'Perhaps they aren't as bad as we
think?'

The Doctor nodded dreamily. Then he frowned.
'What?' he shouted and slapped himself hard on the
head with both hands. 'Of course they are!'

It was diabolically clever, thought the Doctor.
Obviously the Teaching Machines stimulated the
pleasure centre of the brain so that learning was not
only easy but enjoyable, and the 'approval' of the
Krotons a much-desired reward. 'Well, Selris, what
happens now?'

'The Krotons will be waiting for Zoe.'

'Well, they can wait. We're going in there together.'

'Normally the names don't come through for some little time.'

'Mine did,' pointed out Zoe.

Selris nodded. 'Perhaps your performance on the Teaching Machine impressed them.'

Suddenly the gong note sounded again.

'Sounds a bit like a dinner gong,' said the Doctor.

Selris hurried to the message hatch and took out the plastic square. He read out the contents. 'Class three one nine eight. Selected: Male — Doctorgond.'

'Doctorgond!' shouted the Doctor. 'Idiots!'

'It means you anyway,' said Zoe.

There was a humming sound and the door slid upwards.

The Doctor drew a deep breath. 'Well, Zoe, are you ready?'

'I suppose we really do have to?'

'We started this, so we'd better go through with it. We've got to get to the bottom of this somehow, and to do that we have to get inside.'

'It's all my fault,' said Zoe miserably.

The Doctor patted her shoulder. 'Oh, cheer up. I expect it will all be quite interesting really.'

Selris bowed his head. 'I am sorry this had to happen, Doctor. My people will always remember you.'

'What?' said the Doctor sharply. Then he realised. Selris was saying a final goodbye. As far as Selris was concerned, they were already dead.

'Yes, well that's very nice of you,' said the Doctor ironically. 'Stay close to me, Zoe.'

He took Zoe's hand and together they went into the Kroton Machine. The door slid closed behind them.

Jamie came tearing down the steps into the Learning Hall. 'Doctor! Doctor, come back!' But it was too late.

He ran up to Selris. 'What's happened?'

Selris raised his hand to hold Jamie back. Then he laid the hand on Jamie's shoulder, and gave him a look of grave sympathy. 'Your friends are gone. They have become Companions of the Krotons.'

The Doctor and Zoe moved along a darkened corridor. Every so often, a door opened before them, so that there was always only one way they could go.

The last door slid upwards, and they found themselves in a huge control room. The place was in semi-darkness, with strangely designed instrument consoles lining the walls. The only sound was the faint humming and ticking of instruments.

The Doctor had a sudden impression that the whole place was on standby. Waiting. But for what? For them, perhaps.

Zoe looked round. 'It's a space craft, isn't it, Doctor?'

'Yes, I think so, Zoe. But no crew apparently.' He raised his voice. 'Hullo! Anybody here?'

Suddenly a spotlight shone down from somewhere on high. It made a little pool of light, in the centre of which were two simple, functionally designed chairs.

'I think we've just been asked to sit down,' said Zoe nervously. They sat.

The Doctor took his watch and chain from his pocket and handed one end of the chain to Zoe. 'Hold one end of this, Zoe.'

'What for?'

The Doctor pointed upwards. Suspended above their heads was a transparent cone, packed with electronic circuitry. 'That's a force-field generator up there. The chain might help to equalise the power load.'

Zoe looked up apprehensively. 'What are they going

to do?'

Suddenly the cone began descending towards them. It glowed fiercely into life, bathing them in an almost intolerable glare.

'Doctor, I can't move,' called Zoe.

'No,' gasped the Doctor. 'Force field. Try and . . . relax.'

The revolving cone grew brighter and brighter, until it seemed to turn into a great ball of fire suspended directly above their heads.

The Doctor and Zoe writhed against the constraints of the force field, their faces twisted and distorted by the strain . . .

'*Why?*' demanded Jamie. 'Why did you let them go?'

'The Krotons commanded.'

'Och, the Krotons! They just give an order and everyone jumps, don't they? Well, I'm no' just standing here! I'm going to find a way into this box of tricks.'

Jamie began battering on the door.

Inside the Kroton control room, the pressure on Zoe and the Doctor had reached intolerable levels. They were bathed in the fierce white light from the spinning fireball above their heads. It seemed to drain all the energy from both their bodies and their brains.

Zoe was dimly aware that somehow the Doctor was helping her to bear the intolerable strain . . . The gold chain between their hands was twisting and distorting in the power-flow between them.

Inside the forcefield generator, a column of mercury was rising higher and higher. When it reached the top of the column, there was a last blinding flare of light — and everything went quiet.

'Are you all right, Zoe?' gasped the Doctor.

'Yes, I think so . . . What happened?'

The Doctor looked ruefully at his distorted watch chain. 'We were in the grip of some tremendous force . . . '

'It was tapping our mental power,' said Zoe. 'They seem to have found a way of converting mental power into energy.'

'Yes . . . I think they were using it — or rather us — to operate some kind of thermal switch.'

'Doctor, look! Over there! Wasn't there a wall in front of us?'

'Yes, there was. You know, Zoe, I think I'm beginning to understand.'

The wall that had been in front of them had vanished. In its place stood an enormous coffin-shaped transparent tank filled with some bubbling seething liquid.

In the depths of the tank, unseen as yet, a hideous shape was beginning to form . . .

6

The Krotons Awake

The Doctor rose stiffly and went over to the tank. 'Oh dear, Zoe, I think we've been and gone and done it this time!' He peered inside. 'How very curious!'

Zoe came to join him. 'We've gone and done what?'

'Just a minute, I have an idea.'

The Doctor took Beta's medicine phial from his pocket, tipped out the rest of the pills and stowed them away, and used the phial to scoop up a small quantity of the bubbling liquid. He held up the phial and peered at the contents. 'It appears to be a form of slurry, crystals in suspension.'

'What for? What's its purpose?'

'Life on your planet is supposed to have begun in the sea, hmm? Someone once called it primeval soup. Of course, there are many kinds of soup, aren't there? I wonder what this one is?' The Doctor tipped a few drops of the slurry onto a finger, tasted it cautiously and grimaced.

Zoe was looking at the tank. From the bottom there ran two long metallic hoses, each with one end plugged into the tank and the other end free. 'What do you suppose these are? They look a bit like astronauts air-lines.'

The Doctor restoppered the phial and put it in his

pocket. 'Very similar, Zoe. Yes. I think you're right.' He stared hard into the tank. 'Zoe, look!'

Inside the tank a massive shape was beginning to form. It was vaguely humanoid, yet angular and crystalline at the same time. The shape began to stir.

The Doctor jumped back. 'I think we'd better get out of here.'

He looked around. The way by which they'd come was closed now, but the way ahead seemed open. The Doctor grabbed Zoe's hand and dragged her from the control room.

As they hurried away, a huge gleaming arm, ending in a kind of clamp rose from the seething liquid in the tank and began groping vaguely at the air . . .

The Doctor and Zoe came to a corridor junction, and the Doctor paused to get his bearings.

'What are we going to do if we do get out?' asked Zoe. 'We haven't learned anything.'

The Doctor tapped the pocket holding the phial. 'Oh yes we have. Once we can analyse this . . . This way I think. Come along, Zoe!'

The huge gleaming figure climbed ponderously from the tank and stood swaying dizzily for a moment. Reaching down it groped for one of the pipes from the tank and clipped it into a socket in its body.

Immediately the creature seemed to become steadier, more alert, as if the tank was providing strength and nourishment.

Inside the tank, a second huge shape was beginning to form . . .

Jamie had abandoned his futile pounding on the door of the Kroton machine. Now he was trying to pry the doors open with his knife — with inevitably, an equal lack of success.

Selris was doing his best to dissuade him. 'I tell you,

there is no way in.'

'It's a door, isn't it?' growled Jamie. 'If I can just get it open.'

'Nobody can enter unless the Krotons wish it!'

'We'll see about that. What I need is some kind of crowbar . . .'

Jamie hunted through the Learning Hall until he found a storage alcove where a few simple tools were kept. To his joy they included a heavy crowbar. Hefting it determinedly, he strode back towards the door.

Inside the control room the second Kroton, now fully formed, was clipping its nutrient hose into place.

The Kroton Commander was adjusting controls on the scanner. 'The Gonds should be here,' observed Kroton Two in its deep grating voice.

The Kroton Commander adjusted a control on the scanner, and caught a brief glimpse of two fleeing figures. 'They are in the exit shaft.' It spoke in the same flat, emotionless tones as the other.

'Why?' demanded Kroton Two. 'They are conditioned to obey.'

'The conditioning may have failed.' The Kroton Commander jabbed at the controls with its clamp-like hand.

The Doctor and Zoe hurried through the corridors of the Kroton ship, too hurried to observe much of their strange surroundings, though Zoe was vaguely aware of glinting crystalline walls, and weirdly shaped instrument consoles.

They passed through a chamber festooned with a jungle of dangling pipes, through which gurgled multi-coloured liquids, and came at last to an ante-chamber before what the Doctor reckoned must be the rear door of the ship.

The Doctor studied the door, shoving vainly at it.

'It looks as if it should slide,' said Zoe.

'There must be a trip mechanism.'

Zoe pointed to the side of the door. 'There's some sort of photo-electric cell here.' She passed her hand to and fro in front of it. 'It doesn't seem to be working.'

'And if it isn't working . . . '

'The Krotons must have cut the circuit,' concluded Zoe.

'Yes, I'm afraid so.'

'Then we're trapped, Doctor. And they know we're here.'

The Doctor began fumbling through his pockets. 'That piece of mica I picked up in the Wasteland. If I can use it to bridge the gap and trip the switch . . . '

The Doctor found the fragment of mica and began wedging it into the socket of the photo-electric cell.

Zoe looked on dubiously. 'Do you think it'll work?'

'I don't know. The whole ship's built of crystal though, so —'

The Doctor broke off as the door slid upwards with a whine of power, revealing the Wasteland outside.

Desperate to get out of the ship Zoe darted forward.

The Doctor grabbed her arm. 'Wait, Zoe — if we go out there, we'll run into those poison jets . . . '

The Kroton Commander studied the monitor. It now showed the back of the ship and the open door. 'They have re-activated the exit circuit.'

Kroton Two said matter-of-factly, 'Then the dispersion unit will kill them.'

The Kroton Commander reached for the console.

The Doctor and Zoe were still hesitating before the open door. 'We'll *have* to risk it Doctor,' said Zoe desperately. 'We can't stay here.'

The Doctor nodded. 'All right. But jump straight down from the side, Zoe. Whatever you do, don't go down the ramp . . .'

Impassively the two Krotons watched Zoe and the Doctor sprint through the open door, take a flying leap from the side of the ramp and disappear into the Wasteland. They were moving too quickly to realise that the poison spray had not been activated at all.

The Kroton Commander watched them go. 'They are not Gonds.'

'Why did you inoperate the dispersion unit?' asked Kroton Two.

'We need them alive.'

'They have now escaped,' pointed out Kroton Two.

'Keep a watch for them on all scanners. We will order the Gonds to capture them and bring them back.'

The Kroton Commander switched the scanner to the Learning Hall, where a strangely-dressed figure was trying to prise open the ship's doors with a metal bar.

'That is not a Gond either.'

'It is possible that they have evolved.'

The Kroton Commander studied the attacker.

'There has not been time. This is a similar biped animal, but it is not from this planet.'

'It is possible that these superior anthropoids have taken over the planet.'

Selris appeared on the scanner. 'That is a Gond,' said the Kroton Commander. 'Perhaps these new creatures are in alliance with the Gonds.'

'Let us take this one,' suggested Kroton Two. 'Its mind will have the capacity we need.'

Just as Jamie was on the point of giving up, the door of the Kroton ship slid smoothly upwards.

'At last,' said Jamie triumphantly.

'No, don't enter,' warned Selris.

Jamie brandished his crowbar. 'Dinna worry, I've got this!'

Pushing Selris aside Jamie disappeared inside the ship. The door closed behind him.

Like the Doctor and Zoe, Jamie found himself unavoidably led to the central control room. But as he stepped inside, crowbar at the ready, two vast angular shapes bore down on him.

Jamie swung round in amazement. The creatures were enormous, almost twice the size of a man. They had huge barrel shaped torsos, high ridged shoulders and a solid base on which they seemed to slide like hovercraft. The massive arms ended in giant clamps. The most terrifying of all were the heads, blank, many faceted and rising to a point in a shape like that of a giant crystal.

Despite their robotic features there was something crystalline about the giant creatures as though they had been grown rather than made . . .

Before Jamie could even think of resisting, Kroton Two reached out with surprising speed, the clamp-hand fastening about his neck, choking him into semi-consciousness.

The creature moved Jamie effortlessly across the control room and deposited him on one of the chairs.

The two giant forms looked dispassionately down at him.

'Have you damaged it?' asked the Kroton Commander.

'No. It is alive.'

'Animal tissue is fragile,' reminded the Kroton

Commander.

Jamie writhed in the chair, gasping to get his breath back.

'It is recovering,' said Kroton Two. 'Test its mind.'

Jamie regained full consciousness to find himself in the grip of some invisible force. A burning ball revolved just above his head, sucking energy from his body and his mind. Held in the grip of the force-field Jamie's body jerked convulsively, his face distorted with the unbearable strain, while the two giant forms watched his agony unmoved.

The Kroton Commander studied a reading on a nearby instrument panel. 'This is not a high brain,' it observed dispassionately. 'It is a primitive.'

Kroton Two spoke with an equal lack of emotion. 'Then the power will kill it!'

Jamie writhed in the chair . . .

7

The Militants

The Kroton Commander reached out a clamped hand, and touched controls.

The fireball rose higher and faded away, and the invisible force released its hold. 'It is still of value. It can give us information about the other creatures.'

The Commander gestured towards the monitor, which showed the Doctor and Zoe hurrying away across the Wasteland.

As they hurried along, Zoe came to a sudden stop. 'This isn't the way to the Gond city, Doctor.'

'Of course it isn't. It's the way to the TARDIS!'

'The TARDIS? But we can't leave Jamie behind.'

'I need to use the TARDIS laboratory, Zoe. And don't worry about Jamie, he's quite safe. He's looking after Vana, isn't he? Now do come along . . . '

Jamie looked up at the two nightmare figures looming above him.

A voice boomed, 'Where are you from?'

'Och, are you two still here? I thought I'd dreamed you up!'

'Where are you from?'

'What? Oh, Earth.'

'You are of the same race as these bipeds?'

The Kroton gestured towards the monitor screen.

Jamie peered at the screen and grinned. 'Zoe — and the Doctor! Where are they?'

'You are space travellers?'

Jamie was looking intently at the scanner, 'They're in the Wasteland. They got out, then! Good old Doctor — ouch!' He yelled as a clamp-hand closed on his upper arm in a bone-crushing grip.

'Answer!' boomed Kroton Two.

'You're breaking my shoulder!'

'Do not damage the creature,' said the Commander reprovingly.

The crushing grip relaxed.

The Commander repeated the question. 'You and these other creatures are space travellers?'

'Ay, that's right.'

Kroton Two said, 'Look, Commander.'

Both Krotons studied the monitor screen, which now showed the Doctor and Zoe about to enter the TARDIS. The Commander swung round on Jamie. 'What is that?'

'It's called the TARDIS.'

'What is its function?'

'It travels through time and space,' said Jamie. This was the sum total of his knowledge about the TARDIS.

Kroton Two moved to another control console, and suddenly a spinning vortex of light overlaid the two figures outside the TARDIS. 'Range zero seven. Dispersion unit on target.'

On the monitor screen, Zoe was just approaching the TARDIS door, the Doctor close behind her. 'If that object is their space craft Commander, then they are leaving. Shall I open fire?'

Jamie leaned forward urgently. 'They're not

66

leaving. They wouldn't — not without me . . . '

Beta's laboratory was a long, low, cluttered room. It was a curious mixture of the primitive and the technologically advanced — rather like that of a medieval alchemist who had discovered a few basic scientific truths. Barrels and tubs and jars of all shapes and sizes were everywhere.

Beta was busily pouring liquid from a beaker into a hanging bowl, which was suspended over a blazing oil burner, when suddenly he heard the sound of marching feet.

Beta looked up guiltily. He was conducting a simple chemical experiment, and all chemical study had been strictly forbidden by the Krotons.

If someone had informed on him . . .

Suddenly Beta's laboratory was filled with pike-wielding guards. They seemed to be led by Eelek, deputy leader of the Council, and Axus, his chief henchman.

They made a curious pair, thought Beta. Eelek round-faced and bland, with his smooth oily manner, and the fierce, sharp-faced Axus, Captain of the Guard.

Carefully setting down his beaker, Beta looked up. 'You wish to see me?'

Eelek gave his faintly sinister smile. 'Yes. You received my message?'

'I heard only that the Council required my advice. On a matter of science, I presume?'

'No. On a matter of war.'

'War?'

'Against the Krotons.'

'War against the Krotons?' Beta turned away dismissively. 'You must both be out of your minds.'

Axus grabbed his shoulder and swung him around.

'Now just you listen to me, Beta —'

'No!' snapped Eelek. 'We don't have to resort to that — not yet.'

Sulkily Axus let go of Beta's arm.

Beta decided it was time to be diplomatic. 'Of course I'll listen. There's no need for us to quarrel.'

'You're a scientist, Beta,' said Eelek. 'Surely you, of all people, want to be free — free of the Krotons?'

'Free, yes,' said Beta. 'Dead, no.'

'But we can defeat them, Beta.'

'Can we? Our ancestors tried.'

'They were savages, primitive men with clubs and axes.'

Supporting his leader, Axus gestured around the laboratory. 'We're much more advanced now. Look at all this!'

'Are we?' said Beta bitterly. 'All our knowledge was given to us — by the Krotons.'

Eelek smiled. 'Then let us use it against them.'

'You're talking nonsense, Eelek,' said Beta despairingly. 'I tell you, we know only what the Krotons tell us. We don't think, we obey.'

Axus looked disgustedly at Eelek. 'He could help us — if only he wasn't afraid of the Krotons.'

'Don't you think I *want* to be free of them?' shouted Beta. 'Don't you think I'd like to discover truth for myself instead of being fed knowledge as a dog is fed scraps?'

'Well then — will you help us? Make new weapons?'

'To attack the Krotons?' Sadly Beta shook his head. 'I spent some time talking to the stranger — the Doctor. He made me realise how pitifully little the Krotons have told us. Now, if he would help —'

'You can forget about the Doctor *and* his friend,' said Eelek maliciously.

'What do you mean?'

'They submitted themselves to the Teaching Machines in the Learning Hall. They scored the highest results ever recorded.'

Axus said, 'Naturally the Krotons summoned them. They went into the Machine.'

'So, by now they must be dead,' said Eelek dismissively. 'Now, Beta, *will you help us?*'

'Perhaps . . . but you must give me time. There are certain things the Krotons forbid us to study, deadly fluids that eat away flesh, and even metal. In time I could develop a way of attacking them . . . '

'In time,' sneered Eelek. 'Oh yes. It's always "in time" isn't it? Just be patient, just wait for a little more time . . . '

'We've been slaves for a thousand years, Eelek. Do you really think you can free us in one day?'

'Yes,' said Eelek arrogantly.

'At least wait and see what Selris has to say.'

'From now on, you will no longer obey Selris. You will obey me.'

All at once, Beta understood. This wasn't so much a revolution against the Krotons as an internal coup, directed against Selris. Eelek had always been ambitious. Now he was taking over.

The Krotons were staring impassively at the monitor screen, which showed the TARDIS sitting in the Wasteland.

'The space craft may leave at any time, Commander,' reminded Kroton Two. 'Shall I fire?'

The Commander switched off the aiming device. 'No. We cannot kill them. We still need their minds. You will leave the Dynotrope and fetch them back.'

Kroton Two moved to the central tank and unclipped the connecting pipe. From a storage place behind the tank he produced a small portable cylinder, which he clipped in its place.

Jamie was watching all this with the keenest interest. They needed the stuff in the tank to stay alive. If he could cut off their supply . . .

The Kroton moved slowly to the door, pausing by the entrance to take a sort of hand-cannon from a rack by the wall. The weapon fitted on to its hand as an extension.

As the second Kroton moved through the doorway, Jamie turned and looked quickly at the Kroton Commander. It was hunched over the control panel, seemingly forgetting that he was there.

Jamie began sliding cautiously from his chair. There was a second weapon in the rack. Suddenly the Kroton swung around. 'What is the operating principle of your craft?'

'The what? Och, you mean how does it work? Only the Doctor knows that!'

'What is its transference interval?'

Jamie gave the Kroton a baffled look. 'Transference interval? What's that?'

The Kroton turned away dismissively. 'You have no value.'

The voice of Kroton Two came from the console. 'Vision control required now.'

Was there a hint of panic in the grating voice, Jamie wondered? Maybe the monsters weren't happy outside their precious machine. If he could get one in the open . . .

On the monitor screen he saw Kroton Two standing at the top of the ramp, just outside the now open rear door — the one that led to the Wasteland.

The Commander operated controls. 'Vision control on, Proceed.'

Jamie watched as the giant creature moved

cautiously down the ramp and out into the Wasteland, the massive cannon held out before it. It was almost, thought Jamie, as if the thing were nervous . . .

Thara was sitting by the sleeping Vana, when Selris returned. 'How is she?'

'Better, much better, but very tired. I'm sure she'll be all right by morning though.'

'That is good news,' said Selris heavily, and sank onto a couch.

Thara looked up, surprised by his father's tone. All of a sudden, Selris looked weary — weary and old. Thara was used to thinking of Selris as a sort of invincible iron man, and he was shocked to see his father show signs of human weakness.

'Where are the strangers, Father? Still in the Learning Hall?'

'Gone,' said Selris wearily.

'You mean they've left? Gone back to wherever they came from?'

Selris shook his head. 'They went into the Machine. The Krotons sent for Zoe, and the Doctor insisted on going with her.'

Thara stared at him in astonishment. 'And you let them go? Why didn't you stop them?'

'What could I do, my son? It was the will of the Krotons.'

'But why didn't they run? They could have escaped in their machine. They must have known what would happen to them.'

'They did,' said Selris slowly. 'But they also knew what would happen to us, to our race, if the Krotons' order was not obeyed.' He rose. 'I must go. There is a meeting of the Council.'

'That's all you ever think about,' accused Thara. 'Holding meetings, talking . . . How about *acting?*'

'Against the Krotons?'

'Yes! Against the Krotons. You still think of them as our benefactors, don't you?'

'No. I think of them as enemies. As enemies against whom we are completely powerless.'

'Well, Eelek is going to do something about it —'

Vana stirred and moaned.

Thara lent over her. 'It's all right, Vana you're quite safe now.'

'I feel weak,' she murmured. 'So weak . . . '

'It's all right,' said Thara soothingly. 'We're looking after you.'

She drifted slowly back into sleep.

Jamie was watching events in the control room — and awaiting his chance.

The Kroton Commander had its back turned. It was leaning over the instrument console, tracking and guiding the progress of Kroton Two, who could be seen on the monitor, marching across the Wasteland.

Jamie slipped out of his chair and stood up. If he could reach one of the doors . . .

The Kroton Commander swung round. 'Do not move!'

Hurriedly, Jamie slipped back into his chair. 'I was only stretching my legs . . . Look, what are you going to do with me?'

'You are of no value.'

'What's that supposed to mean?'

The Kroton said dismissively, 'You are of no value, therefore you will be dispersed.'

'Dispersed?' thought Jamie. 'What does that mean?'

Then he realised. He wasn't a magician like the Doctor or a genius like Zoe. He could tell the Krotons nothing they wanted to know — so he was of no further use to them.

He was to be dispersed — destroyed. Reduced to ashes that would blow away in the wind — like that first unfortunate Gond they had seen stagger from the Machine . . .

8

The Attack

Father and son glared at each other, over the sleeping form of Vana.

Thara sighed. Despite a very real affection for each other, he and his father seemed doomed to quarrel. If only Selris wasn't so fixed in his opinions, so sure he was always right. Thara smiled wryly. Or perhaps it was because they were so much alike.

It was Selris who spoke first. 'Thara! What did you mean — about Eelek?'

'I meant that you haven't realised what is going on, Father. Eelek is no longer your deputy. He's taken over as Leader of the Council.'

'But he has no authority . . . '

'A vote was taken, Father,' said Thara wearily. 'Everyone in the City knows how the Krotons have been tricking us. Eelek announced it!'

Selris was appalled. 'The fool. The people will want revenge.'

'Exactly. And that's what Eelek has promised them.'

'But can't you see? Doesn't he care what happens to our people?'

'Eelek says he is a patriot,' said Thara drily.

Selris nodded, beginning to see what had happened.

Eelek had always been ambitious — and he was a politician. When obedience to the Krotons had been the accepted line, no-one had been more slavish then Eelek, more insistent on scrupulously obeying every rule.

But now the mood of the people had changed, and Eelek had seized his chance. The people wanted war, and they would only follow a leader who promised to give it to them. Follow him to their graves, thought Selris bitterly.

'It is not patriotism to lead people into a war they cannot win.'

Thara shrugged. 'Maybe Eelek is right. We can't allow the Krotons to rule us forever without putting up a fight.'

'One day, my son, we will be strong enough to fight them.'

'When?' asked Thara cynically. 'After another thousand years?'

'Eelek must be stopped,' said Selris broodingly.

'How? He's not going to listen to you, Father. And nor will anyone else. Our people want this war . . . because of what happened to Vana and the others.'

'And how is Eelek going to fight the Krotons? Lead a march on their machine?'

'Have you got a better idea?'

Selris sat brooding for a moment. Thara was quite right. In their present mood the Gonds wouldn't follow a leader who spoke of peace, of caution and moderation.

So, if there had to be an attack on the Krotons, decided Selris, then he, not Eelek would lead it. It was the only way to re-establish his position as leader. And Selris had ruled too long to give up power lightly.

'There is one way we could fight them,' said Selris at last. 'By not letting them know they were being 'attacked . . . '

The Kroton Commander was still tracking and guiding its fellow Kroton on the journey through the Wasteland. 'Radius one seven nine. Vector five.'

Jamie leaned forward in his seat. 'What about the Doctor and Zoe? What are you going to do with them?'

'They are needed for the Dynotrope.'

Jamie looked around him. 'The Dynotrope? That's this machine, is it?'

The Kroton Commander's attention was back on the monitor screen, which now showed the viewpoint of the second Kroton stumbling cautiously through the Wasteland. 'Radius one six eight. Vector four.'

'Well, why does this Dynotrope of yours need them?' persisted Jamie. 'And why have you been killing off the Gonds?'

The Krotons seemed to have little objection to answering questions, thought Jamie. He might as well gather all the information he could. Besides, if he could keep it talking it might forget about dispersing him, at least for a time.

'The Dynotrope needs high brains for transfer power. The Gonds have no high brains, and despite our conditioning they have not succeeded in evolving them.'

'And that makes it all right to kill them, does it?'

'That is procedure,' said the Kroton flatly. 'Radius one six three. Vector Four.'

Beta was still trying to persuade Eelek to delay his attack on the Krotons. 'Selris should be here before any decision is taken,' he argued. 'He is the leader of the Council — or am I mistaken?'

'You are mistaken,' said Axus smugly.

'But Selris is old and wise. In time of war we need a strong experienced leader.'

'Eelek has taken over,' announced Axus.

Beta turned to Eelek. 'So you've achieved your ambition at last.'

Eelek drew himself up. 'I have the support of the entire Council.'

'I see. It must be quite a change for you to feel popular, Eelek.'

Eelek smiled evilly. 'There is a limit to what I will stand from you, Beta.'

Beta laughed. 'I wonder if you'll still be popular when hundreds of our people have been killed? Do you want to provoke a repetition of the massacre we suffered when the Krotons first arrived?'

'Things have changed since then, Beta,' sneered Eelek. 'Or hadn't you noticed? Today we have fireballs, slings, machines that can smash the strongest buildings to rubble.'

'Have you ever really looked at the Wasteland?' asked Beta wearily. 'Nothing grows there, even to this day. It smells of death. Compared with their weapons we still have only clubs and stones!'

'Come on, now,' said Jamie persuasively. 'What have I ever done to harm you? How would you like to die without knowing the reason, eh?'

He was addressing the broad back of the Commander, who was still busy at the console. As he spoke, Jamie was edging slowly towards the rack from which the other Kroton had taken its weapon.

'Krotons cannot die,' announced the Commander impassively.

'What's that? You mean you can't be killed?' said Jamie in horror. 'You live for ever?'

'We function permanently unless we exhaust.'

'And what do you mean by exhaust?'

'The exhaustion procedure is merely a reversion to basic molecules. But the matter can be re-animated.'

'What about me though?' said Jamie indignantly. 'I can't be re-animated. Why do you want to kill me? What good will it do you?'

'All waste matter must be dispersed,' said the Kroton chillingly. 'That is procedure.'

Jamie edged a little closer to the weapon.

The TARDIS door opened and the Doctor and Zoe emerged. The Doctor was carrying his little phial in one hand and a carpet bag in the other. He handed the phial to Zoe while he closed the TARDIS door.

'So, the life system of these creatures is based on tellurium, eh? Fascinating, isn't it, Zoe? And that tank was obviously some kind of polarised centrifuge.'

'Which *we* activated,' said Zoe bitterly.

The Doctor beamed. 'Oh, you mustn't blame yourself, Zoe. The Kroton Machine must have been there for thousands of years waiting for someone as clever as us to come along!'

'Just like a giant mousetrap,' said Zoe sadly. 'And those poor Gond students have been the mice.'

The Doctor frowned. 'Yes, that's horrible. Still you must admit that the Krotons have found a very good way of surviving through time . . . '

The Doctor went to an outcrop of rock just beside the TARDIS and began sorting through the fragments of loose stone at its base.

Zoe looked on in mild surprise. 'What are you doing, Doctor?'

'There are some rather splendid sulphur deposits just about here.'

Zoe smiled. 'Jamie was complaining about the smell as soon as we arrived.'

'Hydrogen telluride!'

'What? Oh yes, of course. The worst smell in the world!'

'In any world,' agreed the Doctor.

'Doctor — what do you want sulphur for?'

The Doctor looked up almost guiltily. 'What? Oh it might just come in useful. Very useful stuff, sulphur . . .'

Zoe looked round uneasily. There was nothing to see except the bleak grey Wasteland all around. But all the same . . .

'You know, Doctor, I keep getting a feeling we're being *watched*.'

The Doctor was busy throwing chunks of rock into his carpet bag . . .

Jamie could see Zoe's worried face on the monitor screen in the Kroton control room.

'Radius two zero. Vector one. Object in range.'

Which presumably meant that the second Kroton was very close, thought Jamie. He leaned forward urgently, willing his friends to hear him.

'Get back,' he muttered. 'Get back in the TARDIS!' But they couldn't hear him. Clearly it was up to him. Carefully, he lifted the remaining laser cannon from the rack.

The Doctor picked up a chunk of crumbly rock. 'Look at this! Almost pure sulphur.'

'Very nice, Doctor. Can we go now?'

'Very shortly. What do you know about tellurium?'

Zoe's computer-like mind came into operation. 'Well, it's one of the exceptional elements in the periodic table. Its atomic weight is one hundred and twenty-eight, its atomic number fifty-two —'

Suddenly Zoe dried up.

'Go on,' urged the Doctor.

Zoe gulped. 'It doesn't seem to matter anymore. Look, Doctor!'

The Doctor looked. 'My giddy aunt!'

A Kroton stood regarding them from the top of a nearby ridge. It began gliding towards them, covering them with a kind of bulbous weapon — a laser-cannon, guessed the Doctor. And at that range there wasn't the slightest chance of escape.

'You will return to the Dynotrope,' announced the Kroton.

The Doctor rose cautiously to his feet, clutching his carpet bag. 'Er yes, yes of course . . . I mean, if you insist . . .'

'Return!' boomed the Kroton.

The Doctor took Zoe's hand.

The Kroton Commander was totally intent on the scene on the monitor so Jamie seized his chance. He heaved up the massive weapon and trained it on the Commander.

Alerted by the sounds of his movement, the Kroton swung round. 'Stop!'

His fighting blood up, Jamie yelled, 'Now we'll see if you die or not!'

Somehow he managed to find the firing stud in the base of the weapon and the laser beam poured from the muzzle, like flame from a flame thrower.

The Kroton staggered back. 'Stop!' it called. 'St-o-op.' Its voice became slurred like a slowed-down tape . . .

Suddenly the energy blast faltered and began to die away. Immediately the Kroton recovered and began advancing on Jamie again . . .

Jamie stabbed frantically at the firing button but it was no use. Clearly whatever power source charged the weapon was exhausted.

The Kroton bore down on him. He hurled the weapon at it, but with absolutely no effect.

The Kroton came steadily onwards, massive, unstoppable, a living tank. Clamp-like hands reached out. Jamie dodged beneath them, but the sheer bulk of the creature knocked him back. His head thudded into the wall and he slid half-dazed to the ground.

A frantic voice came from the console. 'Commander! Direction point! I have lost contact.'

Turning away from Jamie, the Commander moved back towards the console.

To their astonishment, the Doctor and Zoe saw the muzzle of the laser-cannon wavering to and fro.

The Kroton itself was staggering helplessly. 'Direction point. Direction point required immediately.'

The Doctor grabbed Zoe's hand. 'Quick, Zoe, run. Over there!' He pointed towards an overhanging rock a little way up the slope. They began to run.

The Commander was bringing the wandering Kroton back under control. 'Radius one zero. Vector three.'

'Do I proceed, Commander?'

'The auto-scanner has lost contact with the aliens. You will destroy their TARDIS machine. They must not escape.'

'Direction point?'

'Radius four-one. Vector two.'

Crouched behind the rock, the Doctor and Zoe watched the Kroton's stumbling progress towards the TARDIS. 'Can't it see?' whispered Zoe.

'Apparently not in this light. It was pretty dark in the Machine, remember.'

'It's moving now. Look, it seems to be going towards the TARDIS.'

'Yes . . . yes . . . I rather think it's being directed by the Kroton Machine's scanners. They must have put up a spy satellite . . . '

The Kroton came level with the TARDIS, raised the laser cannon and fired. A stream of fierce white light poured from the muzzle, and the TARDIS was enveloped in a fiery glow.

When the glow faded, the TARDIS had disappeared.

9

The Second Attack

'Doctor,' gasped Zoe. 'The TARDIS! It's gone!'

'Mmm, yes,' said the Doctor absently, apparently not in the least concerned.

'Now what shall we do?'

'Not much we can do, my dear, until that wretched Kroton goes away.'

The Kroton was standing motionless, as if waiting for orders.

The voice of Kroton Two crackled from the console. 'Further instructions?'

'Return to the Dynotrope.'

'Direction point?'

'Reverse previous readings.'

Jamie meanwhile had recovered conciousness and was considering his next move. He raised himself up on one elbow, and saw the Kroton Commander start to swing round.

Jamie slumped down again. The Kroton looked at him for a moment then, apparently satisfied that he was dead, or at least unconscious, returned its attention to he console.

The Doctor and Zoe watched from hiding as the

Kroton turned and moved slowly away, disappearing at last behind the rocks.

Suddenly Zoe heard a strange, unmistakable sound — the characteristic wheezing and groaning of a TARDIS materialisation. And sure enough, the TARDIS was materialising. Suddenly there it was, not in the spot where it had disappeared, but quite close at hand, perched precariously on a spur of rock.

'It's back, Doctor,' exclaimed Zoe delightedly. 'Look, it's all right!'

'Yes, I know . . . Dear me, what a stupid place to land! You can tell the captain's not at the helm, can't you?'

Zoe looked at him accusingly. 'You *knew!* You knew it would come back like that, didn't you?'

'Well, yes actually.' The Doctor smiled. 'Mind you, it only does that if I remember to set the HADS.'

'The what?'

'The HADS, Zoe. Hostile Action Displacement Service. When the HADS is operating, the TARDIS automatically dematerialises, and then comes back when it thinks the danger's over.'

Zoe looked at him curiously, realising how often the Doctor talked about the TARDIS as if it were a living being.

The Doctor stood up. 'I think it's safe to go now.'

'Go where?'

'Well, we must let the Gonds know we're all right, mustn't we? And Jamie will be worried too.'

They moved away.

In Beta's laboratory the argument was still raging. 'I tell you it's simple,' Eelek was saying. 'First we destroy the Learning Hall, then we make a frontal attack.'

'Madness,' said Beta flatly. 'Suicide.'

'What does a Controller of Science know of war?' said Axus contemptuously.

'You came here asking my advice and, as Controller of Science, I've given it. Wait till we can develop effective weapons.'

'And how long will that take?' demanded Eelek. 'I say attack now!'

'No, Eelek,' said a deep, authoratitive voice.

With a sigh of relief, Beta saw Selris stride into the room. 'You'll be pleased to know, Selris, that Eelek has taken your place!'

Selris said scornfully. 'To lead you in an attack on the Krotons?'

Eelek drew himself up. 'That is my plan.'

'I forbid it,' said Selris.

He spoke with such authority that for a moment Eelek was daunted. Then he recovered, his voice loud and angry. '*You* can't forbid anything.' He turned to Axus. 'Order the slings and fireballs to be prepared.'

Axus led the guards out of the room.

Eelek gave Selris a triumphant look. 'We've heard enough of your plans,' he said and followed his supporter.

Beta shook his head. 'Slings and fireballs! They'll never reach the Krotons while they're still in that machine.'

To Beta's astonishment, Selris said, 'Exactly, Beta. Now, I have a plan that will draw them out. Under the Hall of Learning, there are three pillars which support the machine . . . '

Jamie was still shamming dead on the floor of the Kroton control room. He was beginning to wonder how much longer he could get away with it.

Luckily the return of the second Kroton had provided a distraction. For the moment the two Krotons were absorbed in the monitor screen over the console.

'The high brains must be recaptured before exhaust time!' the Commander was saying.

'The alien craft is now dispersed,' said Kroton Two.

'Check exhaust time.' The Commander operated the controls. 'Commence check. Lineal power static?'

'Static.'

'Gravitation feed?'

'Normal.'

'Auxilliary output?'

'Rising.'

Jamie decided that this was the moment. He rose cautiously and crept silently towards the exit. Behind him the voices of the Krotons were still booming out.

'Dynotrope balance?'

'Balance — four.'

The Kroton Commander checked the final readings. He turned to his companion and said emotionlessly. 'The Dynotrope will exhaust in three hours.'

At Selris's house, Thara and Vana were packing food, clothing and equipment into a simple backpack.

'Are you sure you're strong enough for the journey?' asked Thara solicitously.

Vana smiled. 'Of course I am. I keep telling you, I'm all right now.'

And indeed, after several hours more sleep, Vana had woken up more or less restored to normal.

Thara had no idea whether it was the Doctor's hypnotism, Beta's medicine, or simply the restorative effects of sleep. He was just thankful to see Vana herself again.

'I can carry you, you know,' he said tenderly.

'There's no need — I can walk!'

'It's a long way to the hills —' Thara broke off as the Doctor and Zoe entered. 'Doctor, you're back!'

'That's right,' said the Doctor cheerfully. 'Sorry we took so long.'

'We thought you were dead! Selris said you'd gone into the Machine.'

'Oh, quite. Yes, we did actually. But what goes in must come out, you know.' He beamed at Vana. 'You're better, aren't you?'

'Much better, Doctor.'

'Good, good!' The Doctor looked at the supplies. 'Well, I hope you have a nice holiday. It looks as if you're going away.'

'We are. But not for a holiday. Didn't you know? The city is being evacuated.'

The Doctor stared at him, a terrible suspicion forming in his mind. 'Just a minute — *why* is the City being evacuated?'

'Father is leading a party to attack the Krotons. He hopes they'll come out into the open so we can strike back.'

'Oh no!' groaned the Doctor. 'Didn't he learn his lesson last night, when you attacked the Teaching Machines?'

'You don't understand, Doctor. Selris has a plan. They're going to strike the Machine from underneath, attack the supports.'

The Doctor leaped to his feet. 'I don't think that's a very good idea! Come along, Zoe! Thara would you mind taking us to Beta? At once, please!'

Before anyone really knew what was happening, the Doctor had bustled them all out of the room.

Selris had managed to assemble a sizeable team of

workmen from those Gonds still loyal to him. Now he stood in the Underhall watching the results of their work with grim satisfaction.

A team of labourers had lifted the flagstones and dug away the earth from around the base of the main supporting pillar.

Gond engineers had fixed an enormous chain around the pillar. The chain in turn was attached to a primitive but immensely powerful form of winch, used by Gond farmers for dragging out gnarled tree stumps when they were clearing new fields. The winch stood close by with a team of brawny Gond workers ready to turn the cast iron cog-wheel that powered it.

Selris raised his hand. 'We're ready for the stump draver now.'

The labourers bent their backs to their work. The chain around the pillar began to draw taut . . .

Beta looked up from a bubbling retort as the Doctor bustled into the laboratory, followed by the others. 'If you've come to try to persuade me to leave, Thara, you're wasting your time.'

'I haven't,' said Thara. 'The Doctor wanted to see you — and your laboratory.'

'Oh?' said Beta suspiciously.

The Doctor looked round, rubbing his hands. 'Splendid, splendid! My dear Beta, I just wondered if you could do a little job for me?'

He tipped a pile of yellow crumbly rock from his carpet bag onto one of Beta's work benches.

Beta looked at it with distaste. 'What's all this?'

'Sulphur,' said the Doctor simply. He fished a crumpled scrap of paper from his pocket. 'I've written out the instructions here — I don't know if you can follow them?'

He looked on anxiously as Beta studied the paper.

'Yes, I think so,' said Beta a little doubtfully. 'The Krotons have forbidden us to study chemistry.'

'Exactly,' said the Doctor. 'And Beta, did it ever occur to you to wonder why?'

'Where's Jamie, Doctor?' asked Zoe suddenly. She turned to Vana. 'I've just realised, he was supposed to be looking after you. He wasn't there, and he isn't here, so where's he got to?'

There was a moment of silence. Then Thara said, 'But we thought *you* knew where he was. He followed you to the Learning Hall.'

Zoe said, 'Suppose he tried to get into the Machine?'

'Just what he would do,' agreed the Doctor. 'We'd better go and look for him.' He paused in the doorway. 'Beta, you'll let me have a sample of that as soon as possible won't you?' Then he was gone.

'We'd better be going ourselves, Vana,' said Thara.

She shook her head. 'I'm a scientist too, remember. I'm going to stay and help Beta.'

'Oh no, you're not. You're going up into the hills, the pair of you,' said Beta.

But Vana was as obstinate as she was beautiful. 'Don't be ridiculous, Beta,' she said calmly. 'We're not leaving you here.' She sat down on a stool. 'Besides I'm beginning to feel quite faint again, I don't think I could walk another step!'

Beta smiled. 'All right.' He handed her the instructions. 'We'll make a start.'

Inside their control room the usually emotionless Krotons were in a state of panic, so much so that their heads were literally spinning.

'The gravitational feed is dropping,' shouted the Commander.

'The Dynotrope is moving out of balance,' said

91

Kroton Two.

'Switch static feed to full volume.'

'Full volume on!'

Their heads stopped spinning as the Krotons regained control.

'Commence systems check,' ordered the Commander.

When the Doctor and Zoe came down into the Underhall the whole place was shuddering with the movement of the great central column, which was vibrating like a plucked guitar-string.

'Shine a light up there,' ordered Selris suddenly.

The light of a hand toch revealed a huge crack in the hall's upper wall.

'If that goes the whole place will come down,' shouted one of the Gond engineers.

'The Machine will come down first,' said Selris grimly.

The Doctor was horrified at what he saw. 'Stop it! Stop it at once, you idiots! Can't you see what you're doing?'

He ran over to the chain. 'Unhook this thing. You're meddling with forces you don't understand!'

Suddenly there was a low rumbling from above and the whole section of roof around the pillar suddenly gave way.

'Look out, Doctor!' called Zoe.

The Doctor shoved Zoe towards the stairs. 'Run, Zoe run!' But although the Doctor managed to push Zoe clear, he was too late to save himself.

Zoe turned to make sure he was following, just in time to see a shower of dust and rubble cascade from the ceiling, burying the Doctor . . .

10

Battle Plans

Zoe tried to go to the Doctor's aid, but another shower of falling rubble drove her back, and she collapsed at the bottom of the steps, coughing and choking.

Thara and Vana hurried down the stairs into the Learning Hall, and stopped, appalled by the devastation before them. Many of the stone pillars were smashed, great chunks of the floor had simply fallen away, and the Teaching Machines were half buried in rubble. However, the hatch that led to the Underhall was still clear.

Thara turned to Vana. 'You stay here. I must find out what's happening below.'

He began picking his way across between the pile of rubble and disappeared down the narrow stair.

'Be careful,' called Vana, but he was already out of sight.

Struggling to her feet, Zoe found Thara beside her.

'Zoe! Are you all right?'

'Yes, I think so. No bones broken anyway!'

'This way then. I'd better get you out.' He took her arm.

Zoe pulled away. 'No, we've got to find the

Doctor . . . '

'Where is he?'

'Somewhere over there, by the base of the pillar . . . '

They began picking their way through the rubble.

Returning to the Learning Hall to assess the damage, Selris was astonished to find Vana waiting by the open hatch.

'Vana! What are you doing here? Why aren't you in the hills?'

Vana held out a stone phial. 'Thara and I stayed to help Beta make some acid. We were bringing some here for the Doctor when we felt the earthquake.'

'Where is the Doctor?'

'He's probably buried somewhere down there.'

The Doctor had been buried, but, as it happened, not too deeply. Thara found him, just inside the pit at the base of the column fighting his way out from under a coating of rubble.

Luckily the really big chunks of falling masonry had missed him, and although he was dirty and dusty and cross, the Doctor was quite unhurt.

'Here he is,' yelled Thara. 'I've found him!' He jumped into the pit and helped the Doctor to his feet.

Zoe came running up. 'Doctor? Are you all right?'

'Oh yes, I think so. Nothing seems to be broken.'

Thara helped him to climb out. 'Come along, then, you two, we must hurry. There could be another collapse any minute!'

Although the vibrating of the column had lessened, it had by no means stopped and there were ominous creaks and cracking sounds from overhead.

'Yes, I know,' shouted the Doctor. 'If they don't stabilise that machine soon . . . Thara, look out!'

As Thara had predicted there was indeed another collapse. More chunks of rubble showered down from the ceiling, and this time it was not the Doctor but Thara who was the victim.

The falling rubble knocked him to the ground, and a huge chunk of rock fell across his leg, pinning him down.

Now it was the Doctor's turn to be the rescuer. 'Don't worry, I'll get you out!' he called. 'Zoe, give me a hand.'

He began heaving at the rock, and Zoe came forward to help him. With a mighty effort they started to lift the rock free from Thara's leg.

The Krotons were still struggling desperately to restore the equilibrium of their machine.

'Cut auxiliaries!' ordered the Commander.

'Auxiliaries' cut.'

'Feed-in emergency power. Gravitation feed check?'

'Gravitation feed static.'

The flashing warning lights winked out one by one, and the high-pitched scream of the vibration died away.

The Kroton Commander studied the readings. 'Dynotrope balance normal.'

It operated the scanner controls, and the monitor showed a view of the central column. The Krotons studied the pit, now filled with rubble, the half-buried bodies of the Gond labourers, and finally the column itself, which had split clear down the middle.

'The Gonds have attacked the Dynotrope,' said Kroton Two.

The Krotons never had any worries about stating the obvious. Indeed their whole conversation consisted of a series of such statements.

The monitor picked up the Doctor and Zoe, deep in

conversation with Thara. The Kroton Commander said, 'There are the two high brains. Bring them here.'

Helped by some of the surviving Gond workers, the Doctor and Zoe had carried Thara up into the Learning Hall to a clear space by the bottom of the steps, where the wounded were being cared for.

Zoe ran her hands along Thara's leg. 'It could be a fracture, and it's badly cut and bruised. Better keep it still for a while. Give me that wood, will you, Doctor?'

The Doctor watched in admiration as Zoe bandaged Thara's leg, and fixed it in a rough splint. 'Well done, Zoe. But as soon as you've finished we ought to move away from here.'

'You think there'll be another earthquake?' asked Vana.

'That wasn't an earthquake, my dear.'

'Well, whatever it was, the noise was coming from the Machine. It seems to have stopped now.'

'Exactly,' said the Doctor. 'Which means that the Krotons have time to attend to us. Haven't you finished yet, Zoe?'

'No, I haven't. Can I borrow your braces, Doctor?'

'Certainly not,' said the Doctor clutching them protectively. He snatched the bandana handkerchief from his breast pocket and passed it to her. 'I'd much rather you used this!'

Zoe took the big handkerchief. 'That'll do.' She twisted it into a rope and used it to finish binding Thara's leg.

Selris came to join them. Sadly he surveyed the devastation around them. 'We have failed. The Machine is undamaged.'

'I wouldn't be too sure,' said the Doctor gently. 'Just take a look at it.'

Now that much of the Learning Hall had been

96

destroyed, the curved wall at the end could be seen as part of an enormous dome, on and around which the Learning Hall had been built.

A dull black stain was spreading patchily over the done's silvery surface.

'What's happening to it, Doctor?' asked Selris.

'I'm not sure, but I'd say it was no longer functioning under full power. Vana, how is Beta getting along with that acid I asked for?'

'I've just been back to see him, Doctor. He sent you this.' She produced the little phial. 'He only made a small amount to start with.'

The Doctor unstoppered the phial and sniffed at it gingerly.

'Is it all right?' asked Vana anxiously.

'Oh yes, I think so, my dear.'

Zoe took the phial and sniffed it. 'It's sulphuric acid!'

'Basically, with one or two extras added. Don't touch it, it burns!' The Doctor took back the phial, restoppered it and handed it back to Vana. 'Look after it for a moment — it's terribly important.'

Suddenly Zoe said, 'Doctor, what about Jamie? We came here to look for him, remember?'

'So we did,' said the Doctor guiltily. 'I'd forgotten with all this excitement.'

Zoe turned to Selris. 'Has anybody seen him?'

Selris hesitated. 'I thought you knew. He followed you into the Machine.'

'When?' demanded Zoe.

'I'm not really sure. It wasn't long after you and the Doctor went in.'

Zoe looked at the Doctor in horror. 'Jamie wouldn't be any use to them. His mind is completely untrained!'

The Doctor nodded. 'Yes, quite so. And if the

Machine rejected him like the others . . . come on, Zoe!'

Grabbing Zoe's hand, the Doctor almost dragged her up the steps.

By now Jamie had made his way through the noisy and chaotic corridors of the Kroton ship, negotiated the forest of dangling nutrient pipes and now found himself at a dead end — the antechamber before the closed back door.

The door was of course immoveable, and after several attempts to shift it, Jamie crouched down on his heels, very close to despair. Now that the crisis in the ship was over the Krotons would realise he'd gone and come looking for him.

Suddenly Jamie spotted a gleaming fragment of a stone at his feet. He picked it up. It was the Doctor's bit of mica.

Jamie's mind might have been untrained, but he was bright enough in his own way, especially where his own survival was at stake.

He picked up the piece of mica and studied it. It had been lying directly under that circular socket thing just to one side of the door. And if the Doctor had used it to get out . . .

Selris was directing the treatment of the wounded and the clearing up of the Learning Hall when Eelek marched down the steps, his henchman Axus at his side.

Behind them came the usual bodyguard of pikemen.

Eelek raised his voice so that all the Gonds in the hall could hear. 'Well, Selris, are you satisfied now?'

Axus had been checking on the extent of the disaster. 'There are seven of his working party unaccounted for. I think we have four more badly injured. Two of them are probably going to die.'

'The wounded are being cared for,' said Selris angrily. 'I have arranged —'

'No!' snapped Eelek. He gestured dramatically around the ruined hall. 'You have done enough already.'

'You were the one who wanted to fight the Krotons,' said Selris grimly.

Since this was undoubtedly true, Eelek was forced to take refuge in more politician's rhetoric. 'I will fight the Krotons in my own time and in my own way,' he announced grandly.

'My way is better,' insisted Selris. 'The Krotons are invulnerable inside their Machine, but if we can lure them out . . . '

Axus came to the support of his leader. 'You've had your chance, Selris, and look what you've achieved. The Learning Hall is ruined, our people are dead and wounded, and the Machine is untouched.'

Selris pointed to the spreading stain. 'The Machine has been *damaged*.'

Eelek seized his moment. 'Damaged?' he shouted. 'It must be *destroyed!* I intend to launch a mass attack with slings and fireballs. They are in position now.'

'And the Krotons will turn our city into another Wasteland.' Wearily Selris turned away. 'You're a fool, Eelek.'

'And you are a traitor!' screamed Eelek. 'See what your stupidity has done. You were dispaced as Leader of the Council. You had no authority to order this attack.'

'Leadership of the Council has long been heredi-tary. My son Thara will replace me.'

'No!' shouted Eelek. '*I* have replaced you. Guards, arrest him!'

The pikemen moved forward.

'Wait,' protested Selris. 'This is no time to be fighting amongst ourselves. At least let me help you organise the attack.'

'I don't need your help, Selris. You had your chance — and you failed.'

Selris wasn't listening. He was looking over Eelek's shoulder. 'Have I failed? Have I, Eelek?' Selris's voice was grim. 'I said I would bring the Krotons out of the Machine.'

Eelek whirled round.

A Kroton was standing in the open doorway of the Machine.

11

Eelek's Bargain

For a moment Eelek stared at the great silvery figure in awe. Here was one of the gods he had worshipped all his life, the master he had served faithfully for so many years.

He studied the massive silver body, the immense torso and high ridged shoulders, the clamp-like hands and the terrifying blank silver head rising to a point.

One of the hands had a huge bulbous device attached to it, clearly a weapon of some kind. And the weapon was covering their little group.

For a moment Eelek had an impulse to fall down and worship, but things had gone too far for that. Summoning all his courage, he stepped forward.

'Stop!' boomed the Kroton.

Eelek froze. Struggling to keep his voice steady he said, 'What do you want?'

'Where are the two high brains?'

'I don't understand —'

'The two alien creatures are needed urgently. Where are they?'

'He means the Doctor and Zoe,' said Selris quietly. He raised his voice. 'Why do you want them?'

'Unimportant!' boomed the Kroton. 'Produce them.'

Eelek was thinking hard. 'They're not here.'

'Where are they?'

Eelek was nothing if not a politician. He could smell the chance of a bargain, of making some kind of deal. 'You say you *need* them. Why are they so important to you? You've never come out of your Machine before.'

There was a young Gond standing watching events from halfway up the stairs. He wasn't a guard, wasn't even armed, just a too curious spectator.

Before anyone realised what was happening, the gaping muzzle of the Kroton's weapon swung round to cover him. There was a kind of hissing roar and the boy's body glowed brightly for a moment. He gave a single choked-off scream of agony — then he was gone.

'Why did you do that?' shouted Selris angrily. 'He wasn't harming you.'

It was all too clear why the Kroton had killed at random. It was a demonstration of ruthlessness and of power.

'Do not argue with us. You will produce the high brains in fifteen minutes.'

Despite the Kroton's terrifying demonstration, Eelek, courageous in his own way, was still pressing for some advantage. 'If we give you these strangers, will you leave us in peace?'

'The high brains will enable us to operate the drive mechanism of our ship.'

'Drive mechanism? You mean you'll go? You'll actually leave our world?'

'Yes. But if the two high brains are not brought to the Dynotrope you will all be dispersed. Do you understand?'

Eelek's voice was loud and confident, the voice of a leader. 'Very well. If you will promise to leave our world — you shall have them.'

The Kroton turned away and glided back into the ship.

'Why are you doing this?' asked Selris in anguish. 'Only a few hours ago you wanted to fight the Krotons.'

'I wanted to be rid of them,' corrected Eelek coldly. 'Why fight if we can get what we want without bloodshed? You heard what the Kroton said.'

'But the Doctor and Zoe are our friends. They risked their lives for our sakes.'

'I put the interests of our people first.' Eelek looked thoughtfully at Selris, Thara and Vana. All three were friendly towards the aliens. They would warn them if they got the chance.

'Axus, put these people under guard. I'll organise the search for the two aliens.'

Leaving Axus and a couple of pikemen behind, Eelek strode up the stairs.

Jamie was still fiddling irritatedly with the chunk of mica, trying to jam it into the socket and trip the door opening circuit.

He was just about to give up in despair when suddenly he succeeded — at least partially.

The door began to rise — then it jammed, leaving only a narrow gap between door and floor.

Jamie looked at it ruefully. It was a *very* narrow gap. But there was no alternative.

Flattening himself on the floor, Jamie wriggled forwards, trying to squeeze his brawny form through the little space. His head went through all right and then his shoulders, but somewhere around the waist area he stuck fast.

He wriggled furiously. Wasn't there some saying about where your head would go the rest would go — or was that only cats?

Jamie was still thrashing about on the ground like a stranded fish when the Doctor and Zoe came running across the Wasteland towards him.

'Look out, Jamie!' yelled the Doctor. 'Remember the poison spray!'

'Help me!' roared Jamie. 'This door's jammed, I can't move it!'

The Doctor and Zoe came panting up. The Doctor surveyed the struggling Jamie thoughtfully. 'Jammed, eh? That means the power is failing or — yes, that's it! The Krotons must have cut their auxiliary power motors.'

'Never mind all that, Doctor. Help me out!' bellowed Jamie.

'Oh dear, can't you get out? You're getting fat, Jamie. Come on, Zoe, lend a hand.'

They each grabbed an arm and started pulling. Jamie wriggled even more furiously than before and suddenly shot out of the gap like a cork from a bottle.

'Watch out!' yelled the Doctor. All three hurled themselves sideways off the ramp, just as the spray jets opened up.

The corrosive spray was less powerful this time, and by the time it was over the Doctor, Jamie and Zoe were sheltering under a nearby rock.

'What's been happening?' demanded Jamie. 'I thought yon machine was going to shake itself to pieces!'

'No time to explain,' said the Doctor, not for the first time. 'How are you feeling, Jamie?'

'Well —' began Jamie dubiously, about to launch on an account of his ordeal.

'Good,' said the Doctor briskly. 'Now Jamie, I want you to do something very important for me!'

'Not again,' groaned Jamie wearily.

'When we get back to the Gond city I want you to

go to Beta's laboratory. He's producing a special kind of sulphuric acid for me. I want you to tell him to make it in bulk — as much as he can manage — and bring it to the Learning Hall.'

'Aye, but —'

'No time to argue, Jamie. Hurry. When you've finished at Beta's you'll find us in the Learning Hall.'

A Gond sentry came hurrying into the Learning Hall and whispered a message to Eelek.

Eelek smiled and turned to one of his followers. 'The strangers are returning. You two, over there, you with me!'

Thara, Selris and Vana looked on helplessly as the two groups hid in the shadows on either side of the stairs.

'They're going to walk right into a trap,' whispered Vana.

'And Eelek talks about caring for the people,' muttered Selris disgustedly. 'All that really concerns him is power — and his own skin!'

Vana said softly. 'If we could warn the Doctor and the girl, perhaps they could escape in their own space machine.'

Selris nodded. 'Yes, we owe him that at least — a chance to escape . . . '

Faced with the Doctor's orders to make the acid in bulk, Beta simply rigged up a larger version of the apparatus that had produced the first phial.

The lash-up of beakers, burners and tubes was hissing and seething and bubbling on his main bench now, supervised by Jamie and himself.

Both wore cloths about their mouths to protect them from the choking fumes, and neither had very much idea of what they were actually doing.

They were having a series of rather muffled conversations.

'How long will it take?' asked Jamie.

'No idea,' said Beta cheerfully.

There was a hiss of steam and the whole lash-up shook alarmingly. Jamie backed away. 'It's no' going to explode, is it?'

'I don't know!'

'I thought you were supposed to be the scientist?'

'I am, but I've never worked with acids before. The Krotons always used to forbid it.'

He picked up a chunk of sulphurous rock and approached the bubbling cauldron.

'Shall I put in a bit more to speed things up?'

'Why ask me?'

'Let's see what happens,' said Beta philosophically. 'After all, we can only blow ourselves up.'

Beta, thought Jamie, was a scientist after the Doctor's own heart.

Beta tossed the chunk of rock into the cauldron, like a housewife adding another onion to the soup. The cauldron bubbled even more fiercely and a jet of sulphurous smoke spurted out of the apparatus.

Beta turned to Jamie. 'Do you think that was enough?'

'Well it was enough for me!' shouted Jamie above the din. 'Quite enough.'

His words were obliterated by another explosion, and another cloud of smoke.

'Selris, listen,' whispered Vana. 'You try to distract Axus while I slip up the stairs.'

'There are more men posted outside . . .'

'I might be able to get by them. Anyway, it's worth trying.'

Selris nodded. 'I agree. There's just a chance.' He

106

rose and moved over towards Axus, who had been watching the little group suspiciously. 'Axus, listen to me!'

'Well, what is it?'

Selris moved closer so that his bulk loomed over the smaller man, cutting off his view of Vana. 'In the past you've always accepted my judgement, Axus. Believe me, Eelek's wrong. It's a mistake to trust the Krotons.'

'I don't trust them. And Eelek's right. We're doing the only thing we can.'

From the corner of his eye, Selris could see Vana stealing towards the stairs. He edged round, using himself as a human screen, and leaned urgently towards Axus. 'If we surrender the strangers, the Krotons will kill us for certain.'

Axus stared at him. 'Why do you say that?'

'Of course they will. We mean nothing to them, we never have. But while we've still got the Doctor and Zoe we've got something to negotiate with!'

'But if we don't hand over the strangers the Krotons will kill us all for certain,' pointed out Axus triumphantly. 'You're growing old, Selris, your arguments make no sense.'

He moved clear of Selris — and suddenly realised that Vana was missing. Axus whirled round, just in time to see her vanishing up the stairs. 'Stop her! Stop that girl!'

Vana sprinted up the stairs and ran straight into two more guards. She tried to yell a warning just in case the Doctor was near. 'Doctor! Look —'

A hand was clamped over her mouth. The guards grabbed her and carried her, still struggling, to where Selris waited by the disabled Thara.

In the struggle, the stone phial was knocked from Vana's hand and rolled to Selris's feet. Automatically, he picked it up . . .

The Krotons were making final calculations.

'Balance zero plus twelve,' reported Kroton Two.

The Kroton Commander said, 'We have reserve power for twenty-seven minutes.'

'Then we shall exhaust.'

For once there was a hint of emotion, a tinge of sadness in the Kroton Commander's voice. 'Yes. Our function will end.'

The Doctor and Zoe were hurrying down the steps that led into the Learning Hall. They noticed quite a few armed Gonds about, but no-one made any attempt to stop them.

As they reached the bottom of the steps Zoe was saying, 'But what are we going to do, Doctor?'

'To be honest, Zoe, I'm not quite sure. I wish there was some way of getting into that machine —'

The Doctor broke off as Eelek appeared from the shadows.

'Oh, but there is, Doctor.' He gave them one of his peculiarly sinister smiles. 'We'll help you inside.'

'That's very kind of you,' began the Doctor. 'Wait a moment — what's all this?'

At a gesture from Eelek, Zoe and the Doctor were suddenly surrounded by armed guards. The Doctor glared indignantly at them. 'Now then, what are you doing? Look here . . . ' They were herded towards the Machine.

The Kroton Commander studied the scene on the monitor.

'The high brains have been captured. Balance check?'

'Zero plus nine.'

'Exhaust time, twenty-two minutes.'

'Shall I open the Dynotrope, Commander?'

'Yes. But only the two high brains must enter.'

'Take them up to the doors,' ordered Eelek.

'We won't be bullied, you know,' said the Doctor fiercely. 'Don't push!'

But despite the Doctor's protests, he and Zoe were half-shoved, half-dragged to the foot of the ramp.

The Doctor caught a glimpse of Vana hovering in the background. 'Vana!' he called. 'Have you got that phial?'

Vana suddenly realised that she hadn't — and that she had no idea where it was. She spread her hands helplessly.

'But I must have it,' called the Doctor. 'It's vital!'

The amplified Kroton voice boomed from the ship. 'THE HIGH BRAINS WILL ENTER IMMEDI-ATELY.'

The Gond guards levelled their pikes.

'We'd better do as they say Doctor,' said Zoe nervously.

'Yes, I suppose we had. Well, Zoe, ladies first — after you!'

The Doctor was still signalling frantically to Vana but it was already too late.

Zoe and the Doctor started up the ramp and the door began sliding upwards to admit them.

'The high brains are about to enter the Dynotrope, Commander,' reported Kroton Two.

'Prepare for take-off. Initiate Phase One.'

'Phase One ready. Shall I destroy the Gonds now? They are no longer of any value.'

The Commander considered. 'No. The dispersion units use power. We have no power to waste.'

Vana came hurrying up to Selris, who was watching events with an expression of grim helplessness.

'That bottle, Selris, with the liquid Beta made for the Doctor.'

Selris reached inside his tunic and produced the phial. 'It's all right, Vana. I have it safe — here.'

'The Doctor needs it — he says it's vital.'

By now the Doctor and Zoe had passed through the open door of the Kroton Machine and the door had started to descend.

Suddenly Selris began running towards the Machine. Thrusting the astonished guards aside he reached the top of the ramp just in time to throw himself down and roll under the door.

It closed behind him.

Once again the Doctor and Zoe found themselves in the Kroton control room. The Krotons were at their console and the Doctor noticed that both were already plugged into the central nutrient tank.

The Doctor drew himself up to his not-very-considerable height and confronted the two silver giants. 'I gather you wanted to speak with us?'

'You will now assist us with take-off.'

Suddenly Selris burst into the control room. 'Doctor!' he cried.

Selris had just time to hand the Doctor the phial — and then Kroton Two raised its weapon.

'No!' shouted the Doctor.

Selris leaped for the door but it was too late. It had closed behind him.

For a second his body glowed in the laser beam, the Doctor and Zoe heard a bellow of pain — and then Selris was gone.

Zoe buried her head on the Doctor's shoulder. The Doctor patted her back, thinking that Selris had not

110

sacrificed himself in vain. The phial was securely clasped in the Doctor's other hand.

12

Acid

For the Krotons it seemed, the incident was already
over. Thankfully the Doctor realised that their indifference to the motives of lesser beings made it
unlikely they would even wonder why Selris had
sacrificed his life.

It was a mistake, which the Doctor very much
hoped would prove fatal. The Krotons' total ego-
tistical callousness, he decided, made them one of the
least attractive life forms he had ever encountered.

'Set up the intergalactic link,' ordered the Commander.

A strange device rose smoothly from the control
room floor, a sort of four-sided console surmounted by
a huge glowing coil.

Two headsets were linked to the console.

'Take-off, Phase Two,' said the Kroton Two.

'Prepare for take-off!'

'All systems set.'

The Commander turned to the Doctor. 'You will
assist us now.'

'Assist you? In what way?'

'The Dynotrope will exhaust in twelve minutes.'

'That's your problem,' muttered Zoe rebelliously.

'Not entirely, Zoe,' said the Doctor quietly. 'If this

machine runs down there will be a colossal energy release. Enough to destroy us, the Krotons, the Gonds and maybe the entire planet.' He turned back to the Krotons. 'You'll have to explain what you want us to do.' He pointed to the four-side console. 'What's this thing?'

'It is the intergalactic link. It transfers the Dynotrope to our own cosmos. It operates through mental power.'

'You've really discovered a way of transforming mental power into energy?' Even the Doctor was impressed. It had long been known that mental power was the greatest energy source in the cosmos — in a sense, it *was* the cosmos — but no-one as yet had discovered an effective way of tapping it. No wonder these Krotons had such a high opinion of themselves.

Zoe, however, wasn't so impressed. 'And you Krotons haven't enough mental power of your own to make it work?'

'Four high brains are needed in relay. There are only two of us.'

'Then how did you get it here?'

'No more questions.'

'If you want our co-operation, you must expect questions,' said the Doctor.

Kroton Two raised its weapon. 'Unless you do as we order you will be dispersed.'

'Maybe so,' said the Doctor cheerfully. 'But that won't help you much, will it?'

The Commander, it seemed, was prepared to make concessions. 'We are wasting time. The Dynotrope was part of a battle fleet. The other two members of the crew were exhausted by enemy fire.'

'You mean they were killed?' asked Zoe.

The Kroton answered in its own strange terminology. 'They exhausted. They ceased to function. We carried out emergency procedure and landed on the nearest planet. To conserve power, we set the Dynotrope in perpetual stability.'

'I see,' said the Doctor intrigued. 'Then you set up the Teaching Machines to educate the natives up to the mental standards you require.'

'That is so. They were primitives.'

'You still didn't have to kill them!'

'Gond samples were brought in for testing at regular intervals. The Dynotrope absorbed their mental power into its circuits. The waste matter was ejected and dispersed.'

Before the angry Doctor could speak the second Kroton turned from its study of the console. 'Nine minutes to exhaust time, Commander.'

Jamie and Beta staggered into the Learning Hall carrying an enormous glass jar between them. Liquid sloshed about inside and acrid fumes seeped through the cloth stretched over the jar's mouth.

Axus marched officiously up to them. 'Where do you think you're going? What's that?'

'It's something called acid,' said Beta with dignity. 'The Doctor asked me to make it for him.'

Axus laughed. 'He'll have no need of it now. You've been wasting your time, Beta.'

'Where is he?' demanded Jamie.

'He has joined the Krotons.'

Beta gaped at him. 'In the Machine?'

'That's right.'

'And what about Zoe?' asked Jamie.

Vana came hurrying up to them. 'Zoe too. The Krotons wanted them — and Eelek surrendered them.'

'He did *what?*'

Eelek came by just in time to hear his name

mentioned. 'The Krotons needed your friends in order to be able to leave our world,' he explained calmly.

'And you just handed them over, did you?' asked Jamie menacingly.

'If the Krotons will leave our world, they are welcome to your friends.'

Jamie drew back his fist. 'Why you miserable —'

Armed guards moved forward, and Beta put a restraining hand on Jamie's shoulder. 'Careful, Jamie.'

Eelek turned contemptuously away. 'It's time we were all leaving.'

'Leaving?' said Jamie indignantly.

Eelek paused on the stairs. 'Unless you all want to die.'

Beta gave him a puzzled look. 'What are you talking about Eelek?'

Eelek sighed. 'For a scientist, Beta, you are very stupid. This Learning Hall, and for all we know most of our City is built around the Krotons' Machine. And if that Machine goes back into the sky . . .'

Beta blenched. 'This whole place will come down.'

'Exactly. Do you really want to be buried alive?'

'Well, I'm staying,' said Jamie doggedly. 'I'm getting the Doctor and Zoe out of there somehow. Beta?'

'All right. I'll stay and help you, Jamie.'

Eelek looked at Vana. 'And you, Vana?'

'I'm staying to look after Thara. Unlike you, Eelek, I'm not sensible enough to run away and leave my friends.'

Eelek's face was impassive. After a moment he said calmly. 'Very well. Let them stay — and let them die.' Eelek and his men disappeared up the stairs.

Beta gave Jamie a rueful look. 'He could be right, you know.'

'Aye, mebbe,' said Jamie philosophically. 'But at least we can put up a fight.' He tapped the smoking jar. 'Now then, where are we going to put this stuff?'

Beta smiled. 'I know the very place.'

The Doctor and the Krotons were approaching their final confrontation.

The Doctor had delayed with questions and objections as long as he dared, but now the Commander was losing patience. 'Put on the head-sets.'

'Just one more thing,' said the Doctor. 'If you transfer the Dynotrope back to your own world — what will happen to us?'

'You will suffer no harm.'

'How can we be sure you're telling the truth?' argued the Doctor. 'You see, we should die without oxygen — *just as you would die if anything upset the nutrient supply you draw from that tank.*'

The Doctor gave Zoe a nudge — and passed her the stone phial behind both their backs.

Moving forward, he attempted to distract the Krotons while Zoe edged backwards towards the tank, the phial held behind her.

'Take up your positions,' ordered the Commander.

'All right, all right,' said the Doctor. 'I'm only telling Zoe that if, by any chance, something contaminated the contents of that tank, you'd know what it was like to breathe poisoned air.'

'Six minutes to exhaust time,' reported Kroton Two.

The Commander was becoming angry and suspicious. 'You have no choice. Put the head-set on now.'

By now Zoe was standing with her back against the side of the tank. She unstoppered the phial, being very careful to hold it upright, and then swiftly tipped its entire contents into the tank. She looked up, caught the Doctor's eye and nodded briefly.

The Doctor addressed the Kroton. 'Oh well, I suppose we'll have to take your word.' He moved across to the console.

'Set the transfer link,' ordered the Commander. 'Final phase on automatic.'

'Now then,' said the Doctor fussily. 'Where do you want me to stand?'

'Unimportant.'

'Oh, very well. I'll stand over here then.' The Doctor moved to the nearest place at the console. He gave Zoe a meaningful look.

'Oh, *I* wanted to stand there,' she protested.

'My dear Zoe,' said the Doctor. 'In that case, you must stand here, and I'll stand over there.'

In this way they managed to waste several minutes.

'Put on the head-sets at once or you will be dispersed,' ordered the Commander.

The Doctor seemed to be thoroughly confused. 'We're doing our best. Now, which way do they go? This way? No, this way!'

Zoe glanced at the tank. 'Nothing seems to be happening,' she whispered.

'No,' said the Doctor grimly. 'Perhaps in a minute . . . Play for time.' He fumbled with his head-set and managed to drop it. 'Oops! Butterfingers!'

It seemed insane to be clowning at a time of such danger, but Zoe made herself join in. 'Oh, you are clumsy, Doctor!'

'Enough of this!' boomed the Commander. 'Put on the head-sets or you will be dispersed.'

'It's all your fault,' babbled the Doctor. 'You're making me nervous.' He put on his head-set as slowly as he dared.

Zoe did the same, and winced as she felt a sudden tug at her mind. She felt locked in, a part of the

Machine. Had the Krotons won after all?

Suddenly the Commander made a ghastly gurgling sound, staggered back from the console, and crashed to the ground.

Kroton Two tottered back, weaving to and fro, trying to bring its weapon to bear on the Doctor and Zoe. It managed a few words of slurred and gurgling speech: 'What — what have you . . . '

'Down, Zoe!' yelled the Doctor. They threw themselves to one side as the Kroton toppled over backwards like a falling tree. The laser cannon blazed harmlessly at the ceiling.

The Doctor helped Zoe to her feet. 'Are you all right?'

Zoe was staring down at the fallen Krotons. 'Look at them,' she whispered. 'They're — *dissolving!*'

The massive silver bodies were crumbling away before their eyes, collapsing into a kind of shapeless sludge that dribbled away from the decaying figures.

'Yes, they're returning to their basic forms . . . '

Zoe coughed. 'Doctor, these fumes. They're choking . . . '

'I know. We've got to get out of here.' He looked round and then pointed. 'Look, Zoe, the Machine's melting too!'

Great chunks of wall were sliding away, as the Machine mirrored the disintegration of its Kroton masters. The Doctor grabbed Zoe's arm. 'Let's get out of here before we're trapped!'

They hurried through the distorted, dissolving corridors and found the main door already half-eaten away.

A few vigorous kicks from the Doctor disposed of the rest of it and they emerged into the ruins of the Learning Hall.

The place seemed empty . . .

Suddenly they heard voices, shouts and a great deal of coughing coming from below.

They ran down the stairs that led to the Underhall. There they found Beta and Jamie, both with cloths tied over their mouths, pouring the remains of a huge pot of acid into the pit that had been dug by the main pillar.

The Doctor rapped Jamie on the shoulder. 'Hello!' he said, cheerfully.

Jamie turned round. 'Doctor! Zoe!'

Beta looked up. 'What's happening?'

Jamie couldn't believe his eyes. 'Are you all right, both of you? Are you hurt?'

'Just a little shaken, Jamie. But believe me we're much better off than the Krotons!'

In the corner of the Learning Hall, Thara was being nursed by Vana. Suddenly he pointed, 'Look, Vana. Look at the Machine!'

By now the whole dome was disintegrating, caving into nothingness. 'It's working, Thara,' said Vana joyfully. 'Look, it's working!'

Jamie, Zoe, Beta and the Doctor came hurrying up the stairs to join them.

'What made you think of pouring acid on the Machine?' asked Zoe.

Beta laughed. 'We reckoned if the Doctor thought a few drops were so important, we'd see what a few gallons would do!'

Zoe turned to the Doctor. 'And how did you know that the Krotons and the Machine would dissolve, Doctor?'

'Mmm? Well, the Machine was about eighty per cent tellurium, you know, and tellurium is soluble in sulphuric acid.'

'But the Machine wasn't pure tellurium . . .'

'Well, the acid wasn't pure sulphuric acid,' said the

Doctor cheerfully. 'Anyway, it worked, didn't it?'

Beta and Vana and Thara were all talking excitedly.

The Doctor nudged Jamie and Zoe. 'Come on you two, I hate goodbyes.' They slipped quietly up the stairs.

'Well, it's finished now isn't it?' Vana was saying.

'Yes, it's finished,' said Thara. 'The end of the Krotons. We're free at last.'

Beta frowned. 'There's still Eelek to deal with.'

Thara smiled grimly. 'That will be my pleasure. I shall succeed my father as leader of the Council — *whatever* Eelek thinks.'

'And now we can develop our own sciences,' said Beta eagerly. 'The Doctor will help us.' He looked round. 'Doctor?'

'They've gone,' said Thara gently.

'But I wanted to ask his advice,' protested Beta.

Thara smiled. 'There are no Krotons now, no Doctor. We shall have to find our own answers, Beta. Just us!'

In the Wasteland only the dying echoes of a faint wheezing, groaning sound remained to show that the Doctor and his companions were on their way to new adventures.

DOCTOR WHO

	TERRANCE DICKS	
0426114558	**Doctor Who and The Abominable Snowmen**	£1.35
0426200373	**Doctor Who and The Android Invasion**	£1.25
0426201086	**Doctor Who and The Androids of Tara**	£1.35
	IAN MARTER	
0426116313	**Doctor Who and The Ark in Space**	£1.35
	TERRANCE DICKS	
0426201043	**Doctor Who and The Armageddon Factor**	£1.50
0426112954	**Doctor Who and The Auton Invasion**	£1.50
0426116747	**Doctor Who and The Brain of Morbius**	£1.35
0426110250	**Doctor Who and The Carnival of Monsters**	£1.35
	MALCOLM HULKE	
042611471X	**Doctor Who and The Cave Monsters**	£1.50
	TERRANCE DICKS	
0426117034	**Doctor Who and The Claws of Axos**	£1.35
	DAVID FISHER	
042620123X	**Doctor Who and The Creature from the Pit**	£1.35
	DAVID WHITAKER	
0426113160	**Doctor Who and The Crusaders**	£1.50
	BRIAN HAYLES	
0426200616	**Doctor Who and The Curse of Peladon**	£1.50
	GERRY DAVIS	
0426114639	**Doctor Who and The Cybermen**	£1.50
	BARRY LETTS	
0426113322	**Doctor Who and The Daemons**	£1.50

Prices are subject to alteration

DOCTOR WHO

	DAVID WHITAKER	
0426101103	**Doctor Who and The Daleks**	£1.50
	TERRANCE DICKS	
042611244X	**Doctor Who and The Dalek Invasion of Earth**	£1.50
0426103807	**Doctor Who and The Day of the Daleks**	£1.35
042620042X	**Doctor Who – Death to the Daleks**	£1.35
0426119657	**Doctor Who and The Deadly Assassin**	£1.50
0426200969	**Doctor Who and The Destiny of the Daleks**	£1.35
	MALCOLM HULKE	
0426108744	**Doctor Who and The Dinosaur Invasion**	£1.35
0426103726	**Doctor Who and The Doomsday Weapon**	£1.50
	IAN MARTER	
0426201464	**Doctor Who and The Enemy of the World**	£1.50
	TERRANCE DICKS	
0426200063	**Doctor Who and The Face of Evil**	£1.50
	ANDREW SMITH	
0426201507	**Doctor Who – Full Circle**	£1.50
	TERRANCE DICKS	
0426112601	**Doctor Who and The Genesis of the Daleks**	£1.35
0426112792	**Doctor Who and The Giant Robot**	£1.35
	MALCOLM HULKE	
0426115430	**Doctor Who and The Green Death**	£1.35

Prices are subject to alteration

DOCTOR WHO

	TERRANCE DICKS **Doctor Who and The** **Hand of Fear**	
0426200330		£1.35
	Doctor Who and The **Horns of Nimon**	
0426201310		£1.35
	Doctor Who and The **Horror of Fang Rock**	
0426200098		£1.35
	BRIAN HAYLES **Doctor Who and The** **Ice Warriors**	
0426108663		£1.35
	Doctor Who and The **Image of the Fendahl**	
0426200772		£1.35
	TERRANCE DICKS **Doctor Who and The** **Invasion of Time**	
0426200934		£1.35
	Doctor Who and The **Invisible Enemy**	
0426200543		£1.35
	Doctor Who and The **Keeper of Traken**	
0426201485		£1.35
	PHILIP HINCHCLIFFE **Doctor Who and The** **Keys of Marinus**	
0426201256		£1.35
	DAVID FISHER **Doctor Who and The** **Leisure Hive**	
0426201477		£1.35
	TERRANCE DICKS **Doctor Who and The** **Loch Ness Monster**	
0426110412		£1.25
	CHRISTOPHER H BIDMEAD **Doctor Who – Logopolis**	
0426201493		£1.35
	PHILIP HINCHCLIFFE **Doctor Who and The** **Masque of Mandragora**	
0426118936		£1.25
	TERRANCE DICKS **Doctor Who and The** **Monster of Peladon**	
0426201329		£1.35

Prices are subject to alteration